I0663960

The Paper Chase

A Chief Inspector Pointer Mystery

By A. E. Fielding

Originally published in 1935

The Paper Chase

© 2015 Resurrected Press
www.ResurrectedPress.com

All rights reserved. No part of this book may be used or reproduced in any manner without written permission except for brief quotations for review purposes.

Published by Resurrected Press

This classic book was handcrafted by Resurrected Press. Resurrected Press is dedicated to bringing high quality classic books back to the readers who enjoy them. These are not scanned versions of the originals, but, rather, quality checked and edited books meant to be enjoyed!

Please visit ResurrectedPress.com to view our entire catalogue!

For news and updates, visit us on Facebook! Facebook.com/ResurrectedPress

ISBN 13: 978-1-943403-04-2

Printed in the United States of America

Other Resurrected Press Books in *The Chief Inspector Pointer Mystery* Series

Death of John Tait
Murder at the Nook
Mystery at the Rectory
Scarecrow
The Case of the Two Pearl Necklaces
The Charteris Mystery
The Eames-Erskine Case
The Footsteps that Stopped
The Clifford Affair
The Cluny Problem
The Craig Poisoning Mystery
The Net Around Joan Ingilby
The Tall House Mystery
The Wedding-Chest Mystery
The Westwood Mystery
Tragedy at Beechcroft

RESURRECTED PRESS CLASSIC MYSTERY CATALOGUE

J. S. Fletcher
The Herapath Property
The Rayner-Slade Amalgamation
The Chestermarke Instinct
The Paradise Mystery
Dead Men's Money
The Middle of Things
Ravensdene Court
Scarhaven Keep
The Orange-Yellow Diamond
The Middle Temple Murder
The Tallyrand Maxim
The Borough Treasurer
In the Mayor's Parlour
The Saftey Pin

R. Austin Freeman
The Mystery of 31 New Inn from the Dr. Thorndyke Series
John Thorndyke's Cases from the Dr. Thorndyke Series
The Red Thumb Mark from The Dr. Thorndyke Series
The Eye of Osiris from The Dr. Thorndyke Series
A Silent Witness from the Dr. John Thorndyke Series
The Cat's Eye from the Dr. John Thorndyke Series
Helen Vardon's Confession: A Dr. John Thorndyke Story
As a Thief in the Night: A Dr. John Thorndyke Story
Mr. Pottermack's Oversight: A Dr. John Thorndyke Story
Dr. Thorndyke Intervenes: A Dr. John Thorndyke Story
The Singing Bone: The Adventures of Dr. Thorndyke
The Stoneware Monkey: A Dr. John Thorndyke Story
The Great Portrait Mystery, and Other Stories: A Collection of Dr. John Thorndyke and Other Stories
The Penrose Mystery: A Dr. John Thorndyke Story

The Uttermost Farthing: A Savant's Vendetta

Arthur Griffiths
The Passenger From Calais
The Rome Express

Fergus Hume
The Mystery of a Hansom Cab
The Green Mummy
The Silent House
The Secret Passage

Edgar Jepson
The Loudwater Mystery

A. E. W. Mason
At the Villa Rose

A. A. Milne
The Red House Mystery

Baroness Emma Orczy
The Old Man in the Corner

Edgar Allan Poe
The Detective Stories of Edgar Allan Poe

Arthur J. Rees
The Hampstead Mystery
The Shrieking Pit
The Hand In The Dark
The Moon Rock
The Mystery of the Downs

Mary Roberts Rinehart
Sight Unseen and The Confession

Dorothy L. Sayers

Anybody but Anne
The Bride of a Moment
Faulkner's Folly
The Diamond Pin
The Gold Bag
The Mystery of the Sycamore
The Come Back

Raoul Whitfield
Death in a Bowl

And much more!
Visit ResurrectedPress.com
for our complete catalogue

FOREWORD

The period between the First and Second World Wars has rightly been called the "Golden Age of British Mysteries." It was during this period that Agatha Christie, Dorothy L. Sayers, and Margery Allingham first turned their pens to crime. On the male side, the era saw such writers as Anthony Berkeley, John Dickson Carr, and Freeman Wills Crofts join the ranks of writers of detective fiction. The genre was immensely popular at the time on both sides of the Atlantic, and by the end of the 1930's one out of every four novels published in Britain was a mystery.

While Agatha Christie and a few of her peers have remained popular and in print to this day, the same cannot be said of all the authors of this period. With so many mysteries published in the period, it is inevitable that many of them would become obscure or worse, forgotten, often with no justification other than changing public tastes. The case of Archibald Fielding is one such, an author, who though popular enough to have a career spanning two decades and more than two dozen mysteries, has become such a cipher that his, or as seems more likely, her real identity has become as much a mystery as the books themsclves.

While the identity of the author may forever remain an unsolved puzzle, there are some facts that may be inferred from the texts. It is likely that the author had an upbringing and education typical of the British upper middle class in the period before the Great War with all that implies; a familiarity with the classics, the arts, and music, a working knowledge of modern European languages, an appreciation of the finer things in life. The author certainly had also traveled abroad, primarily in the south of France, but probably to Belgium, Spain, and Italy as well, as portions of several of the books are set in those locales.

The books attributed to Archibald Fielding, A. E. Fielding, or Archibald E. Fielding, are quintessential Golden Age British mysteries. They include all the attributes, the country houses, the tangled webs of relationships, the somewhat feckless cast of characters who seem to have nothing better to do with themselves than to murder or be murdered. Their focus is on a middle class and upper class struggling to find themselves in the new realities of the post war era while still trying to live the lifestyle of the Edwardian era. Things are never as they seem, red herrings are distributed liberally throughout the pages as are the clues that will ultimately lead to the solution of "the puzzle," for the British mysteries of this period are centered on the puzzle element which both the reader and the detective must solve before the last page.

A majority of the Fielding mysteries involve the character of Chief Inspector Pointer. Unlike the eccentric Belgian Hercule Poirot, the flamboyant Lord Peter Wimsey, or the somewhat mysterious Albert Campion, Pointer is merely a competent, sometimes clever, occasionally intuitive policeman. And unlike, as with Inspector French in the stories of Freeman Wills Croft, the emphasis is on the mystery itself, not the process of detection.

Pointer is nearly as much of a mystery as the author. Very little of his personal life is revealed in the books. He is described as being vaguely of Scottish ancestry whose father was a Coast guardsman on the Devon coast.. He is well read and educated, though his duties at Scotland Yard prevent him from enjoying those pursuits. In an early book in the series it is revealed that he spends a week or two each year climbing mountains, his only apparent recreation, though before becoming a policeman he'd played football for the All England team. His success as a detective depends on his willingness to "suspect everyone" and to not being tied to any one theory. He is fluent in French, German, and Italian and familiar with those countries. He is, at least in the first two books, unmarried, and sharing lodgings with a bookbinder named O'Connor, in much the manner of Holmes and Watson, though this character is absent in the later works. Yet in *The Paper Chase* he still shares the lodgings with someone though that figure is absent.

One intriguing feature of the Pointer mysteries is that they all involve an unexpected twist at the end, wherein the mystery finally solved is often not the mystery invoked at the beginning of the book. *The Paper Chase* is no exception. Fielding introduces numerous red-herrings and subplots to confuse the reader while still largely playing fair with the reader. When Fielding wrote *The Paper Chase* the series was already ten years old, the book being the fifteenth novel to feature Chief Inspector Pointer. The author's style had matured and been refined over that period. Gone are the over reliance on disguises and other dramatic gimmicks that mark some of the earlier books. There is much more reliance on solid detection, the interpretation of clues, and judging the validity of the testimony of those involved. Yet, the Pointer mysteries have a certain flair that separates them from the "humdrum" school of mysteries that were starting to appear at the same time. Stylistically, they fall somewhere between the works of Christie and those of Ngaio Marsh or E. C. R. Lorac.

The Paper Chase begins with a group of strangers on holiday at a winter resort in the Italian Tirol who are drawn together by an love of winter sports such as tobogganing. The five males in the party form a bobsled team to compete in the local race, and the two women form romantic entanglements with several of the men. After the race, they all return to Britain intending to maintain contact, but within hours of arriving in London, one of the women is found shot to death in the flat of one of the men, a man who has gone missing. It is at this point in the story that Chief Inspector Pointer is brought in. He quickly suspects that what at first appearance was a love affair gone wrong, is instead related to the fact that one of more of the party was passing very high quality counterfeit five pound notes. The question then becomes, what were the involvements of the murdered woman and the missing man in that scheme.

The author takes full advantage of the politically unsettled nature of Europe at the time. The South Tirol where the story starts had been part of Austria before the war, but was moved to the Italian side of the border afterwards, a move that pleased few of the local residents. The Fascist government in Italy and the rise of the Nazis in Germany are alluded to as is the recent civil war in Spain. Part of Pointer's task in *The Paper Chase* is to rule out any role of espionage in the case.

In typical Fielding fashion, *The Paper Chase* confuses the reader with false clues and plot lines that prove to be dead ends. Faced with a victim who was not what she seemed and with at least one of the other members of the holiday party with secrets to hide, Pointer faces the task of uncovering the truth while presented with only a meager set of clues, though, of course, with his usual tenacity he manages to solve the mystery of *The Paper Chase*. The real question, is can the reader do the same?

Despite their obscurity, the mysteries of Archibald Fielding, whoever he or she might have been, are well written, well crafted examples of the form, worthy of the interest of the fans of the genre. It is with pleasure, then, that Resurrected Press presents this new edition of *The Paper Chase* and others in the series to its readers.

About the Author

The identity of the author is as much a mystery as the plots of the novels. Two dozen novels were published from 1924 to 1944 as by Archibald Fielding, A. E. Fielding, or Archibald E. Fielding, yet the only clue as to the real author is a comment by the American publishers, H.C. Kinsey Co. that A. E. Fielding was in reality a "middle-aged English woman by the name of Dorothy Feilding whose peacetime address is Sheffield Terrace, Kensington, London, and who enjoys gardening." Research on the part of John Herrington has uncovered a person by that name living at 2 Sheffield Terrace from 1932-1936. She appears to have moved to Islington in 1937 after which she disappears. To complicate things, some have attributed the authorship to Lady Dorothy Mary Evelyn Moore nee Feilding (1889-1935), however, a grandson of Lady Dorothy denied any family knowledge of such authorship. The archivist at Collins, the British publisher, reports that any records of A. Fielding were presumably lost during WWII. Birthdates have been given variously as 1884, 1889, and 1900. Unless new information comes to light, it would appear that the real authorship must remain a mystery.

Greg Fowlkes
Editor-In-Chief
Resurrected Press
www.ResurrectedPress.com
www.Facebook.com/ResurrectedPress

CHAPTER ONE

VIPITENO, on the Brenner Pass, is better known to travellers in summer than in winter, and better known even then under its pre-war, Tirol name of Sterzing. In summer it has been haunted by German artists until there is a Sterzing school, not unlike our own Newquay school. It is a pretty enough hamlet when the days are warm, with its thickset houses, its overhanging eaves, its flowers at the windows and in front of the many wayside crucifixes. But of late it is making headway as a winter resort—for those who do not mind wind. It has the longest natural ice run for bobsleighs in Italy, and it was this fact which had brought Hugh Winslow here.

He had ricked a knee at tennis, but with a horse or a sleigh to pull him and his bob up from the end of the run, and with a railway station at hand, he found it troubled him very little. He had been out a week by now, and intended, if he could get a crew together, to enter for the bobsleigh race in another ten days. His would be the only English bob, and would have to beat some good men from Munich and the neighboring Alpini garrisons, but the cup would be given this year for the winning five-man bob, and he still hoped that he might enter for it.

He and his cousin Ursula went on down at seven o'clock to meet the Dolomite Express. Most of the passengers went on to Meran, especially, so it seemed to both of them, the useful-looking ones, but you never knew your luck. Winslow was on the Stock Exchange, and that was one of his slogans. He was short and thin, ugly but clever looking, with something eager in his eyes, and something reserved. In age he was under thirty. His cousin Ursula was just over that boundary. She had a frank, interesting face, and a knack of looking well dressed, however simple her clothes might be. Trimness was her chief characteristic. She avoided frills even in speech. The two were the best of friends. They were both of them orphans. Brought up by bachelor uncles in a quiet country house, they had adopted each other silently as brother and sister years ago. Their affection had remained unaltered in quantity and in quality.

The train was late, which meant that it would wait but a second, and that in its turn meant agility on the part of alighting passengers. Some carabinieri with their cloaks swirled around them stood a little to one side like a group of crows. They met every train. Quite a little knot of people got out this evening and were carried off with their luggage by the porters. Hugh and Ursula discussed them at dinner afterwards.

"We must have the big man," she said in her quick, positive fashion. Hugh looked at her interrogatively.

"I like his looks," she said to that.

"Do you?" He himself seemed dubious. "Looked a bit of a Lord Almighty to me," he went on. "I thought he was going to brain me with a bag, because I didn't move out of his path quickly enough."

"Yes, I don't think he'd stand much of that," she agreed with a smile; "but for a member of your crew—I think he looks a winner."

"Then there's the tall fair lad who nearly got carried on," Hugh said next. "He's staying here. His name— perfect, isn't it?—is Captain Kidd. He's sure to join in. And there was a third man who looked English—or American—to me. An older man with creases down the corners of his mouth, he might do. . . ." Hugh did not sound enthusiastic.

"I should prefer your overbearing friend in an emergency," Ursula said to that. "He'd do things, while your stout one was merely goggling at them."

Winslow laughed. "As long as I get the men, I don't care much what they do, or not do, provided they come along on my bob and race for the Cup. There's only this chap Lightfoot whom we found here, so far."

"The trouble with him is that, like me, he's skinny," she murmured thoughtfully.

"Oh, no, the trouble is that he's not there half the time. I suppose it's the artistic temperament. He's an artist, it seems."

"Yes, but he must be a very poor one," Ursula said. "I told him that I painted, and would be glad of his company, and he hurried into a speech about being really an engraver. Personally, I think he's a photographer, and ashamed to own that he gets his drawings that way, for when I said that photography was an enormous help in getting correct outlines—for you can work from it in all weathers—he positively beamed and said that was just what he had found."

"I can't imagine him positively beaming," Winslow objected. "Absent-minded beggar is my name for him. Ah, there's the lad with the pirate's name."

A very tall, slender young man, who looked a bare twenty, had come in and was waiting a trifle shyly for the head waiter to show him to a table. His eyes rested on Winslow and his cousin with a glint of rejoicing in them. Plainly he recognised fellow countrymen.

"I'll go over and introduce myself over coffee," Ursula went on, "and I'll see if I can rope in the big man. I saw that he was going to the Drei Kreuzen." Ursula rose.

"Tre Croci, unless you want to be arrested by the fascisti," Winslow corrected' her. "And you *will* call the porters *trager*, instead of *faccini*. As for the names of the places around—you'll learn in prison what they're called now, unless you have a change of heart, my girl."

"Mr. Lightfoot always calls them by their old Tirol names," she said to that.

"Not in the hotel lounge. He even calls the proprietor here, whose name it seems is Landsmann—Signor Contadino."

"Yes, and they both roar every time he says it."
Ursula was lighting a parting cigarette.

"Look here, you're not going after those two beggars
now?" he asked in horror.

"How crude you think me. I shall wait till a good
dinner is over and boredom approaching," she assured
him. "Don't you say anything if one or other of them
blows in here. Leave it to me—"

"Said the serpent," he finished as she really left him.

The man of whom they had spoken, Lightfoot by
name, came through the hall. He did not see her and
went on to the hall porter's desk, taking out a bulging
note-case. "I want larger notes instead of this basketful of
small ones." He laid the wad on the counter.

The hall porter promptly reached for his note-case.
Ursula had noticed how obsequiously all the hotel staff
waited on Mr. Lightfoot. He was evidently an old habitué
of the place. Catching sight of Ursula, he came forward
now, and began to talk to her of the weather outlook,
which was good. Ursula switched on to skiing, of which
she was very fond. The porter had told her only that
morning that Lightfoot was quite first class at this
branch of winter sport. She was rather piqued that he
had not asked her to accompany him on any excursion.
Now on her leading up to it very tactfully, as she thought,
he quite definitely slid out of her suggestion that they
should make up a party, and try for one of the many
excursions over the snow to which Vipiteno lends itself so
admirably. He was a very tall, very thin man with large
dark melancholy eyes. Haunted eyes, she had called
them, when she first saw them. He had a whimsical
mouth and unexpectedly forceful jaw. His hands were
artistic hands, sensitive and long fingered. He was a
marvellous bridge player. Hugh was good. So was Ursula,
but after one rubber, they both had a healthy respect for
Lightfoot's brains and memory. He might not be all there
on a bob, but he seemed able to play cards automatically.
The stout man, whose arrival she and her cousin had

noticed, came down the stairs at this moment and was shown into the restaurant. So he, as well as Captain Kidd, was staying here. That would make it easy for Hugh to tackle them immediately. She watched her cousin for a moment through the glass panel of the door. He and this Captain Kidd seemed to be getting along splendidly. What a gay young man the newcomer seemed! His eyes, if they were small—and they were—danced all the time. He seemed to be agreeing enthusiastically with whatever it was that Hugh was saying, and Ursula, feeling that two of the crew were already bagged, went on out into the cold night. At the Tre Croci she asked the newcomer's name. He was English, as they had guessed, and his name appeared to be Edward Moffatt from Manchester. She waited about, looking at picture postcards, until she saw him establish himself near one of the big radiators with his black coffee and a cognac, then she asked the waiter to tell him that an English lady would like to speak to him—Moffatt—in the writing-room. There was something very distant in his look, and reserved in his manner, as he came into it, but when she explained her errand, he thawed. Privately, he thought that he had never seen a prettier picture than she made in her deep blue velvet frock and tangerine cloak, with a huge white fur collar like a snowdrift, out of which her dark face and bright eyes showed well.

As for Ursula, the more she talked to him the more she liked him. His cool manner did not put her off. She went by his steady gaze and air of complete self assurance. She judged him to be courageous and forceful, both characteristics which she liked. That he was not hail-fellow-well-met with everyone was a point in his favour with her. Ursula shared that attitude. He had an infrequent smile which she thought rather nice, and it was with a feeling of pleasure she let him see her back to her own hotel and come on in for a word with her cousin.

They found Hugh and the three other Englishmen all talking around the big log fire in the comfortable lounge.

Captain Kidd was delighted at the idea of racing down a new ice run. He certainly was good looking, Ursula thought, studying him at closer range, and he appeared a mere boy, until you caught a look in his eyes that made you add at least ten years to his seeming age. The stout man's name was Priestley. He looked rather like an actor, Ursula thought, or a singer. Moffatt showed to less advantage when with men than women, she decided. His eye was again remote and chilling.

"Supercilious devil," was Winslow's instant reaction. "Looks as though he were wondering which of us would bring him a chair first." But the ice was soon broken all round, and, in talking, Moffatt showed himself as an amusing, cynical, well-travelled man of the world.

"I thought I had seen a bit of everywhere," Priestley exclaimed after they had chatted, some half an hour, "but you certainly win, when it comes to the number of countries which you know well"

"I'm a commission agent," Moffatt said to that, in the timber line particularly. "Perhaps I should put it clearer by saying that I'm a sort of conference arranger, and general mediator between people who live at the ends of the earth and want to meet."

"And I'm a begging letter-writer," Priestley put in with a smile. "I mean it. I'm a writer of thousands of appeals to the charitable public to help deserving causes. By the way"—he turned to Kidd—"are you, by chance, any relation to Sir Geoffrey Kidd? I heard you speak of Dover just now, as though you knew the country around it well."

"I'm his grandson," Captain Kidd's silly haw-haw rang out again. He seemed to find everything a joke.

"Really? The old General used to be a tower of strength when it came to the Miners' Children Fund. He left them quite a nice legacy."

"He left me quite a nice little one, too," Kidd said. "That's why I've sent in my papers. I know how to use it. Out in China I came across a wonderful kind of transparent rice paper which is going to revolutionise all sorts of things, and I bought the patent. Marvellous stuff. Can be used for glass windows, for straw hats, for—well, there's no end to its usefulness."

"We shall have to introduce him to the nunkies," Ursula said to Hugh. She explained. "Hugh and I own a couple of uncles who make paper."

"Joliffe and Joliffe," supplemented Hugh casually.

Captain Kidd's face showed that he knew the name. "Really? I should like immensely to show them some of the stuff. They head my list of the firms with whom I wanted to get into touch."

"If you help Hugh here win the cup, I'll take you down in person and introduce you," Ursula said, smiling. "They brought Hugh and me up. We used to live there practically next to the works as children. I felt it acutely. Like living over one's shop—" And she, too, laughed with Kidd at the snobbishness of the very young.

"I shall hold you to that promise," Kidd said with one of his unexpectedly business-like glances.

"You never need hold me to my word," she said a trifle coldly; and with that the talk turned to China, and then to Japan, and to the outlook for textiles. Priestley had a good deal to say, and said it well. Moffatt had little to say, and said it better. Kidd sat listening as though enjoying the talk immensely.

"Is that transparent paper you're interested in any use for photography?" Lightfoot asked Kidd under cover of the general talk. He had been sitting huddled together in his chair. His evening clothes were creased and shiny, though well cut.

Kidd said in the expansive, optimistic way of the born salesman that his transparent paper would be magnificent for films. He overflowed with chemical details which apparently were too much for Lightfoot, who only repeated that he wondered if it would do . . . and edged deeper into his chair.

The men were weighed on the hotel scales. Winslow must know how to balance his bob. He himself had to be steerer on account of his knee, which prevented his flinging himself sideways. Otherwise he would have preferred to be brake. However, perhaps he was better in front. The brake should be heavy and strong, as well as agile, and Winslow was slight and short. Kidd, on the other hand, seemed to have all the necessary qualifications, provided he had the necessary quick wits. Winslow would have chosen Moffatt but for the greater length of Kidd's legs and the young man's agility. As things were, Winslow hoped to be able to make a flying start instead of the standing one to which he had resigned himself. But Moffatt, who would sit second, and Kidd, should both be able to jump on the running bob, and so gain perhaps as much as two seconds on the day of the race.

Then and there the bob squatted on the floor of Lady Browne's sitting-room and practised. "Left—Back. Right—Back. Left—right—left," until they moved like automata. Lady Browne was a pleasant woman of around forty, with whom Ursula lived, and who had come out here, ostensibly to take part in winter sports, but in reality to sit in her warm and comfortable sitting-room and play bridge, just as she did in Town. She played by herself when there was no one to join her; but as a rule the hotel proprietors or managers could usually find other bridge fiends to make up a table.

"How funny you all look," she said, now gathering up her cards. The other players did not speak a word of English; and Lady Browne's French was a tongue in itself, so they were reduced to signs. "Fancy doing that sort of thing, when there's a pack of cards within reach." And she swiftly dealt, holding up two fingers and pointed to her diamond brooch, which meant two diamonds.

The men finally got up, the timing had been perfect. "I don't think we shall skid if you do it like that in the morning," Winslow said, well pleased, and the party broke up after an absent-minded nod from Lady Browne, who was murmuring, "Let me see, did he point to the shovel or not? Yes, four spades, I think."

"We've made a good haul," Winslow told his cousin as they went on up to their rooms. "I detested that big chap Moffatt at first, but he seems a very decent fellow, really."

Ursula said that she thought so, too.

"Let me see: yes, three sweaters each, plus-fours, elbow pads, knee pads, steel knuckle plates on their leather gauntlets, crash helmets, spikes in their boots, and rakes screwed on the toes . . . I don't think I forgot to give them any instructions as to how to rig themselves out—" Winslow was the engrossed skipper looking over his ship for possible weak places. "That young fellow Kidd is a distinct acquisition."

Ursula said that she thought so, too. "And he'll help to eke out Mr. Lightfoot's weight," she reminded him.

"We may be able to pick up some other chap in Lightfoot's place," Winslow thought aloud. "Anyway, young Kidd's an acquisition. Can't think of him as going into business, though. He's such transparent paper himself." And, laughing, the two separated.

It was the next afternoon. The morning's trial had gone off well. They had driven out to Calice up on the Giovo Pass road, started their bob down the four mile long run, and wound up in fine fettle at Cacateia sixteen hundred feet below. The three new men had worked in well. Lightfoot, for once, had not been dreaming, and the timing had been satisfactory. Now Hugh was off on a small but very swift ice-run some distance from Vipiteno. He was feeling very fit. His knee was much better. The *Speedwell*—that was the name Ursula and he had chosen for his bob—was really going to be able to give a good account of itself.

The Brenner Pass was looking beautiful in his eyes as he laid himself down lovingly on his skeleton. He was glad that Ursula had persuaded him to try the place. She sketched well, and knew it of old, in summer time. He gave a tug to his gauntlets, grasped his front bar tightly, hugged his elbows, to which thick leather pads were strapped, to his side—a touch at full speed on the ice might draw blood—and let himself over the sheer drop of the little run holding on a second by the steel prongs fastened to the toes of his stout boots. It was only a short run, this, but a good one. That initial drop gave a pace which many a better run lacked. There was only one high corner to it, and that was the second one. He loved that one. With the ring of the steel runner like wine in his ears, the glorious upward rush—like nothing else—up—up—up in a swirl around the well-built curve of ice, then another swoop along the sinking run, another swirl or two, not nearly so good, and then the slowing down to a tame finish in a snowfield. It was not the Cresta, but it was fine while it lasted. He was on the rim of the curve lifting his machine with his light heart and the up-pull of his body. He might look like a fly on a wall, but he felt like air itself.

True and straight he lay on his machine. True and straight he took the curve. Even the downwards slither of his runners was "right" as he got into the straight again afterwards. At the end he got off with a sigh of satisfaction, whistled to the St. Bernard dog which "worked" this run, tied his toboggan to its collar, and with one hand on his back walked slowly up again. At the top would be sugar for the dog. He did not intend to go down again; he had some letters he must write. He stopped. Someone else was on the little run. How oddly, she was lying on her toboggan. Surely she didn't intend to go down even this short run like that? He called out a warning, but she was off over the drop. A cry reached him. It sounded like the cry of a shot rabbit. The toboggan was rocketing from side to side in a way that brought his heart into his mouth. Any good rider would go down that little run straight in the middle; but this girl—the light shone on her bright curls. Again a cry reached him, a cry of sheer terror, and then—what happened came in a flash. Off to one side of where the second curve in the run had been made ran a brick wall enclosing an orchard. Winslow had already told himself that to make the run absolutely foolproof the brick wall should be moved farther back just there, so that if any utter beginner, by some exceptionally bad work, were to be whirled over the edge, he might escape with only cuts and bruises. As it was, he stood clear of his own toboggan, and the dog waited. She had wobbled and rocked going down the first sheer drop, and wobbled up when making the curve, but now, like an arrow shot from a bow, she was flung over the rim and through the air on her steel toboggan straight for that brick wall. She was lying far forward on her toboggan. Her head would crash into those bricks. It was all a matter of a split second. Winslow did not think that he could save her, but he could not stand gaping and shuddering while a young girl was brained before his eyes. He jumped for her, and by a flying tackle, a miracle of young eyes, young muscle, and rugby football training, he caught her and came down heavily with her on the snow, while her toboggan whizzed by his ear so close that he felt the scorch of its rush. Then came a crash like thunder.

He struggled to his feet. He had come down under the girl, he knew, but she rolled away motionless with her little face almost as white as the snow it ploughed up. He snatched off her gloves and rubbed her hands. To his great relief a pair of deep-blue eyes opened wide. It had only been a faint.

"You saved my life! You saved my life! You saved my life!" she babbled. Then she stopped herself, and, to Winslow's horror, began to cry. That too she stopped almost at once, and then began to laugh. By this time she was standing, and he was knocking the hard lumps of snow from her white woollen breeches and jumper. She was like a little white teddy bear, he thought, as he finally got her free.

"It looked so easy—I watched you do it." Her breath still came in gasps. She had a common intonation, but she was exceedingly pretty. "I've never been on a toboggan before—"

"I guessed that," he said dryly, but looking down at her with genuine pity. It must have been a dreadful second, over that drop, down that glass-smooth narrow little run, up what would look to her like an impossible wall of ice. "Let's see what's become of your machine." The front bar was wrenched out of the true, one runner was bent, and a fine hole was knocked in the brick wall. She laughed a little shakily. "But for you, that hole would have been in my head, and my neck would have been like that bar there. I've never been on a toboggan before, and I damned never will be on one again!"

But Winslow would not hear of this. Having had a crash, she must get her nerve back again. He took her to the foot of the run. She had no spiked boots, but here they did not matter; the toboggan at best could only just move along, so slight was the slope. He lent her his. He showed her how to lie on it, how to hug it, how to lift it, how to touch one foot or the other to the ground to alter its course, how to "brake" with both feet, how to swing them high over her back when she wanted more speed. She did quite well. So well, that finally he asked her to try from the top again. She clung to his arm breathlessly in the bit of deep snow, and laughed up into his face, an adorable laugh, he thought it, with those big baby eyes.

"You can't go wrong," he assured her. "Hold your machine as you do now, and let the ice-run do the rest."

"I'll go down it," she said, tossing her head and setting her teeth rather grimly. "I'm no quitter. I came out to do it, and I'll do it!" She stretched herself as he had shown her, hugged the toboggan tightly and was off. She came through with flying colours, and gave a crow of triumph as he and the dog joined her at the foot.

"What made you try it all by yourself?" he asked as they started up the slope with the dog in front.

"I saw that girl who was talking to you men so hard last night at the hotel go off on one this morning. What one woman can do, I can!" The last came with quite a vicious snap.

"You mean—you're staying at our hotel, the Bar?"

"No. It's the Orso," she corrected, as though the other name had no meaning.

"Same place. One's the old Tirol name—German—the other's the Italian."

"But Bear's English," she protested. Evidently her education was not quite up to honours standard. He explained. She was not interested.

"Who is she?" she asked instead. "I mean that tall young lady with the black hair and sunburn?"

"She's my cousin. You might call us brother and sister." To think that he had not even noticed this charming little vision last night.

"You and Ursula will like each other. Are you with friends?"

To his surprise she said that she was out by herself.

"I sent my maid away at Paris," she explained very carefully. "Of course, I had to start off with her from Town, or people would have been no end surprised. I never stir without her, not really. But I felt that I wanted to be simple, and just—well—off on my own." She laughed. She had a common laugh, but she looked enchanting. They started back to Vipiteno in his sleigh, greatly pleased with each other. Then a dreadful thought occurred to him. Was she going to tell all the world of this adventure of theirs? Was he to be labelled here too as a lifesaver? For, as it happened, he had fished a very elderly lady out of the river on his last vacation, and the jokes on it, and her own overwhelming gratitude, had made him a marked man, and completely spoiled his holiday. This must not happen here. He said a few imploring words as to keeping her little accident to themselves. To his joy, he found her more than willing. She said frankly that if there was one thing which she did not care to be, it was a fool, and she had been one. And but for him a dead one. She would never forget it, she said, with a quick squeeze of the arm nearest her, but she saw no reason to boast of it. They dropped the subject by mutual consent then, with no faintest notion of the part the accident would play in the very near future.

Fay Starr—she told him her name, and they were Fay and Hugh at once—was a most amusing chatter-box, and for the rest, her prettiness and her youth, and the sunshine and his youth, made up the magic. Winslow felt more than ever certain that he was going to enjoy his stay. Fay was promptly introduced to the little circle, and Captain Kidd as promptly showed that he considered her a delightful addition. Lightfoot and Priestley also fluttered round the gay little candle. Moffatt, however, was not to be diverted from his talk with Ursula. It seemed to be a "case" there. Winslow wondered if it was just the usual winter-sports affair, or something deeper. Good old Ursula deserved the best of life, and so far, well, life had not offered her anything very wonderful. Or she had not taken it. Oddly enough, she and Fay quite definitely did not care for each other. And it was more Fay's doing than Ursula's. Winslow wondered at that. Fay had seemed such a charming little angel. Why this freezing hauteur towards the older woman?

CHAPTER TWO

A WEEK passed. The bob ran better and better as crew and machine grew more intimate. But Ursula and Fay did not get on the better for a longer acquaintance with each other. Quite the opposite. Hugh was surprised at the waspish temper that the pretty Fay showed whenever it was a question of his cousin. By herself, or with only other men present, Fay was the most amusing of kittens, but let Ursula be so much as spoken of, and she showed teeth and claws. At first the older woman took no notice, then she gave as good as she got, then she carried the war into the other girl's territory, and soon reduced Fay to impotent fury.

"She's always jumping on me anything I say at table d'hôte," complained Miss Starr to Hugh with a pitiful upward glance at him. "She makes me say stupid things from sheer nervousness, and then calls attention to them. Of course, I didn't listen to my governesses as much as I should have done—no one would, who had such a gay time at home as I've always had—but I don't see why she should try to make fun of me! And the questions she asks. I've always been taught that questions are rude. I was presented at the Drawing-room Court two years ago, when I came out, as I told you all, and she wanted to know, when I was talking to Captain Kidd about how, wonderful it all was, who presented me. As if I could remember in all that crush!" Winslow nearly swallowed his cigarette, his grin was so wide; but he only pressed her arm consolingly. "Never mind Ursula, except when she gives you tips on how to do things—"

"I can ski as well as she can—nearly."

This was not quite true, but Fay was proving unexpectedly good at all the sports she tried, obviously for the first time. The girl had no end of pluck and a good eye for speed and distances. "There's nothing she can do that I can't do," Fay now repeated hotly.

He laughed down at her. "Not always—any more than she can do what you seem to be able to do so easily."

"And what's that?" she asked.

"Make a fool of any man who looks at you." She laughed as though greatly pleased. "Ursula's not a bad sort," he wound up ill-advisedly.

"So Mr. Moffatt seems to think," said Fay meaningly.

"Well, why shouldn't he?" Hugh teased. He liked Moffatt better and better these days, and he rather hoped that he and Ursula were coming to mean something in each other's lives. Moffatt never seemed to be aware of Fay Starr's existence, except when he could not help himself, though the girl tried to attract his attention. As for Kidd, she seethed to have completely bowled him over, and Winslow was amused at what looked like streaks of real jealousy among the nonsense they all talked to and of each other. He considered Kidd a great addition to the party, and he did not intend losing sight of him after they left this place. That transparent paper of his really did sound a good thing. Being on the Stock Exchange, Winslow knew how often new patents made fortunes for the men who could handle them aright.

It was only Lightfoot whom he did not like any better now than at first, about whom there always seemed some odd little mystery. Winslow would find him now and then sitting in the *gaststube*—it still bore its German name— where usually only farmers and countrymen stepped in for a drink of Blumauer beer, or an *achtel* of the local wine, or a plate of *gulasch*, or a true Tiroler *knödel*. Deep in talk, Lightfoot would seem, his pointed nose almost in the other man's plate, or glass, and yet twice he had gone out of his way to mention having been at quite another locality, altogether during their evening chats. "In America, a short time ago, I should have taken him for a rum-runner," he said to Ursula.

"The proprietor here spoke tremendously highly of him when bringing him up to play with Brownie," she countered.

"He takes jolly good care to keep out of Lightfoot's way himself," Hugh pointed out, and Ursula had to agree, but then Mr. Lightfoot also appeared to avoid talking to the proprietor. In a little hotel hemmed in by snow there were hours when a chat in the big warm lounge and hall was almost unavoidable; but if the proprietor and Lightfoot were left together, they would fade away as though mutually anxious to be gone.

Hugh was staying till the week after the race. As for Moffatt, he intended being out here as long as Miss Winslow stayed. He did not flatter himself that she would promise to marry him after so brief an acquaintanceship, but he did hope to get on a footing which would ensure his continuing to see her in Town. Fay Starr had spoken of a fortnight. Captain Kidd would have to leave the day after the race; something had cropped up in connection with his paper patent which meant that he must rush back to England. Lightfoot, too, said that he was only remaining on until after the Cup race. But for his place on the *Speedwell*, no one would miss him. Now, Mr. Priestley, on the other hand, had become a sort of institution. He did not profess to care much for sports or bridge, but he was so kind, so helpful, so good a listener, so good a talker, too, that he was promptly put by Ursula and her cousin on their visiting lists. Ursula and Hugh had been of service to him, too. He had rooms in Pont Street which were suddenly to be cleared out to make way for an hotel. Ursula knew from Hugh that the suite above his own in Lowndes Square was vacant, knew that the service of the house and the house itself was all that could be desired, and she suggested to Mr. Priestley to get into touch with the lady—she was a lady—who lived in half the house and let the two top stories as two bachelor service-suites. Hugh's account of his rooms so charmed the older man that he exchanged letters with Mrs. Clarke, and finally gladly took on the empty top floor, sending a cable to the housekeeper of his present rooms to have his things shifted at once. Thanks to Hugh, he was even able to send written instructions as to how to place them, and he expressed himself as more than grateful to the Winslows for having saved him from the necessity of cutting short his holiday and looking up possible chambers. Hugh was not afraid of seeing too much of him. Priestley appeared to be a very busy man even here at Vipiteno. An honorary secretary of six charities, to each of whom he gave his services for one day in the week, was not likely to want to kill time by dropping in for fireside talks. His week-ends he generally spent at various hotels and spas lecturing for his protégés. Only once a year did he take a fortnight absolutely without thought of money, and that would soon be over. As Kidd was going back so shortly before the time when he himself must return, Priestley decided to travel with him as far as Dover. The others noticed that neither of the two men suggested that Lightfoot should join them. Evidently they, like the two Winslows, felt that something odd, peculiar, un-frank about the man.

Then came the day but one before the race. It would be closed the next day so as to give the workmen time to have it in perfect condition. Lightfoot spent the morning on the run, and, judging by Ursula's careful timing, they had a very good chance for the Cup. It was a wonderful day. The air was dry, the wind quiet, and the sun glittered along the snow-laden fir branches as though heaping up gold there, enough gold for all the poor of the whole world. The bobsleigh course was alive with running bobs, the crews yelling for sheer joy of living, flinging themselves right! left! almost out of their bobs, with hands flung out as though in greeting to some Hitler of the ice world. It was four glorious miles of rush and wind and roar of steel runners and yells of cheering crews.

"If you can do it like that day after to-morrow you should win," Ursula said, putting up her stopwatch. "It's your way of taking the banks low down that does it, Hugh."

"It's Kidd's splendid braking," Hugh said warmly. "He lifted the toboggan back into the straight more than once when we came out of a bend."

"It's Lightfoot's magnificent sweeps," Kidd laughed back. "Once he was hanging on by his boot spikes only; all the rest of him was extended on the ice bank. And as for Moffatt, the way he raced along beside the bob till the last fraction of a hemi-semi second and then got on straight was magnificent."

It had been a most difficult and very well-done performance, and all the crew said so.

"Hasn't anyone a kind word for me?" asked Priestley in a tearful tone. "Where would you be without my weight? It's my breathing that does the trick. I breathe in going up, and breathe out going down, and lift her along with me."

In high good humour they each of them began to brag of the part that some imaginary help which they had given had played in the good time they had made. Finally they hung on to the sleigh in which Ursula and Fay were sitting and drove back for a late lunch. After a short rest, Winslow took them on to Bressanone, where, quite outside the little town of steeples and priests and nuns, was a very swift bob run, with a couple of catchy banks rather after the battledore and shuttlecock style of the Cresta. Twice down the run and the training was over. They wound up with coffee at the small hotel close by. It was but half open, with one young man to act as receptionist, hall porter and cashier, and at the same time continue his own holiday hobby of photography. No one stayed at the hotel in the winter, and he was given his food and lodging in return for looking after the few servants and any stray visitors who might drop in. He was a pleasant young Swiss, delighted to discuss the superiority of his own country's sports with the *Speedwell* party. He came from Interlaken and, as it was near there that Ursula had learnt to ski, the two became quite friendly. He showed them some of his excellent photographs. They were to be exhibited, he hoped, at a coming photographers show at Interlaken. He was hard at work, as he talked, fixing some of them. Other strips of films hung around to dry like black and white Chinese street signs swinging in the breeze.

They finally left him to it, and tramped on to the farther end of the verandah. There they spent a restful three-quarters of an hour drinking cups of hot coffee topped with cream, and eating quantities of a cake ordered by Ursula, which she called *kaffekuchen* but which the one waitress corrected into *foccacia di café* with a faint titter, and strolling in and out and round the little inn. Afterwards came the usual discussion as to who should pay. Winslow insisted that as skipper it was his right. Moffatt told him that he was only the steerer, and far too unimportant to be allowed the privilege. Kidd claimed that as brake he was the one; Priestley laid pathetic weight on his age. Lightfoot had not offered to stand treat. He never had done so on any of their little outings. Just as he never had been seen to tip. He took up every centesimo of change, Hugh had already noticed. He sometimes wondered why the man stopped at what was the most expensive hotel in the town, for his clothes and his way of living, apart from that, suggested straitened means.

Just then Kidd had his way. They tossed for it. He and Moffatt against Priestley and Winslow. Kidd won the toss, and then he and Moffatt tossed again. It fell to Kidd to pay, and, laughing as always, he made for the door in the partition which divided off their end of the verandah from where the young Swiss was at work.

"He's not here now, but he's left some stamps out—" And Kidd strode over to the counter. Winslow, stepping out after him, saw him peer over, as though suddenly catching sight of something on the other side, saw him, with an exclamation, rush around the end, and then, Winslow following, saw him bending over a body sprawling on the floor.

"He's fainted! He's on the ground here," Kidd said. Moffatt had followed Winslow, and the three of them tried to raise the young Swiss in their arms. He was very heavy; and his face, when they caught sight of it—it had been turned away from them—was so dreadful, that Winslow, for one, nearly let him slide out of his grasp again. There was a suffocating smell, too; and something seemed spilt on the boards back here.

"Don't let the girls see him," Moffatt said at once. "He's dead. Where's the 'phone? What's the Italian for doctor—*medico* or *dottore*, isn't it?

The Boots passed just then, and came forward, at first from civility, and then with a gasp of horror. He took control. Lightfoot seemed to have been with him. At any rate he, too, was here now, peering down at the dead man, for on a gesture from the Boots the men had let the young Swiss gently down on to the floor again.

Moffatt was talking to the hotel man, neither Italian nor German came easily to him, and Winslow turned to Lightfoot, intending to suggest that he should do the explaining, he who seemed to speak all languages with ease. But Lightfoot was kneeling beside the Swiss, staring down at him with so concentrated an expression that Winslow felt sure he would not hear him, even if he called him by name. As he had turned he could have sworn that he saw Lightfoot do something too swift for the eye to follow with his hand. It looked as though he had picked something off the dead body and put it into his own pocket. As he did so his eyes met Winslow's, and for a long second Lightfoot stared into Hugh eyes with the most enigmatic expression, or lack of it. It was like meeting the stare of a cat. Then Lightfoot's face altered, he looked away and then back with an expression of shocked concern.

"How did it happen? Were you here when he—died?" he asked in a hushed voice, looking at the bottle which the Boots had picked up from beside the dead man.

Kidd, too, sniffed at it. "Surely that's spirits of salts," he said. "Hydrochloric acid? We use it for my transparent paper.

Priestley had now come out, and was adding his notes of shocked horror to the other sounds.

"Go back and keep the girls from coming out," Moffatt said urgently; but for once Mr. Priestley paid no heed.

"Is he dead? Dear, dear! A stroke of some kind, I suppose—though he seems so young. Heart failure, possibly?" He looked with an expression of deep pity on the blue, distorted face with the swollen mouth. Then he said, "We ought to send for a priest. If he's a Roman Catholic—"

"He's not," Lightfoot said almost absentmindedy. "But look here, you chaps, the Boots here says the police must be sent for. He'll wait till we're off the premises. Suppose we hurry. There's no use in being mixed up in this sort of thing. The sleigh's outside. He's had it brought round. What about getting off at once?"

Hugh thought that the sooner they started the better. The men could put it on the fact of having the two girls with them if comments were made on the heartlessness of the rush back to Vipiteno, and, as he said, when dealing with foreigners, the less one was mixed up in anything odd the better. And odd this death certainly was. Priestley said nothing, nor did Moffatt, but they were the first to hurry Miss Winslow and Fay into the sleigh. That done, the men jumped on the bob, grasped the towing rope, and were off. The crew was very silent, the two young women full of laughter and chatter.

"I hope it won't interfere with the race," Kidd said to Hugh, as they clambered stiffly off the bob at the shed where it was kept near the Bar Hotel.

Winslow hoped not, too. "We must be prepared for its doing so," Moffatt said gloomily, and for a lot of fuss and bother."

"Why that poor young fellow should have committed suicide just this afternoon!" Kidd went on, shaking his head. "If only he'd waited an hour."

The local paper which came out in the late afternoon was bought as soon as it appeared by the *Speedwell* crew. But there was no hint of the tragedy at the little hotel outside Bressanone in it. That was understandable, but Winslow was amazed when the next day the only mention of it was a short paragraph to the effect that a certain Fritz Seiler had been found dead, from a mistaken drink of some corrosive acid, it was feared.

There was no mention whatever of any visitors to the hotel at the time. On the contrary, everything suggested that there had been no guests there since midday.

Winslow was poring over it in the smoking-room with a dictionary to help him, when a hand touched his shoulder. It was Fay Starr, and the hand felt very cold and shaking.

"Is it true that something happened to the cashier at that place yesterday?" she asked under her breath, her eyes enormous. "To the cashier?" she repeated, as Winslow made no immediate answer. Lightfoot and Moffatt came on in after her.

"Yes, the poor fellow died in a fit," Lightfoot said, coming up to the table where Winslow had spread out the sheet paper. "Subject to them all his life, it says here."

"Did you know the man?" Moffatt asked her. "I thought you had never been to Switzerland, and it was his first trip away from his own country—"

"Oh, I've never been to Switzerland," she said hurriedly; her colour was back in her face again. "Of course I didn't know him. A cashier! But it seemed so ghastly. I didn't know that he was supposed to have died in a fit—"

"Apparently he had them constantly, poor chap," Lightfoot repeated, and Winslow admired his aplomb, and the way he tapped the newspaper as though to say that a long, detailed, medical report of the dead man's health lay there. Miss Starr could not read German or Italian. She gave a sigh of relief. "I'm superstitious; and it seemed unlucky for the race," she said, and left them.

Winslow thought it unexpectedly nice of Fay Starr to show so much feeling. He had had an idea, once or twice, that under all her pretty ways she was a hard little thing.

"It's a bit of a shock." Kidd had now joined the group, evidently sharing Winslow's feeling about Miss Starr's words. "She had been buying postcards off the poor fellow just a few minutes before. Does it say why he did it?

"It says he was engaged," Moffatt said dryly, "but that was a distinctly good idea of yours, Lightfoot." And he passed it on to Kidd, who also approved of it unconditionally.

"You were buying something from him, too, weren't you?" he said, turning to the originator of the Bright Idea. Lightfoot made no reply, but his eyes, as he turned and left the room, shone for a moment in the sunlight, and to Winslow's surprise they were bright red—a real suffused crimson.

Now Winslow's uncle had once been forced down in a 'plane near the Arabian Gulf close to Rub-el-kali, the great desert, and he used to tell how the tribesmen's most flattering term to a man out there was "*O, red of eye*" as a preface to a request, or some further piece of adulation. They used it as equivalent to "*O fearless one.*" Was it a mark of courage? Was Lightfoot then a courageous man? Oddly enough, the other day when they had all had a rusty spill into a snow bank—and death in a snow-bank is a matter of split seconds if you cannot get your mouth or nose up—Lightfoot had not turned a hair. Winslow wondered whether there might not be unexpected qualities hidden underneath the tall thin man's dreamy manner. And then, immediately on that, came another of those odd, disturbing little occurrences which seemed to mark his acquaintanceship with Lightfoot. He went up to his room for a pipe which he had left in a pocket, and, passing through the lounge, saw Miss Fay Starr standing by a table writing an address on an envelope. At the same moment Lightfoot came out, did not see Winslow, who was in the shadow, and passed close to Miss Starr, looking over her shoulder at the envelope as he did so. She turned in a flash. Turned with something white and tense in her face. Lightfoot smiled pleasantly at her. "Sorry I startled you. I was looking to see whether by any chance I left my fountain pen here just now. It's of no value except a sentimental one."

"Surely that's the only value that matters," she said smartly, leaving her envelope lying out as she looked about her. Winslow went on up. Lightfoot's explanation made his odd action quite simple. And yet—as he put his pipe in his pocket, Winslow suddenly remembered that Lightfoot's feet had made no sound whatever on the hardwood floor. A shadow could not have moved more silently. Coming down again through the lounge, Hugh saw Lightfoot alone, looking up some trains. The other members of the crew had drifted out and were chatting together, still with the newspaper in their hands. The hotel proprietor passed out from his room, made as though to join the little group, caught sight of Lightfoot, and, after a second's hesitation, merely gave the stiff formal bow which was his, and passed on. But Kidd called to him, "Signore! Have you heard about the death of the young Swiss at the Stella d'Oro? Was it a fit?"

"A fit?" The man seemed to hesitate. He was a tall, wooden-faced, thin German, with something tired and exhausted looking in his features. It was the type of face that, before the War, was rarely seen out of Russia—the face of a man who lived among enemies, who had learnt to watch his very looks as well as his words. He spoke good English, rather a rare accomplishment in the Tirol, but he had taken honours in modern languages at Vienna. "I do not know," he said now gravely, and added hurriedly, "I hear my telephone ringing. Excuse me, pray, gentlemen."

Lightfoot joined the others. "I only spoke of fits to keep Miss Starr from feeling it too much, but it says here in the paper"—he pointed to a back paragraph—"that he died from hydrochloric acid poison. We smelt spirits of salts, you remember; and that bottle beside him—" Taking the paper again, Lightfoot read in a low tone, translating as he read, "The latest information we have about the unfortunate young Swiss at the Stella d'Oro at Bressanone is that he must have made a mistake in the bottles about him, one of which contained distilled water. He evidently intended to drink from it, and took instead a fatal draught of poison. The bottle, with the stopper out, lay on the floor, too."

"Nasty way of ending up," Moffatt said. "Could anyone make such a mistake?" Kidd asked doubtfully.

"Pitiful story!" Priestley shook his head. "Hydrochloric acid must burn frightfully. Terrible end!"

"I wonder he didn't cry out," Kidd persisted.

"Probably had no voice with which to cry," Winslow said to that. "Ghastly." He was anything but superstitious, yet he felt an odd, new sense of something dreadful hovering over him. It was as he stood there in the bright clear lounge as though grey fog filled the room, chilling him to the bone. He told himself that it was ridiculous to feel like this because of the death of a stranger, however tragic the death was, but the odd thing about his feeling was that it did not seem to concern the past, but the present —the future.

"Does he leave a family?" Moffatt asked. "Frightful shock for them."

"It says that he was engaged to a young Brixen lady, was greatly liked in the little town on his own account, and was the only son of Friederich Seiler, the much respected head cashier of the Bankverein at Interlaken." Lightfoot folded the paper and put it away in his pocket.

"Odd that there's no mention of us in all this," Winslow said, feeling that perhaps speech would lift from him this sensation of not having any concern in the talk about him. It was ridiculous that he, who was racing for the Giovo Pass Cup to-morrow, should feel as though all this were but a dream, from which he was about to wake to something that would be—what this was not—real and important. He shook himself quite visibly, and to his relief the feeling left him as suddenly as it had enveloped him. "I'm thankful for the silence about it," he went on.

"We all are!" threw in Moffatt.

"But it's so different from the way we do things," finished Priestley.

"Don't crow too soon," Moffatt warned them. "We may hear enough, and to spare, about it yet!"

But the next day came the notice of the funeral and further words of sympathy to the family and the young man's fiancée, and a general unmistakable tone of the matter being finished. And from first to last not a word about the bob, and the sleigh, and the party having coffee on the verandah. That meant that the Boots, and the waitress and the sleigh driver had all of them said nothing. Odd, Winslow thought. Was someone seeing to it that there should be silence about them? If so, who, and why? It was lucky, but most inexplicable.

CHAPTER THREE

"YOUR cousin and the Starr child seem very much taken with one another," Moffatt said to Ursula late that same afternoon.

"Just a winter resort case," she replied. "Luckily. The uncles are as old-fashioned as hansom cabs, and they would have seven fits, one for each day of the week, if it were anything serious."

"I hope they don't feel like that about you, too," he said rather awkwardly.

"They wouldn't like me to be engaged to Fay Starr," she replied with a heightened colour, but an attempt at a joke.

"Would they object to your engagement on principle? I mean, do they want you both to keep single and dance attendance on them?"

She laughed outright this time. "I spend a weekend now and then with them. I'm devoted to them, and they're fond of me, but as to expecting me not to marry on their account! The last thing they want is a woman, young or old, about the place. They live for the Works. There's a special way into their offices from their rooms, and they move in and out like nice, dear automata. Hugh couldn't stand the life. He tried it for a year and gave it up. I run down to see them constantly, as I say, but—well, we have very little in common. But I do hope Hugh won't lose his head."

"A man has to lose his heart first," Moffatt said to that, "and, personally, I don't think he has lost either of them."

And Moffatt was right. Winslow had not. He was as certain as Ursula what the uncles would say to Fay Starr, and he had no intention of letting it come to that. She was a most enchantingly pretty creature to look at, and flirt with, but as for anything serious—he never contemplated it. Nor, he was certain of it, did she. Now Kidd talked as though he really were in love with her. He was jealous, too, though, being such a good-natured lad, Winslow thought his jealousy only amusing.

Came the day of the Giovo race. A perfect day. No wind; sparkling sun; glittering snow. Each breath one drew a gift from God, as it were, divine, quite unlike the breath you had drawn before, and the next breath waiting for you to take. The *Speedwell* had been sandpapered and oiled until she shone like silver. The crew in their white woollies and broad blue sashes across their breasts looked very smart. They drew the fifth place. An Italian team, the *Risorgimento*, had unenviable first place, first after the official bob which would declare the track open and the tapes in perfect order. Italian officers helped with the arrangements at the starting-point. Winslow had no idea there were so many up here. The people all around had turned out, too. Dark, very plainly-dressed, stoutish women, and sturdy men. They seemed a race apart from the nervous, slender Italian women, wives and daughters of the equally slender and tall Italian officers. The two groups did not mix. Winslow saw that there was some sort of disturbance among the people of the place—the Tiroler, as he called them still. They seemed deeply stirred about something, and something that angered them, he thought. Sullen and resentful were the faces of many of them, and then, after a while, he found these same people making preparations to drive home again.

He was notified by a pleasant, smiling young Italian Master of Ceremonies that the *Speedwell* had been moved forward to the fourth, instead of the fifth, place. Winslow was not pleased. Every bob ahead meant smoother ruts in which to run. He asked the reason for the change.

"The bob ahead has scratched, or been scratched." Lightfoot, standing by, translated the swift reply, swift, and yet rather ill at ease, Winslow thought.

"What happened?" he asked, studying his card. The bob ahead had been a Munich bob, a crack team, the *Edelweiss*.

Lightfoot said that he did not know. Some accident to the bob, he understood.

Winslow wondered if the anger that he had felt among the people around could be connected with this scratching. Certainly the crowd of onlookers here at the starting-point was large enough, but not so large as it had been. Perhaps they thought that the rules had been over-strictly enforced. But, except that ventre-a-terre racing was forbidden, as it is everywhere except at St. Moritz, there were practically no rules. The Coppa this year was for a five-crew bob, but whether it was wood, or iron, like the *Speedwell*, rope steered or wheel, was left free. He wondered if the people around bet much on the race. Lightfoot shook his head. No, the Tiroler wasn't a betting man as a rule, and his wife didn't have enough money allowed her to waste it.

Winslow dismissed the whole little affair. The second bob was the *Swastika*, also a Munich crew.

The time drew near. The hour arrived. The wooden barriers were moved aside. The official bob swept down, an Italian bob, to open the course. A telephone message came up to say that all was in order. The Italians had decided on a standing start. Evidently they had not had time to practise together. With what looked like twice the ordinary number of legs, they pushed her over the brink, broke the tape, and with a wild yell were off. Three seconds to wait and the second bob started, then the third, an Austrian bob. The *Speedwell* now moved into place. Helmets on, steel-knuckled gauntlets on, thick elbow and knee pads on, Winslow and Priestley took their places. Lightfoot, Moffatt and Kidd would stay off the bob till the last second, running beside her and flinging themselves on with careful timing, a much more difficult feat than it sounds.

The signal came, Winslow and Priestley scraped her over the edge, the three running members of the crew worked to perfection. The flying start was a success. They flew down the first sweep with a glorious feeling of ice and sun and good fellowship and racing blood. On they went, Winslow restraining his love of taking his banks high, for every inch of ice run meant a fraction of time between tape and tape. About half-way down, as they swung out of the first part of a difficult hairpin bend, they came on an overturned bob; the Viennese one, the third of the race, had come to grief. Snow-wreathed forms were trying to right her, but two men lay out on the ice run in the very centre of the track.

Should he keep on straight, and chance just missing those prostrate figures? Winslow knew that he ought to miss them by nearly three inches. If he swerved it would set the *Speedwell* wrong for the back end of the loop, though Kidd might be able to straighten them out. He glanced over his shoulder.

"Straight!" yelled Moffatt.

"On!" yelled Lightfoot. "On! Don't swerve!"

"You'll clear 'em!" roared Moffatt. But the weight of the bob altered. Far out over the side Priestley and Kidd were straining, and their shifted weight slewed the bob to one side. Winslow's steering followed the swerve. After all, it would be a close pass, and the men might wriggle. Three inches between steel runners and a man's head. . . . There was a hail of ice splinters and the sound of runners slithering. It was a nasty skid, but they straightened, and Winslow set himself to make up the lost time and to get back into the middle of the run.

"That's done us!" yelled Moffatt. "You've lost us the race, you fools!"

"On!" came from Lightfoot as though in a sort of ecstasy, "straight on!"

The corner was taken none too well. The bob was now in the centre again, but that gathered accumulated speed, the speed of an arrow, which only comes from straight all the way, was gone, and nothing would make up for it, Winslow feared. They were bumping and rocketing now. But he told himself there was nothing you couldn't get back by sweating for it. And the crew sweated. Like madmen they yelled and pulled, and swung her round the curves, lifting her by will-power as much as by muscular effort.

"Right . . . Back!" came Winslow's call; and out to the right and then back to the centre the crew fell and rose as one body. Even he swayed a little to the direction. He took every risk. "*Left! Right! Left!*" came more than once without a pause to straighten in between. He felt that he had to justify himself in the eyes of Moffatt and, oddly enough, of Lightfoot.

"Brake!" yelled the watchers at the bends, "brake!" For braking is allowed on the Giovo Pass run; no sawdust is put at the bends to slow up the bobs. Kidd did not touch his brakes. Not a man touched foot to the ice. It looked as though the lot of them must fly off the course altogether in one wild leap towards the sky, and the crash altogether into the snow. But not a man braked. A touch of the steel of their gauntlets, but no one braked. Priestley tried it lower down at a really awesome bank, but Moffatt behind him jerked his legs up and he did not try again. Like a force of nature, they swooped down and up and flew along and round after round of clapping and bravos as they broke the thread at the end of the course greeted them. They had broken the record for the ice run. They were one mass of frozen snow, but they clumped happily to the recording instrument. They had beaten the *Risorgimento* and the *Swastika* handsomely; and the people congratulated them warmly. A German bob came next. Midway down they beat the record of the *Speedwell*.

"You lost us the race there!" Moffatt declared harshly when the good figures that the Germans were making came through.

"It doesn't do to think of anything but one's objective," Lightfoot declared, like a master instructing a little boy.

"Once you begin to sympathise with the obstacles, you're done."

Winslow said nothing. He felt sore enough about it, and yet three inches was too little; he knew that now in cold blood.

A little later, and the German bob ceased to be a peril. Their total time was nearly half a second longer. Once again, and by a Kitzbuhl bob, they were nearly beaten, but once again their figures lengthened towards the close, and the *Speedwell's* were not reached. And when all were in, they knew that they had won the Coppa for this year, and their hearts rejoiced with that joy of primitive man in a combat, not against his fellow men half as much as against nature as well. Against the ice on the ground, the wind of the sky, the inanimate steel of the machine, the will of man had triumphed and won out. And the victory pleased everybody. The Tirolese would not have welcomed an Italian win. The Italians would not have cared to see Germans, let alone Austrians, win, but the *Speedwell*, innocent of political tinge as her pretty name, passing away like the flower, and leaving no traces behind her in the place, had no enemies.

In the evening the Coppa dinner was given by the winners to the crews of the other competing bobs who could be present. Some had gone back, or on to other runs.

The big dining-room was all lit up. The dinner was long and rich. Ursula had once said to an American tourist that the scenery around them was heavenly, and he had agreed, adding after a pause with a sigh, "But the cooking's devilish." Winslow rather agreed with them, but they can make one good soup, liver-dumpling soup which would tempt an anchorite on a fast day. And for a sweet they had mounds of sieved chestnuts, powdered chocolate and whipped cream, into which the women waded. Zabaglione followed, which tasted all right to the English people, but at which the Italian officers raised their eyebrows in private. They were handsome fellows, these officers, Winslow thought, but then he liked their race. They kept rather to themselves, until Ursula and Lightfoot thawed them by their knowledge of their tongue. Fay Starr won them merely by her looks. What there was of her evening frock was shining gold, and her bright face and hair seemed to flame out of it. Moffatt devoted himself entirely to Ursula, who, in her deep-blue frock with an amber band on her dark hair, looked very well. The *Speedwell* was toasted amid general acclamations. The host himself, as well as the head waiter, drank it. Winslow had to reply. He promised to come back and run her again. Promised to return every year and race. Promised to come out in the summer. Promised . . . Ursula pulled him down amid general laughter.

It was a sort of farewell banquet, too, to the three men who were leaving so shortly. When coffee was served, Moffatt said to Winslow, looking across the room, "I'm rather surprised that Kidd is actually leaving—and leaving Miss Starr. Somehow, I thought—eh?"

"I don't suppose it's a life-long separation," Winslow said solemnly. "Kidd does occasionally come up to Town. To attend church, Priestley would say. But he might manage to get a glimpse of Miss Starr as well You're staying on, aren't you?

"Yes. It's too good to leave," Moffatt said; and he gave Winslow a direct look, and a smile that the other liked.

"I quite agree with you," Winslow said promptly. "You have my best wishes, if they're any good to you."

The party broke up early. Drives through the snow at night are not particularly pleasant. Lightfoot excused himself before the others had gone, saying that, as he was leaving by the night express, he had some final packing to do.

Winslow was in his room changing into easier slippers when the door opened without any semblance of a knock. Lightfoot came in. He came so close that Winslow had to move his foot, or it looked as though the other would step on it.

"Look here," Lightfoot said in a low, hurried voice, "I wonder if you'll do me a small favour, Winslow?"

Winslow could not refuse anyone to-night. He asked what was wanted.

"I've got an envelope here which should be handed over, and I haven't time to deliver it myself. It's a small collection some people I know have made for the local Guides' Orphanage. I offered to hand it over, and, what with one thing and another today, I've completely forgotten it."

"Of course I'll pass it on," Winslow said promptly. He thought it very decent of Lightfoot to care for the kids, and said so. "What do I do?"

"Just go to the post office, ask for the postmaster; his name is Weiss, now Blanco, of course. Ask for him personally. There's some local feeling about the orphanage, especially among the Italians. They want a higher percentage of Italian children taken, I believe. So if anyone's around just ask Signor Blanco for a personal interview about a guide you want for some skiing, and hand him this envelope when you're alone. The postbags were opened last time and it's as well to be careful."

Winslow set out at once. The post office, the usual ugly building all the world over, was not far. He asked for the postmaster of the only man still on duty. The man said that he was Signor Blanco. Winslow handed over his envelope, was taken into an inner, room, and there it was opened. Somewhat to his surprise, Winslow saw a wad of big notes, English bank-notes among them. The postmaster took a paper, wrote a receipt and handed it over with a hearty *Vergelt's Gott*, for Winslow had added a note of his own to the pile.

On the way back, Winslow saw a little figure ahead of him just stepping out of one of the hotels.

She walked fast, stamping through Vipiteno's one and only broad street as though treading something down into the crunching snow. Her hair was bare, the snow powdering it in a charming way. It was Fay Starr. He touched her on the arm as he overtook her silently in his rubber overshoes. She turned on him and swore at him. Then, seeing his startled face, she explained that some man, a stranger, an Italian, she thought, "Dago anyway," had taken to following her about lately, and she was tired of it.

Winslow fell into step beside her, tucked her arm in his, and began to talk about the dinner party, but her words had shocked him profoundly. The girl must come from the lowest classes to have such language at her tongue's end—and the devil's own temper! She seemed to read his thoughts, for she looked up at him in her most enticing way.

"You aren't shocked because I swore just now, are you? I learnt it from our groom at home. He's a dear old man, but he does use dreadful language; and when I was little my nurse, who afterwards married him, used to always take me down to the stables when I was supposed to be out in the park. When I'm angry those old words seem to rise up without my thinking—just like tears when you cry. And of course I was angry at being spoken to in the street—by a perfect stranger, as I thought."

He nodded and talked again of the dinner and the race. Her explanation was on a par with her references to her mother's diamonds, and the family mansion in Park Lane, and her own two Rolls-Royces. What a girl of her intonation was doing in such exalted spheres was a bit puzzling. She said that she hunted, too, and got frightfully out of her depths when Ursula at first innocently put her through her paces.

"Poor little kid," Winslow thought; "she probably comes from some shopkeeper's comfortable home, and has come out here to make smart friends. It was a pity that she had been so rude to Ursula; who could have helped her socially a good deal." Privately, Hugh thought her open dislike of his cousin rather flattering, and rather comic at the same time. Now and again he would catch her watching Ursula with a look of real fury in her blue eyes which made them look more like an ugly doll's than a pretty baby's. As for himself, he thought that she flirted with him more to vex Ursula than from any real attraction to him. There was a stone-wall end to her flirtation, he had found.

Her eyes and her smile might lead you on, but it would be up the garden path.

Back at the hotel, he found that Lightfoot had already left, but there was a note from him, saying that in case Winslow was not back before Lightfoot's train had gone, would he post him the receipt—followed the number of a house off Cromwell Road.

Winslow posted the receipt promptly, and thought no more of the matter for the moment.

Two days later he got a cable from his partner.

Could he come back as soon as possible? The partner's father had had a stroke, and he wanted to be free to rush off to him in the north of England.

Winslow cabled back that he would start by the next morning's Dolomite Express and be in Town the following evening, and at the office by half-past nine the next morning. This was the best that he could do, as no other train left Vipiteno any earlier.

He wished the cable, if it had to come, could have reached him the day before, when he could have had Priestley and Kidd as fellow travellers. Winslow explained matters to the head waiter, asked for his bill, and, after settling it, decided to see if he could change a twenty-pound note for four flyers.

Kidd and Priestley had each paid in English notes, he knew, and it ought to be quite easy to oblige him. The cashier unlocked the safe, and took out quite a little wad of English notes. Stripping off the top four, he handed them over.

"Dear me, what wealth!" said a light voice behind him. Miss Starr was looking beyond Winslow into the big safe.

The proprietor made some dismal—and truthful—remark about Italian taxes. Fay wheeled sharply. Winslow had moved off down the corridor beside them, as though she were invisible. She caught him up at once. "What's wrong? What have I done now?" she asked, smiling confidently and coquettishly at him. "I only went to the station because—" She stopped her sentence. She stopped her smile. "What's wrong?" she repeated in a very different tone.

"Come in here!" was Winslow's reply, opening the first door beside them at random. It was a rarely-used writing-room. He closed the door. His face was very pale under its new tan. Fay now saw that he still held the notes in one hand. He held them out to her.

"Look at these! Do they seem all right to you?"

"Why, of course!" She took each of them in turn, holding it to the light and feeling it.

"These three are forgeries," he said. "That one's all right."

"Forged!" she repeated. "You mean—they're no good? Fakes?"

"Just exactly what I do mean. They're good imitations. Would probably deceive ninety-nine out of a hundred."

"Oh! They changed some money for me only last week. How about these?" She rummaged in her bag and produced a handful of Italian notes. Winslow shook his head. He could not help her when it was a question of Italian notes. But his uncles were the makers of the paper used by the Bank of England for their notes. He had worked a year in their factory. He knew the right from the wrong stuff at a touch—by a sort of instinct. He stood silent a moment. Reaction had come. He deeply regretted his outburst and his words to her—the first person to meet him while still under the shock of the discovery. This was far too serious a matter to be babbled about.

"I don't believe you're right!" she said again, looking first at one note and then at the others. "They're all just the same."

He said nothing, and went back to the proprietor. He stepped with him into his private room.

"Look here," he began. He had decided to say nothing here, but to wait till he got home and let the Bank handle matters. He felt himself on too dangerous ground to care to take even a step alone. "We like our notes signed by each person who passes them on. Whom did you get these from?"

"Impossible to say with certainty." The man was amused. "But they all came from you gentlemen, and ladies staying here."

"You mean Captain Kidd and Mr. Priestley?"

"And you yourself, Mr. Winslow, you too pay in English notes. So does your cousin and Milady Brown. So does Miss Starr. Look, this note here with the tear in it is one she paid in this morning. I took it myself, and tore it in squeezing it into the rubber band. And this one with the dirty finger mark on it, Mr. Lightfoot paid that. These others I can't tell apart."

"You're certain that he handed in this one, and Miss Starr this one?" Winslow laid the two notes in question on one side.

"I am. Ah, there is Miss Starr!"

Through the glass upper part, Winslow saw that Fay was standing just outside the door, very close and still. Oddly enough, something in her attitude suggested Lightfoot's when he had stood behind her peering over her shoulder—for his fountain pen, he had said. And it suggested something else—also connected with Lightfoot. He had it! Lightfoot in the lounge of the little hotel at Brixen staring down at the dead young Swiss behind the counter.

"Then she at least can initial hers." He spoke lightly as he beckoned Fay back again into the little writing-room, still empty.

"The proprietor says you handed him in this note this morning," he began, holding it out. "I haven't said a word to him about any of them being forgeries, of course; nor must you! Remember! But, now, try to think where you got this."

"That's not the note I paid with," she said promptly. "Mine had a—"

"It's your perfume," he said, sniffing at it. "No one else uses your stuff."

Personally he disliked the smell, but he knew from her many references to it that it was exceedingly expensive, and therefore, to her ideas, very exclusive.

She pressed her nose to the note. She had a very pretty, rather imperious little nose, and nodded rather sullenly.

"Well, what of it?" she snapped. "If I was taken in, like you were, what of it?"

"My dear girl, I'm not blaming you," he almost laughed at her anger; "but try to recall where you changed it—whether at the bank, or in the hotel here, or—"

"I know!" she interrupted, "I got it changed by that poor young man who drank from the wrong bottle. The one in that place with the name that always recalls Brixton to me."

Winslow was startled.

"Brixen! You're sure? Though this is just between ourselves, one has to be very exact in these things."

"Of course I remember! I bought a painting of one of the castles, a pretty little thing, made me think of my own old home—the Park, you know. It was frightfully dear. I paid with a note, and said I'd like half in English money. He had just got this one from Mr. Lightfoot. He's the one to question, not me. Though I can't think why you bother. It's nothing to do with you. Or is it?"

She stared almost fiercely at him. He did not notice it.

Lightfoot. . . . The other bad note with the dirty smudge on it came from him. Lightfoot, of the odd, furtive ways, the many meetings in little obscure places where money so often seemed to change hands. He felt very much tempted to question Fay about the cashier at Brixen, or Bressanone, as he generally called it, but he did not want to rouse her curiosity still further about the notes. This news that she had changed a note there— there where the young Swiss had been found dead in such dreadful circumstances—Winslow resolutely put behind him all speculations as to whether there could be any connection between the forgeries and that death. He could not spare the time to start on that inquiry. He must get back as quickly as possible and put the matter into competent hands. The rest of the day Fay was very distraite though she tried to appear as gay and lighthearted as usual. Winslow was both touched and a little annoyed at the way she took the fact that he was leaving. She surely could not have mistaken his quite evidently casual attentions for anything deeper? He liked her; he would not hurt her or any woman's feelings, for that matter. Winslow never spent a more uncomfortable day. Ursula and Moffatt were off with some acquaintances from the hotel on a skiing expedition which would bring them back, if on time, early next morning. He hoped to see them before he left, but, in any case, he had no intention of telling them about the notes. Not unless he found that they, too, were the owners of any of the forgeries on which he had stumbled so unexpectedly. The one chance of locating the forger was to let him think that his work had not yet been detected, lull himself perhaps in the idea that it was undetectable.

CHAPTER FOUR

WINSLOW had dreaded saying good-bye to Fay, so, under the plea of perhaps missing her next morning, he decided to get it over that same night.

She surprised him by the calm with which she parted from him. His rather vaguely-expressed determination to see a lot of her in Town was met with still vaguer murmurs of, "Yes, it would be nice."

Winslow felt vexed with her.

Early next morning, as he was shaving, a knock came on his door. He hoped it was Moffatt, for whom he had left an urgent message. But in answer to his "*Entri!*" Ursula came in.

"I hear you're going home," she said. "Is anything wrong?"

He explained. "And incidentally I shan't be sorry to get some new treatment for my knee; it's rather tiresome since the race."

"I'm sorry to hear that, Hugh," she said, perching herself on the table, "and is the Starr girl part of the new treatment? "

"Starr girl?" came frothily from Winslow.

"She has settled her bill, and is arranging for her luggage to be taken over, ready for the Dolomite Express. I saw it placed by the lift as I came in. Such luggage! The cook would be ashamed of it. Look here, Hugh, don't let her go home with you."

"Business of yours?" he asked with a cold glance at her over his white-flecked cheek.

"None, I know. In one way. But—it's not interference, Hugh, it's—I don't know what to call it—a certainty that you'll be sorry for it, if you let her into your life." She spoke gently.

"Excuse my foaming at the mouth," he said, wiping his lips,"' but it's to her that you ought to talk like that, not to me." He grinned.

She waved a careless hand. "That's not what I'm thinking of. No, I'm half-minded to come, too."

"And leave Moffatt?"

She blushed, a real blush that made her look years younger.

"You have changed already under her detestable influence," she said warmly.

"You two girls do love each other!" He folded away his shaving tackle and dropped it in a bag.

"She's definitely a liar," Ursula retorted.

"Granted. But you might be, too, if you hadn't a couple of thousand a year of your own. Nothing to make you have to lie. Fay has had a hard fight for existence, or I'm much mistaken. Personally, I always feel flattered and touched when people take the trouble to lie to me. Shows how much they value my good opinion."

Ursula made a face at him.

"As long as you don't think she's in love with you, you may come through all right; for she's not. You do know that, don't you?

He did, since last night. And, anyway, that was the last thing that he wanted. But he did not care for Ursula to be so certain on the point. He turned her out of his room with cousinly lack of ceremony, on the plea of wanting to finish his dressing. Downstairs, he looked sharply about him, and did not know whether he was glad or not when he could see nothing of a slim little figure.

Lady Browne rather bewildered him by saying, "I ought to be vexed with you for stealing my pal from me. But it's only for a short time. I'm going back myself next week. Three hearts, partner," and she touched her heart while holding up three fingers. He understood what she meant when at the station he found Ursula and Moffatt watching their luggage being hauled along by two maids and a Boots.

"I decided I should be lonely without you, Hugh," Ursula said, looking around her. "Where's the Starr? Isn't she here?"

Winslow shook his head. "For once, Miss Marple, you were mistaken!"

"Oh, well—anyway, I wanted to come home. And it's nice being able to travel with you. Lucy Browne is a darling, but I do get so tired of playing double dummy. Besides—" She hesitated and flushed. "I wouldn't tell you this morning, but—" She actually dimpled.

Moffatt strode up just then. He drew Winslow on one side. "I hope you don't mind my coming back, too; but I— well, we settled it yesterday on the Schlern. She's wonderful!" The two men shook hands.

Hugh told the other that he was getting the best girl in the world, and Moffatt said he knew that. "That's why I'm not letting her out of my sight," he went on a trifle awkwardly. "I don't often make hasty decisions, but when she said she wanted to go back with you—I think she's afraid you may find it hard to shake off a certain young lady. Why, well—" Moffatt finished with the effect of a shrug. "The place wouldn't be the same without her," he finished.

Hugh was delighted that he was coming, and said so. Just now he wanted to be alone, and since Ursula was coming, too, he was thankful that she would be taken off his hands. He wanted all the time that the journey would give him to turn things over. He had not yet made up his mind just what to do, or rather, he had not yet settled on the right sequence. Scotland Yard? The Bank of England? His uncles? The latter were clearly indicated, of course. The question was, should he tell them the facts at once, or when there was more chance of finding out who the forger was? It was not their paper that had been used. In a way, that suggested the Yard or the Bank, but, when Hugh had left his uncles, it had been partly because of a difference of opinion over an action of his which they had considered foolish. Time had softened the feelings on both sides, but Hugh had not forgotten the mistaken judgment on his powers. He would show them how he, by his own brains and deductive work, had found out the provenance of those forged notes.

"I wonder if you could change me a twenty-pound note into four fivers," he asked as they stood alone in the little waiting-room. Each promptly produced a note-case. Ursula had three five-pound notes, Moffatt only one. They were all genuine, and finding that out, Winslow changed his mind, decided that he would rather keep his one note after all, and not risk incommoding them.

He decided to send a cable to his partner, telling him that he was actually starting. Turning away from the telephone table, he almost ran into Fay Starr in a wonderful geranium-coloured tweed with a collar of natural fox.

"I've got to return home, too," she said without any flirtatious glances up at him. She spoke almost crossly.

"Too bad, when I'm enjoying myself so much! That Count Jacky—I call him that because I can't remember these Italian names—is a dear, and quite devoted. Much more so than you ever were! But I, too, have had a wire, and I can't stay out here any longer. It's most annoying; but, there, what has to be has, to be!"

Her manner, her indifferent eye, calmed his first feeling of intense vexation. For it was, as Ursula had once said, one thing to flirt with Fay out here, another to be landed with her in Town. He fancied that she had few friends of a class with which she cared to associate nowadays.

"Going home to your people?" he asked conversationally.

"Yes," she said to that. "I'm thankful you're coming home at the same time. I hate travelling by myself. It was a mistake, not bringing my maid Antoinette—" They were in the common waiting-room now, and she shot a defiant, yet uneasy, glance at Ursula and Moffatt by the fire.

Ursula met her very blandly. But there was a derisive twinkle in her eye and curl to her lip. For a moment Hugh thought that Fay Starr was half minded to throw up her return-journey project and go by another day's train; go by herself; he read it in her face. So it was genuine, that recall to England. But, after a second's struggle, Fay seemed to decide to leave things as they were. She turned to Moffatt with a smile. He did not smile back. He stared at her in almost visible disapproval.

"I had no idea that we were going back four strong—" he began with his most superior air.

"No, I expected to be quite alone with Hugh," Fay said sweetly, and Hugh grinned. Ursula refused to reply in words; and Moffatt, after some palpably untrue remarks about the more the merrier, went off to see to some papers.

"I thought you were off skiing with Count Giacomo," Ursula said at last to fill in a rather tiresome silence.

"I had no idea I should have to go home!" Fay replied, and something angry showed in her blue eyes. "But if people make fools of themselves, someone has to help them out." With which oracular statement she began to jot down her expenses in her little travelling note-book.

The journey was not a happy one for Winslow. Ordinarily a young man and a pretty girl do not bore each other, however brainless either, or both, are. But this was not an ordinary occasion, for Winslow just now was not—mentally speaking—a young man, but a hunter starting out on a hunt. He had only the top surface of his mind free with which to talk to his companions, or rather to hear them talk. During the day, he and Fay were left to themselves, the train was almost empty, and Ursula and Moffatt made themselves comfortable in another carriage; and Fay, too, was not herself. The Starr did not shine at

all brightly. She was distinctly peevish. She more than
once hinted that she was giving up a great deal for his,
Winslow's, sake, that she had counted on at least another
fortnight of her delightful holiday. Not that she said this
plainly, but it ran as an undercurrent very close below
the surface at times. And she asked him about the forged
notes with a veiled persistence that startled him.
Something deep inside him rang a cold clear note of
warning when she returned to the subject over and over
again. He began to think over the whole of her journey to
London with him. Why, since she seemed to regret it,
since she often forgot that she had said that a cable had
summoned her back, was she here at all? There was no
trace of any desire to flirt with him, or even make herself
ordinarily pleasant. On the contrary, he seemed to feel
that grudge against himself as genuine. Once when he
was pretending to be asleep he caught her gaze suddenly,
and thought how unfriendly was her eye. At the moment
he believed it was vexation at his drowsiness, but . . .
Winslow was really quick and clever-witted. This
flattering idea did not fit in with her lack-lustre attempts
to meet his efforts at passing the time. But the next day,
running towards Calais, she changed. If ever a pretty girl
tried to swing a young man off his balance, she tried. But
though he played up well, she did not succeed. In point of
fact, he paid little heed to her. He was thinking over his
plan of campaign. He must not slip up on this. If he found
that he was getting out of his depth he would call in
Scotland Yard, or perhaps a private investigator, but he
did not think that he would be out of his depth. He would
go at once to Lightfoot, and on his replies would build his
plans. He determined to find out the truth—the whole
truth. We are all of us born detectives. From the
housewife buying eggs, to the young man inspecting a
second-hand car, or the gardener intent on slugs, we are
exercising the same native faculty. It is only because we
are the descendants of those who were quicker than the

other fellow to detect the hollow branch from the sound
one, a friend from a foe, that we are in existence at all.

Lightfoot was seldom out of his thoughts for long.
Lightfoot, with his absent-minded manner which could
change at times to such over-intense emphasis. He had
not cared for the chap, but between that and thinking
him implicated in passing off forged banknotes was a
bigger step than he cared to take before he had heard
what he had to say. But Lightfoot had been at
Bressanone, and if Fay was right the dead cashier had
had a bank-note handed to him by him; and that packet
which he himself had passed on to the postmaster. . . .
Deep down in his heart, though he was not conscious of it,
here lay the real reason why he had decided not to go at
once to the Yard or to the Bank of England, who had their
own detectives. Had he, Winslow, lent himself to a
fraud—a fraud connected with those very notes to which
his uncles' firm was in its turn linked? He stirred at the
sting of that idea. To be broadcast as the fool who had
lent himself to the swindle by passing on dud notes—! His
face flushed every time that he got as far as this. And
every time he vowed that he himself, unaided, would
ferret out the truth. Then, if his blunder came out at the
trial, as it certainly would at least it would be his brains
that had got on the track of the counterfeiters. The last
would more than offset the former. He was not conscious
of this reasoning, but he knew that he intended
singlehanded to locate the man and the place where he
worked. Later, he might need help, and would ask for it,
but not at first.

The crossing was appalling. It looked for a while as
though they would have to put back to Calais, but they
finally got in. Ursula promptly decided to stay at the Lord
Warden. Moffatt said that he must go on up to Town,
since, unfortunately, he had wired to a business man to
expect him. But they would meet next day in her flat in
Mayfair. She had wired to Kidd and Priestley to be there,
at a *Speedwell* cocktail party; Lightfoot, too, had been

asked. Hugh, of course, must be present. He nodded, each time with reservations which he kept to himself. He might or might not be able to come. Fay seemed to have felt the sea's effects very little, though she looked older and harder and less pretty on landing, Hugh thought. From something she said, he took it for granted that she, too, would spend the night at Dover, then, at the last moment, she jumped on to the train.

He did not see her get in, but after a few minutes she walked into his compartment, having apparently persuaded a young lad there to change seats with her. She was pale, Winslow noticed. Her pallor became her much better than her roses, or was it some change in her expression? He thought that she looked a little tired, and, odd though it sounded, sad. He was touched. She did care for him a little, after all. The parting evidently went deeper than he had thought. He made her a sign to bend forward, and, leaning over towards her, murmured something about not being able to take her out this evening, but hoped that they could arrange something for tomorrow. She had not been asked to the lunch by Ursula, he knew.

"To-morrow!" She gave the equivalent of a little shrug. "You talk as though you were sure of having one. I'm not. No one is." And she fell silent for a moment before she insisted on saying good-bye there and then and going back to her own compartment. She explained that she hated saying good-bye and pointing out her luggage at the same time, and her friends would be sure to have sent their car and footmen to meet her. He was too delighted to demur more than as the merest formality and again grew absorbed in his own thoughts. The train had made wonderful time, but it was past nine as they neared Victoria. Well, nine or later, he would go at once to Cromwell Road. There was a chance of finding Lightfoot in. If so, he might make a start this very evening. Yet such is human nature, that he found himself looking out for Fay at the Customs, but she was not to be seen;

though as he was driving off in a taxi he could have sworn that he saw her jump into another one farther down the rank. If so she had no luggage with her. Whoever it was had cleared the pavement in practically one leap and disappeared inside the taxi as though anxious not to be seen. He thought of the friends' car and the footmen, and gave a half laugh. Then he dismissed her from his mind. He might not have done so had he known that she was following him at a very safe distance—following him as one does who knows the other's destination.

He found the address off Cromwell Road to be a large gloomy-looking house, greatly in need of paint. He rang the bell. There was a long wait, then the door was opened by a very superior-looking manservant in very rusty clothes. The man eyed Winslow closely.

"Your name?" he asked, speaking with a strong French accent when Winslow asked if Mr. Lightfoot were at home.

Winslow gave it and repeated his question.

"I think he is in," came the reply. The eyes were watchful. Clever eyes, Winslow thought; but not the eyes of a manservant. He would have guessed them to belong to an artist or a sculptor.

"Will you please take my name to him, and say I would be much obliged if he would spare me a few minutes. The matter is very important, and very urgent."

Something crossed the man's face before his features assumed an expression of absolute stolidity. But for a fraction of a second Winslow would have said that he had frightened the fellow.

"This way," he murmured, leading the way into the room nearest them, a room that gave on the street. Winslow walked to the window and stood looking out with unseeing eyes, looking straight at a taxi in which sat Fay Starr, had he known it. But his thoughts were entirely on the coming interview, and her taxi was some distance down the road with another stationary one nearer to Winslow.

He drew a deep breath as the door opened and Lightfoot came in, closing it quietly behind him. "I came about a five-pound note," Winslow said after the barest of greetings, "that was handed in by you at the Hotel Orso. It's a forgery. Could you tell me how it came into your hands?"

Lightfoot had a cigar in his hand; he twirled it a second between his fingers without speaking. The silence grew rather long.

"And there was another one, at Bressanone. That, too, is believed to have been paid in by you—to the Swiss who was found dead. It, too, is a forgery."

Lightfoot was looking at his cigar with an almost negligent air. When he finally replied his tone was casual almost to carelessness.

"Have you the notes with you? May I see them?"

"I didn't bring them. You can see them at my rooms, with pleasure."

"I think you must be mistaken," Lightfoot said now, speaking as though the matter hardly concerned him either way. "I changed my money at Basle on the way out to Vipiteno, at the station. I think I should have detected any forged notes." His eyes were intently fastened on Winslow, but his manner was easy.

"They are forgeries, none the less," Winslow repeated. "You got them at Basle Station, you think. But surely the money-changers there are from the local banks? "

"I may be mistaken as to where I got them," Lightfoot threw in, "just as the people may have been mistaken who thought the notes were handed in by me, just as you may be mistaken—for all your certainty in thinking them wrong 'uns." Here he smiled into Winslow's troubled eyes. "I'll look it all up in my diary. I have the numbers noted down, of course, and also where each was changed. I'll let you know in the morning."

"I'm afraid I must press you to look into the matter at once," Winslow said gravely. "By to-morrow the whole affair will be in the hands of Scotland Yard."

He thought it as well to jostle Lightfoot out of his calm and indifferent way of taking the matter. In a way he, Winslow, was immensely relieved, but in a way he was not.

"Well, then"—Lightfoot looked at his watch, an ancient, rather battered-looking affair—"shall we say an hour from now? Half-past ten at your rooms? If you'll let me have your address. I think I can look up my facts in an hour. But I haven't unpacked my notes made on the journey yet."

Winslow thought that he taking the matter very well. Some men might have flown into a temper.

"Won't you have a drink?" Lightfoot now asked him, but Winslow had had all the drink he wanted on the train. He thanked the other, and said as much.

"Very well, then, half-past ten or eleven—to allow for delays." Lightfoot smiled quite pleasantly. As he opened the door for his guest, both of them saw the man who had let Winslow in, presumably the butler, standing with his arm around a very well-dressed lady of about his own years. She was patting his cheek affectionately and trying to get a flower to hold behind his ears. A young man in shirt-sleeves and a cloth in his hand stood by grinning broadly—and familiarly.

Lightfoot instantly closed the door again with a snap.

"My butler and his wife are rather a nuisance," he said shortly. "She's on the films. They're leaving next week. French people never learn our ways. I suppose I shall see you to-morrow at Miss Winslow's *Speedwell* lunch?"

Winslow replied in kind, and after a word about the race, Lightfoot once more opened the door. This time the butler was standing stiffly to attention by the street door, and handed Winslow his umbrella with an obsequious bow. He looked rather disturbed, Winslow thought, as well he might.

Inside the house that he had left Lightfoot was saying:

"Yes, a pity that you two couldn't have waited a minute before hugging each other. Oh yes, he suspects all right. More than suspects! Which is why he came. Now you and Madame must be off at once. Wales, I think. Umberto can go on to the place we've arranged in Derby. The Professor must leave within a quarter of an hour. I don't think the house is being watched yet. You, Umberto, see to the printing presses. We have till eleven at any rate. Probably till half-past eleven. He's hardly likely to move till then."

"And you?" asked, the man who had acted as butler.

"I stay behind and play for time." Lightfoot tossed his cigar away. He spoke in a cold hard voice. "And I shall see to it that we get it." No one, who had only met him casually, looking into Lightfoot's face as it showed under the electric lights just now, would have recognised him, unless they had seen him, as Winslow had, the day of the race when it was a question of pulling out farther and possibly losing the race.

"And now hurry!" He looked at his watch again. "Though I think he means what he said, and won't move till the time is up." And with that the group broke up.

Winslow, meanwhile, drove on to his rooms in Lowndes Square. He had his key ready, but he rang the bell for the man to get in the luggage. It also occurred to him for the first time that he had not cabled to say that he was coming back earlier than he had expected to. However, he had his keys, and the rooms would be sufficiently presentable. As no one answered the bell he unlocked the door. As he did so, someone jumped out of a taxi farther down and ran up the steps after him.

"Hugh! Hugh!" came his name, softly but urgently. He wheeled in the half-open door. Fay rushed up to him.

"Let me come in with you! Quick! I must have a word with you," she said in an urgent whisper as she reached up and gave his cheek a kiss, as hard and quick as a bird's peck.

He stepped back from the door in sheer bewilderment. His mind was full of the notes. He hardly recognised Fay, so deeply absorbed was he in more urgent matters.

"Quick, quick!" she repeated breathlessly. "Open the door of your flat, and I'll wait there until you've had your luggage brought in."

"She's going to ask me for a loan," he thought glumly as he looked into her pale and desperate face. She ran beside him up the stairs and was in at his door, as he opened it for her, like a bolting rabbit.

There seemed to be no one about the house. After one call down the kitchen stairs, Winslow had the taxi driver bring up his bags and let him go. Then Fay, who had been standing by the electric fire which she was turning on, came forward. Out of her handbag she was tugging something small, shining, deadly. It was a revolver. "You fool!" she was almost stuttering. "You blithering fool, to force me to do this!"

CHAPTER FIVE

MRS. CAPSTICK was rolling pastry. Swift, competent, fat hands had Mrs. Capstick, and as she rolled she talked to her husband, who was reading the paper, seated opposite her in his shirt-sleeves.

"I'll make the tart now so as it'll be cold for her return." ('Her' was always Mrs. Clarke to the two Capsticks.) "And you'd best step out for some cream later on, and the cheese she likes. Fillets of veal and smelts and a tomato soup." Mrs. Capstick was working the dinner backwards. "That ought to do. After all, she's only been away since morning, and won't expect a banquet. Let me see, that new gentleman, Mr. Priestley, will be back on Monday morning. Don't forget to order grapefruit for his breakfast. Lor, there's the front door bell!"

Capstick got into his coat and went upstairs. Mrs. Capstick, who had followed to the bottom of them, listened to what sounded like the yapping of excited terriers. Going on up, she found her husband gazing down at a couple of little boys aged about eight, one of whom, very red in the face and big of eye, was speaking in a shrill falsetto.

"Please, I didn't mean to crack it! I had no idea I could throw so far. I never thought I could hit it! But mother says I'm to come over and tell you I did it, and please what are you going to do about it, and I never thought the ball would go that far!"

"Cracked one of our windows," Capstick, heavily official, turned to his wife. "Case for the police, I think! Clear case for the police, yuss." And he glared officially at the two little boys. Their mother had sent them over to have a lesson; he, Capstick, would do his duty—and hers, too.

"If it's that policeman at the corner of the Square, he caught my Dandie for me last week. He's ever so nice!" came in a shriller squeak still from the second, and younger boy. Capstick reflected bitterly that the police weren't what they were. A little more, and they would cease to be of any help in bringing up kids.

"What window have they cracked?" Mrs. Cap-stick asked promptly.

"Mr. Winslow, from what I make out. I'll have to go up and see. Now then, you two young shavers, go home and tell your mother that the lady of the house is away till to-night, and that she'll write over about it as soon as she comes home. And don't you go flinging no more balls about—"

"I was batting on the balcony!" explained the boy, "just showing Ernie here how to do it, and I'd no idea the ball would go so far." Conscious pride again struggled through. "And, please, I'm ever so sorry!" he added politely.

Capstick eyed the flushed little faces grimly. "I'll have to have a word with the policeman about this. Very serious thing, cracking window-panes. Why, it's agin the law. Now then, you go home and wait for what Mrs. Clarke says to your ma."

The two crestfallen children went off. Husband and wife made their way up the stairs.

Capstick unlocked the door on the second floor. What had been two big rooms and a small room had been turned by Mrs. Clarke into a three-roomed suite with its own entrance door and little lobby. Out of the latter two doors opened. The sitting-room straight ahead, and the bedroom to the right. A bathroom had been constructed in between the two, with a door into both rooms.

"I thought I left this door closed," Mrs. Capstick now said, pushing what was ajar fully open. "Why whatever—" Mrs. Capstick had taken one step into the room, then she moved back so suddenly that Capstick all but ran her down.

A young woman, very smartly dressed in a tight fitting geranium red tweed coat and skirt and a hat to match, was sitting with her head on her breast, her feet stuck straight out ahead of her under the table. It was not a graceful attitude, but it suggested deep sleep. And she had not stirred at their entrance; nor did she now lift her head.

"May I ask—are you a friend of—?" began Mrs. Capstick, ruffling a little. A hand clutched her shoulder. It was Capstick.

"Go downstairs, Mattie!" he ordered, his lips pale. "Go outside!" he repeated; and, giving his wife a quite unconscious shove well to the rear, away from the seated figure, Capstick reached it in two long strides and then turned his head to say again in a tone that Mrs. Capstick had never heard him use, "Get downstairs, I tell you!"

But Mathilda Capstick stepped forward.

"Mind that blood on the carpet!" called her husband again, who seemed quite at home in the scene, and very much in command.

Mathilda gave a jump with both feet back on to the parquet surround. Capstick bent over the body—for it was only a body—of a young and very pretty woman, whose mouth was dreadfully open, as were the dull eyes of what, in life, he rightly fancied, had been a bright blue.

Without touching her, he saw that all over the back of her coat between her narrow shoulder blades was a dark stain, the same kind of a stain as was on the carpet below her chair.

"Oh, my lord, Henry, what's this! What's this! Oh, the poor young thing! Oh, run for the policeman at the corner! Run! Run! Or the doctor. Oh, what will Mrs. Clarke think we've done while she's been away!"

"I won't leave you alone with that! Not likely," Capstick said firmly. "Who done one in might do two in," he added darkly.

"Nor I won't telephone from this room, neither," in answer to his wife's eyes on the instrument by the window. "Finger-prints, my lass! Don't you touch nothing, or you're for it! Now then, you come along of me!"

"But—but where—how did she get in?" asked the wife.

"That's not our business. You come on downstairs now!" And Capstick by sheer force of personality took his wife off with him. Downstairs she stood by while he telephoned to Scotland Yard.

"But they're umberellas—" protested his wife, no reader of newspapers. "This is murder, Henry! Call the police in!"

"It's Scotland Yard what has the first call," Capstick spoke, as though he were conferring a favour. "We're in the metropolis, and that means that we telephones to the Yard. A Superintendent or the Commissioner himself will be round directly. What about a clean apron? And I could do with a fresh collar." His wife gaped at him. And this was the man whom she thought she had completely under her thumb? She felt humbled.

"But who is she? Where's Mr. Winslow? It's his suite of rooms. Then where is he?"

"Never you mind. That's their affair. Mr. Winslow's in Italy, still. That young get-up there—perhaps she's a friend of his. More like a friend of a friend to whom he'd lent his key. We shall know all about it very soon." Mr. Capstick spoke in a tone of certainty only to be matched by a saint upon his deathbed.

"But you don't know that he isn't in there still!" came protestingly from his wife as Capstick led her to their room and began to get out a fresh collar.

"I locked the door and took the key," Capstick said, "besides leaving the door at the head of the stairs above open." The two busied themselves improving their appearances.

"Henry," called his wife suddenly as she was making for the kitchen again. "Did you see the cracked pane?"

A grunt was the only reply. Henry had not. "Nor did I, neither," his wife confessed. "Drove it clean, out of my head."

"They'll find it!" came from her husband with assurance. "There's nothing they won't see!"

A ring came at the front door. Capstick approved of that ring. Clear enough to be insistent, and yet not noisy.

The first of a group of men who came quickly up the steps was a tall, erect figure with a grave sunburnt face, pleasant enough in expression, but not the face of a man with whom you could take liberties, Capstick decided. Nothing easy-going about it. Yet the chief inspector's fine gray eyes looked capable of compassion, Mrs. Capstick thought.

It did not take the two servants long to state the facts. Their mistress away for the day, a suite upstairs whose owner was in Italy enjoying himself at winter sports, the two children with their tale of the broken window, and their own entrance into the suite, and what they found there.

Capstick led the way upstairs and was then asked to wait outside.

Chief Inspector Pointer stood in front of the body, and then behind it, studying it attentively. He judged her to be around twenty-five. She had been sitting when shot, he thought, and had not been disturbed since. Sitting with her back to the door, facing the window—which had a cracked pane in it—and the big writing-table. Directly behind her was the door leading into a pretty bath-room, through which a door led into the bedroom. Over the bathroom door was a velvet curtain which covered it about three-quarters across. Had anyone wanted to, it would have been exceedingly easy to step in there, or hide there, and fire from the curtain's side. The brown carpeting which was uniform through all three rooms showed no marks; but it was old and fairly thin of pile.

The broad surrounds of parquet showed marks of feet towards the door, and a broad place in the dust which looked as though something oblong had been stood down there. It was roughly the size of a couple of large suitcases stood side by side. In the bedroom one drawer of the writing-table looked as though it had been pulled out recently. There was no dust on the outjutting ledge. Except for that, the room did not look as though it had been entered. The photographer had finished, and Pointer returned to the first room, the sitting-room. The doctor was just putting a thermometer away.

"About how long has she been dead, would you say?" Pointer asked.

"Somewhere round eighteen hours. Perhaps less. Not more, I should think, though it's impossible to say with certainty. Unlike the cause of death. Bullet has penetrated the heart. Fired from fairly close range; no singe, though."

"About the distance of that velvet curtain?" Pointer asked meaningly.

"Distance and direction would fit. Man's rooms these, aren't they? Well, the story won't be difficult to piece together, I take it. Where's the owner?" asked the doctor.

"Off in Italy—apparently."

"Ah, apparently!" And the doctor helped to lift the body off the chair and lay it on a stretcher now brought in. The stretcher was taken into the bedroom. A couple of women detectives would go over the clothes and see if they gave any help in finding out who the dead girl was. No handbag was to be seen anywhere, nor any weapon. Pointer had Capstick come in again, and asked him to look carefully around and see if anything was missing, or out of place. Capstick thought not. From him Pointer learnt in a couple of minutes that a Mr. Hugh Winslow had had the suite for over two years; that he was on the Stock Exchange, and that his office was in Queen Victoria Street; the man gave the number. Unfortunately, being Saturday afternoon, the office was shut. Pointer made a gesture towards the mantel with its many photographs. Was Mr. Winslow's picture there? Yes, in that one of the

Old Rugbeians Club. Capstick indicated the face. Mr. Winslow was at the moment in Italy in a place called Vipiteno. He was expected back in about ten days to a fortnight. He, Capstick, would be sure to have a wire or a letter to say when he was coming; though once before, when he had rushed back for some Stock Exchange work, Mr. Winslow had forgotten to send any word and had just blown in one evening. As to character, Capstick gave the young man a very good one. Quiet, pleasant, unassuming, reserved. No, there was no one particular friend who came a great deal to see him. Mr. Winslow belonged to a good club, and generally saw his friends there. He generally dined there, too. As for lady visitors, Mr. Winslow occasionally would have ladies in to tea or dinner. His cousin, Miss Winslow, came oftener than anyone else; she usually turned up about once a month. Did he, Capstick, know her address? He did not, but had an idea that Mr. Winslow and she and the lady she lived with in town were off together for a holiday. As for keys, Mr. Winslow had one, of course, and Capstick the other. Pointer went to the telephone, and sent the Yard what sounded like a grocery order. It requested that a wireless be sent to Vipiteno in the Alto Adige, Italy, and that all possible inquiries there and here in Town be set in motion about a certain Hugh Winslow who had been at Rugby, was on the Stock Exchange, had a suite of rooms in a certain house in Lowndes Square, where a dead girl had been found, and was himself absent.

That done, Pointer had Capstick show him over the rest of the house. He heard about a Mr. Priestley who had taken the top floor very recently, had arrived a few days ago, and had gone off into the country. He was coming back on Monday, and had been "sent" them by Mr. Winslow.

And he learnt what Capstick and his wife knew of Mrs. Clarke, which was very simple. She was the widow of a barrister. The Capsticks had been in her husband's employment and had stayed on. About three years ago

Mrs. Clarke had suddenly found her income drop away, and had decided to turn the top part of her house into two suites for bachelors. This apparently had worked well, as since then she had not talked any more of leaving Lowndes Square.

Pointer did not care for the two servants much— possibly because of his inspection of the house. He thought them shirkers at their work. But they seemed to have a very straightforward story to tell, and to be only greatly excited, not frightened, at what had happened. Capstick himself was an ex-marine. Just what was it that had happened? Both the Capsticks were sure that they had neither of them seen the dead girl before. Both seemed certain that Mr. Hugh Winslow could have had nothing to do with her end. Capstick said that he thought Mr. Winslow had lent his key to some foreigner whom he had met abroad, and that this was the consequence.

Pointer's women detectives had told him that almost everything she wore certainly came from London. Besides, she looked English to the chief inspector. As to last night, the Capsticks had had a "late pass." As Mrs. Clarke was out with friends till past one, they had not returned till after twelve. They had heard nothing, but as they slept in the basement, it would have had to be a very loud noise which would have wakened them. Capstick assured the chief inspector that Winslow's key had not left his pocket at any time; which was why he felt so sure that Mr. Winslow had lent his flat, and had either written, and the letter had miscarried, or had meant to do so, and forgotten. Probably the former, Capstick thought.

The finger-prints expert had finished by this time and left. Pointer went up to the suite again, where now a plain-clothes man stood on guard. The photographer had not yet finished. Pointer went first to the bedroom this time and worked back to the sitting-room. The drawer of the bedroom, which was not pushed home, and on whose ledge was no dust, contained papers only. Receipts, apparently, chiefly from cleaners, and for a very moderate amount of spirits, and a good many cigarettes. The entire contents were emptied into one of Pointer's cases and put aside for careful inspection. But for the moment their interest lay in the fact that it had been, apparently, only the drawer with papers in it which had interested someone last night, or early this morning, for the Capsticks had not opened up the house until what they called seven, which Pointer suspected of being nearer eight. Mrs. Clarke breakfasted at nine, and they did not look early risers. The remainder of the bedroom showed nothing interesting, until, on opening one of the built-in cupboards he found, tossed back on a shelf, an elbow-pad. He picked up the oblong of leather stuffed with horsehair with straps top and bottom. He recognised it at once. Pointer was fond of the Cresta, he was as good at tobogganing as most sports, though ice-boat sailing had his especial liking. This pad had the unmistakable feel of leather that had been in recent use. Nor, was it dusty. It even felt distinctly dampish to his fingers. On one of the straps were the initials E.L. This, too, went into his case. For this looked as though someone from a winter sports centre, where tobogganing was done, had been here. You don't need that sort of thing when coasting down Hampstead Hill. He left the bedroom without any further finds. In the bathroom he touched the soap. It was cracked and dry. Tub and basin were coated with dust. He went on into the sitting-room, and worked that room over inch by inch. He knew for certain, when he had finished, that, as he thought, there had been no struggle in here, that whoever came in had had fairly dry shoes. Not walked any distance last night, that meant; and that the desk, at any rate, had already been thoroughly searched. Paper by paper the chief inspector thought, or he was—what he was not often—much mistaken. The search had not been hasty. Quite the contrary. It might have been done by Mr. Winslow himself. Just the way a man would look through his papers who wanted to make sure that he had not left anything dangerous, anything in the nature of a signpost behind. There were plenty of finger-prints in the room, and they were duly photographed.

Barring them, the only thing which might turn out to be a direct clue was a small carved knob of some dark wood which Pointer found on the floor near the writing-bureau. It had a hole in it, into which a flat-topped wooden peg had apparently been glued. Nothing in the suite was minus a knob. Nothing matched it. The wood and the carving were peculiar. They did not suggest Swiss or Italian wood in the least. Nor was it new. There was no paper lying around, in which it might have been wrapped. Had it belonged to something which had been carried into the room, say in a bag which had been opened on the table in front of the dead girl? But the table top was covered with a film of dust, unbroken, except where her elbows had made little marks, and where her hands seemed to have rested. The knob lay so close to the writing-table that it was hidden by the latter's shadow. Pointer had an open mind about it. It would fit many things, but he would not be surprised if it turned out to be the knob from someone's umbrella crook. There was one faint, rubbed mark on it which looked very recent, such as might have been made last night by having got caught in one of the drawers. As has been said, it had rained last night. The dead girl had no umbrella with her, she seemed to have nothing with her, but a man might have had.

Pointer handed his find to the photographer, who was just preparing to leave.

"Make me a copy of that in No. 1 paste."

No. 1 paste was a quick-drying and hardening preparation much used by the Yard for small models of things from which casts could not be taken for fear of smudging finger-prints. This little knob's blurred patch might yet prove definitely to what object it had belonged.

Yardly took it, gave a smile that said that the job would be easy and swift, and went to the window, where he opened a box he had with him, rolled a piece of what looked like dark putty between his fingers into a ball, dusted some powder stain over it and rolled again, measured the two balls with callipers and pared his model down to agree with the other. Then with his penknife he carved the few simple details on it. Finally he stood a capital copy beside the original to dry. In another two minutes it would be stiff enough to handle. Pointer meanwhile had examined the lobby and front door. In the lobby was a place where something had been set down which matched in size the marks in the sitting-room—suitcases, very likely. As for the lock, it showed no sign of having been tampered with, though a Yard locksmith was even now hurrying who would settle that question definitely. If there were no scratches on the wards it would look as though the right key had opened the door, whether used by the right person or not. Pointer went back into the room, took over the two knobs and let the photographer hurry off home. He stood by the cracked window staring at the chair which the dead girl had so recently occupied. Why had she come? Beyond taking off her gloves, she had not tried to make herself at home. They were tucked into the chair on which she sat. Pretty gloves with a perfume that went with all her things, a Chanel perfume, and with a couple of small pinkish stains on them, strawberry stains, apparently. Her, hat was a ridiculous little saucer perched on one eyebrow, with a veil that stuck stiffly out at the sides. There had been no love-making with that hat on. Why had she come? For a talk, one would have said, had she been a man. Not a hair was out of place of all her beautiful smoothed waves and curls left free down one side of her head. Winslow was said to be away at winter sports. This girl had certainly been in some such sun, too. Her skin, fair and delicate, was blistered and burnt. There was what looked like a faint bruise on one cheekbone. Under the tan. Had she been away with him? Come back with him? How many people had been in that little room?

CHAPTER SIX

POINTER asked for Capstick again. He questioned him as to the luggage which Mr. Winslow had taken away with him. Two expanding suitcases, he was told. A third similar one was in the attic, which had not been needed. He brought it down in length and, when expanded, in breadth, it corresponded with the marks left in the dust. And they were longer than the usual suitcases. While talking to him, Pointer dropped the little knob—the copy—from his pocket. It rolled towards Capstick, who picked it up and handed it back to the chief inspector with the unmistakably casual glance of a man looking at something which is not of the slightest importance or interest to him.

A car could be heard drawing up. Capstick made for the door. "That'll be Mrs. Clarke!" he said eagerly. Coming down with him, Pointer saw a taxi draw up, and out of it climbed a tall woman of early middle age. She was handsome in a way, but her features were too sharp for Pointer's liking.

"I'm glad to see you back, Madam!" Capstick said almost gushingly. Mrs. Clarke looked at him with a hint of a raised eyebrow.

"Take my bag into the morning-room and pay the man." She looked inquiringly at the chief inspector.

"He's from the Yard, Madam, that's just it!" came from Capstick, who was not Jeeves, and felt completely out of his depth at the coming interview.

"It's Mr. Winslow, 'm," put in his wife, who had come up, too. "He's not here, and there's a dead body in his rooms! A young girl."

Mrs. Clarke turned her head from one to the other. Then she looked at the chief inspector. "I don't suppose

they are mad," she said briskly. "But they sound like it.
Will you come in here with us? Now, then, Capstick, pay
the taximan and explain yourself. One at a time, Mrs.
Capstick, please."

Capstick was back in a moment, and told what had
happened until he called in the Yard. Mrs. Capstick,
trying to confuse matters by her comments, was quickly
sent down to the kitchen by her mistress. Then she asked
the chief inspector to let her know how matters stood at
the moment. That, too, only took a minute.

"I'll come up and see the body, of course," she said,
and led the way up the stairs. He folded back the sheet
from the face.

"No, I never saw that face before. Poor, pretty child.
She's a mere girl, as Mrs. Capstick said. She spoke as
though genuinely moved. "And you found her—and no
one else—in these rooms and no clue to how it was done?"

"Oh, yes," Pointer said, "we know how it was done."
And he explained this. "But not who did it. Not yet."

"Well, obviously." She paused. "Mr. Winslow's not in
the least a criminal type," she went on. "They quarrelled,
I suppose, and there was an accident, and a gun went off
which had only been pointed in a moment of fury and
never been intended to use. I'm only afraid that Mr.
Winslow has been foolish enough to leave England at
once and return abroad. As I say, he's definitely not a
criminal—definitely. But that's the worst of the modern
way of careless living. Sooner or later the bill comes in,
and each one of them thinks they can dodge payment. I
suppose that poor child wanted something definite,
perhaps that he would marry her, and because of what
was begun in foolish lightheartedness, she's dead,
whoever, she is—poor little thing—and he's ruined for
life. It's very sad—very."

Pointer asked her if she knew of any friendship on the
part of the missing Winslow for any girl in particular.
Mrs. Clarke said that she knew practically nothing of Mr.
Winslow, except what could be gleaned by meeting him

perhaps once or, twice a month on the stairs. He was the son of an old friend of hers, but she had purposely not treated him as a friend herself.

"I prefer business to be business, and not mixed with friendship," she finished.

"Did you hear anything last night?" he went on. "Your room is the other side of the house, I know, but you might have heard some sound."

"I not only heard, I saw Mr. Winslow leaving early this morning," she said composedly. Pointer wheeled around.

"Oh? When, pray?"

"About five. My cat was shut out last night; the tiresome creature is always getting shut out, and it miawed so long this morning that, finally, I got up, put my gown on, and went to the front door to let it in. As I got nearly to it I saw Mr. Winslow just stepping out. I opened the door after him to say something—I thought he was still in Italy, of course—but he was just turning the corner to the right. I meant to speak to Capstick about it, though as a rule I leave the two suites entirely to the servants; but I got a telegram at breakfast about a house I'm buying in the country which made it slip my mind."

Pointer questioned her closely, and got her to go into details and minutes, and where she stood and just where Mr. Winslow was . . . and even asked for particulars of the telegram. She seemed to be quite frank and straightforward. The telegram she handed to him. It was to the effect that the party wall which she wanted cut through was, etc., etc. . . . It fully explained her absence for the remainder of the day. She was not to be shaken in any of her statements, and promised to sign a typewritten copy later on. Alone in the suite, Pointer stood a full minute looking at his shoe tips. So Winslow had been back himself. He had not lent his key. Mrs. Clarke returned with an address for which he had asked her; but Miss Winslow was abroad, she explained, had gone with

the lady whose flat she shared, and her cousin, to Italy
for a holiday.

Moffatt and Ursula looked at the very pretty buffet
table which she had arranged.

"He's sure to turn up," Moffatt was saying easily.
"Knows it's in his honour, so to say, and he's sure to come.
That's why he hasn't telephoned."

"But why isn't he in his rooms? I've tried late last
night and early this morning and he hasn't turned up at
his office. Mr. Effingham says he sent him word at Calais
that his father was better, and he needn't come on, but,
as we know, Hugh did. I saw him get the wire, but he
didn't say a word about there no longer being any rush to
reach Town."

"He didn't say to you, or to me," Moffat said dryly.

"Well, where is he? I want to send word to the uncles
about our all going down there together next week.
Captain Kidd is to motor us; it'll look less formal that
way, and yet give him a chance to show his paper. Hugh
said he'd telephone me first thing after breakfast, and it's
now past six."

"It's possible that he isn't in Town at all," Moffatt said
to that.

"You mean Miss Starr?" she asked bluntly. In that
case he's started for Iceland, perhaps," he went on.

"Iceland?" she queried.

"Once when I had to step into their compartment I
heard her talk as though she might be going on there."

Ursula digested this in gloomy silence.

"My dear, you worry yourself quite unnecessarily
about those two," he said firmly. "Miss Starr doesn't care
a brass button for Hugh, really; at least not in my
opinion. Now, if it were young Kidd, I wouldn't bet on it."

She shook her head.

"Perhaps she doesn't know herself which she likes
best, in which case both are safe," he went on.

"Perhaps. But I think she knows her own mind unusually well." Ursula took up and put down a toboggan laden with potato chips. "She strikes me as having tremendous determination. Simply tremendous! I feel as though nothing but death would make her give up anything on which she had really 'set her mind."

"Possibly." Moffatt suppressed a yawn. "You know her better than I do."

The party was a great success. Ursula never flopped. Lightfoot did not turn up, but Captain Kidd did, and Priestley came in, too. The rooms were full of the usual talking, laughing, smoking, drinking, eating crowd. Suddenly a waiter came up to Ursula.

"You're wanted on the telephone, miss."

Ursula excused herself. Outside the man explained that a gentleman was there who wished to speak to her, and had told him to deliver the message in just that way. Something about it being connected with Mr. Winslow, the gentleman had said. The name he gave was Pointer— Mr. Pointer.

The name conveyed nothing to Ursula. Looking back afterwards, she felt, as had many another before her, that life broke in two at that place. Before and after she had met the chief inspector represented two quite different existences.

"You come from my cousin, Mr. Winslow?" she asked, going into the little breakfast room where Pointer had been shown. It was heaped with the chairs and articles that had been taken out of the other rooms.

"There's been an accident at his flat," Pointer said. "We want to get into immediate touch with your cousin. Is he here?"

Ursula looked frank bewilderment, then growing apprehension.

"An accident? To whom? To him?"

"Perhaps you'll come back to his rooms and help to clear up just what has happened," he said pleasantly, "and if you've any guests here—you have a cocktail party on, I gather? "—the din could only mean that—"who were at Vipiteno with Mr. Winslow, perhaps you'll bring them, too?

"It's a very urgent question of identification," he repeated, and added, "Please be as quick as you can."

He went downstairs and out to his car. He knew that she would be swiftly on his heels, and he did not want to explain further.

Ursula made a sign to Moffatt, who followed her out.

"Hugh's had an accident. At least—he wants anyone who was at Vipiteno to come to his rooms—"

"Sounds more like a party to me," Moffatt said.

"Oh, no, no! Something dreadfully wrong. Someone, a doctor, I think he must be, has just run in to bring the message. Now can you get hold of the Kidd and Mr. Priestley? I'll speak to Mrs. Marchmont, she'll carry on for me perfectly."

In three minutes they were downstairs and bundling into Kidd's car. Another five and they were on the steps of Lowndes Square. Capstick was standing there on the look out for them. The chief inspector had waited to see them start, and had then cut round a corner in his own little car. The four had not exchanged a word on the way. "Mr. Winslow?" Ursula asked the man at once. "What has happened to him?"

"Will you all come this way, please?" was his only reply, as, acting on instructions, he led the way up to the suite. They were shown directly into Winslow's bedroom. Ursula recoiled before the covered stretcher on the floor.

"It's not your cousin!" Pointer said instantly, stepping forward. "I ought to introduce myself more fully. I am a chief inspector from New Scotland Yard. Pointer is my name. We were summoned here by the manservant a short time ago. He had reason to enter this suite, and found a young girl sitting by the table in the other room, shot dead. Mr. Winslow is nowhere to be found. I want you to tell me if you can identify the dead girl for us?"

He had given her time to get herself in hand, and to prepare her for what she would see. The chief inspector did not think Ursula Winslow had had a hand in this or any crime, she struck him as emphatically "straight" by nature and by training.

He now folded back the sheet from the face. They all stared down at it. She lay with that curiously faraway look on her face that the dead so often wear —they who are really so far away.

With exclamations of horror they all bent down as though unable to believe what they saw.

"Fay Starr!" "Miss Starr!" came from all four in a gasp.

Pointer had the name now.

"You all recognise her?"

"Oh, certainly!" Ursula was speaking in a low tone of horror. "Certainly we do. Oh, the poor little thing! The poor little thing! When. . ." She broke off.

"Where did you meet her?" Pointer asked.

"She stayed at our hotel in Vipiteno," Moffat explained. "The man who lives in this suite, Mr. Winslow, Captain Kidd here, Mr. Priestley "—he indicated him, too—" and I all were there on a holiday. Miss Winslow was there, too, with a friend, a Lady Browne. Winslow, Miss Winslow, Miss Starr and I all came home together. Miss Winslow stayed in Dover, my car met me, but Winslow came on by the boat train; so apparently did Miss Starr. They would have got to Victoria around nine o'clock yesterday evening. So you can imagine the shock this is!"

Ursula advanced towards Pointer. She was very pale. They were all of them pale.

"Where's my cousin? You say this girl was found here—shot—dead—here in his rooms. Then where is he?"

Pointer led the way into the sitting-room. "She was found dead in that chair," he said simply. "Shot from the back through the heart. The doctor thinks she may have been killed around ten last night. We can find no weapon. Apparently it was a 3-inch Colt."

Ursula stared at him blankly. "I don't understand what you're saying," she said finally. "You're not trying to tell me that you think my cousin Hugh Winslow had anything to do with this—with her death? Why, he was a great friend of hers. Nor is he the kind of young man who shoots people, let alone women. Please tell me once more just what happened here." She spoke almost impatiently.

"I wish I could," Pointer said simply. "That's still to find out. You say she is a Miss Starr. Where does she, live? Who are her people?"

They explained how little any of them knew of the dead girl.

"But my cousin?" Ursula repeated. "Where is he? How did that girl come to be here, and he gone?"

Again Pointer only wished that he could tell her. Looking at her with open and real sympathy and hidden watchfulness, he thought that she was telling him the truth so far as she knew it. That she had no knowledge of Miss Starr beyond what she said, that she did really believe her cousin to be entirely innocent. Truth, like love, is divine, and each can at times make itself felt by some means independent of words. Pointer felt its presence here.

He asked several questions about Vipiteno, about the journey home, about the other visitors at the hotel. There was only one which interested him so far—that was Lightfoot. No one knew his address, they said; but Pointer, remembering the elbow pad, had his man try for E. Lightfoot in the telephone directory, and in a few minutes he was told that Mr. Lightfoot had been located, but that they could get no reply. A telegram was sent him, asking him to come to Mr. Winslow's rooms and to communicate with Mr. Priestley as soon as possible. Mr. Priestley suggested this, and Pointer accepted with pleasure.

The chief inspector questioned each of them as to their addresses, occupations, and whereabouts last night. Not one, not even Ursula, had an alibi for the hours from ten onwards. The only hours that apparently counted. According to what Pointer was told by each, Kidd had gone to bed early, as it chanced that he had been up the two nights previously. He lived in service chambers, where no notice was taken of whether the inmates were in or out.

Priestley had been down in the country speaking on behalf of one of his many charities, but as it happened, he, too, had put up at a station hotel last night, and had gone to bed shortly after ten. The place was within half an hour's drive from Town, and the station hotel was one that kept open all night. Moffatt had had an important piece of business on hand; he furnished the names of the two men with whom he had had a sort of preliminary conference.

It, too, had stopped at a little past ten, and he claimed to have gone to bed after it, but as his manservant lived out, he, too, had no alibi.

While Pointer talked to each of them, he had placed the little ball which he had found on the table beside him. None of them paid it the least attention.

"Is Mr. Winslow engaged to be married?" Pointer asked Ursula finally.

They were in the drawing-room downstairs now, talking alone together.

"No."

"He was in love with Miss Starr, wasn't he?" Pointer went on, guessing.

Again she shook her head.

"They were the merest of hotel friends. Winter-sports friends. But that upstairs"—she raised her eyes full of horror to the ceiling—" there's only one possible explanation to that, chief inspector. My cousin had lent his rooms to Miss Starr and to—whoever it was that shot her. He and she parted at Victoria Station, if not earlier.

He must have told her that he didn't intend using his rooms last night, and lent her his key."

"But surely he would have sent word to the butler here," Pointer objected.

There was a short silence. What she had said was what Pointer himself thought might prove to be the case, but for Mrs. Clarke having seen Winslow leaving early this morning. She had said that she saw his face quite clearly—that there could be no possibility of a mistake.

"Then it looks to me," Ursula went on, "as he said nothing to the servants here, as though he had only lent her the key for a short time. Say she wanted to have a very private talk with someone for an hour or so . . . and he knew that he would be somewhere else. . . . It looks to me as though he had asked her to leave it for him on the hall table, or send it on to him by hand, or he's met with an accident on his way here from Victoria—or in the boat train."

"Have you any other relations who might know where he is, or how to get into touch with him?"

She explained about her uncles who were their sole relatives. "It won't be any good asking them," she went on, "for I've been telephoning to them only this morning, arranging a visit we intended to make, and they hadn't heard from him. Besides, my cousin and they don't meet often. Once a year at most."

Again she fell silent.

There was just a chance, a bare thousand-to-one chance, that Winslow had lent his key to Miss Starr, had had his luggage left overnight in the flat, had stepped in to the lobby, or sent a man up for it, and taken it off to some other place, coming back himself for some forgotten paper and letting himself out early when Mrs. Clarke had seen him, which would mean that he had only gone into his bedroom and not stepped into the sitting-room at all. It would take a very complicated explanation to meet all the difficulties of the problem; but it was possible, barely possible, that Winslow had been seen leaving the house at five this morning, and yet had no idea that a dead girl sat by his table in his sitting-room.

"If you're right," Pointer said finally, "and he's conscious, then he'll get into touch with us as soon as the papers are out."

CHAPTER SEVEN

BUT when Moffatt came in a moment later, he found her sitting with her head sunk in her, hands.

"Edward." She lifted what was a very pale and frightened face to his calm one. "There's some dreadful mystery here! Of course, I wouldn't let that man from Scotland Yard guess how I feel; he's much too clever for one to give him the hundredth part of an inch. But what really happened? Why isn't Hugh anywhere around?"

Moffatt said nothing, only held her hand firmly in his own broad one.

"'We must find him," she said suddenly.

"No one can find him if he doesn't want to be found," Moffatt said to that.

"But it's ridiculous, Edward, our talking like this! Of course he can't know anything about—that." She looked miserably at him. He avoided her eyes and kept silent, until seeing that she wanted an answer he said at last, "I can imagine anyone losing their head and their nerve if they had killed someone by accident—say."

"I can't imagine Hugh losing his," she said slowly. "I can't imagine him being such a fool as not to see that, however bad things were, they would get infinitely worse if he didn't go at once to the police."

Moffatt pursed his lips and frowned thoughtfully.

"You say you love me," she said suddenly, and as far as he was concerned unexpectedly. "Well, then, do something for me. Do this for me: help me to find Hugh and bring him to reason!"

"My dear girl!" Moffatt looked, and felt, appalled. "How can we find him? Where are we to look?"

"Surely we can do what the police can do," was the indignant answer. "You've plenty of spare time just now, having come back from Italy sooner than you meant to. Use it with me, Edward; use it for me!"

He held out for some time, but finally she had her way, and he saw her into a taxi for her flat, and went ruefully back into the room where Priestley and Kidd were now waiting for him. Kidd looked quite excited.

"I say, Moffatt," he broke out, "why not let's handle this thing ourselves; find out the answer to that conundrum upstairs."

Moffatt groaned aloud.

"Ursula has just set me that enchanting task. She wants me to help her find Winslow."

"Well?" Kidd asked, his eyes alight.

"She doesn't want to find Winslow really," Moffatt continued bitterly. "What she wants is to find a spotless lamb bearing his name. Can't be done. Whatever the solution to the mystery is, personally I think it's a very simple one; it's not one that will bring Winslow back to his family with a halo round his head."

"What do you think happened?" Priestley asked, coming out of a brown study.

"Well," Moffatt gave his half shrug, "at the best, an accident with a pistol and a lost nerve, and a young man in safe and secure hiding. Not at all the sort of case for fools to rush in and find him."

"Oh," Kidd looked rather taken aback, "of course there is that," he finally agreed. "There is that. . . ."

"I don't see what else there is," Moffatt said, "if either of you can suggest a better idea, pray let me have it. For Ursula's sake. She's quite at a loss."

There was silence in the room. Kidd smoked his pipe furiously. Then he took it out with an air of triumph.

"You know," he addressed the two silent men," if we just go by facts and clues, we're only tailing after that clever chap upstairs, who'll get there first any day. He's Yard trained. But if we go by psychological clues and ideas, we ought to be able to take some short cuts he won't see. We score, too, by knowing both Winslow and

poor, little Fay Starr." He turned and looked out of the
window for a second, his back to the others, then be
turned round to face them again. "Now I have a theory
that fits the facts and fits the character of Winslow as
well—"

"I have one, too," Priestley said, blinking at him.

"Then let's have yours first," Kidd said instantly.
"Frankly, I think mine is a winner; you may have hit on
the same idea—struck by the same brain-wave."

"Well, say there was a genuine accident with a pistol,
and that Winslow dashed out of the house for a doctor
and has been run down by someone's car."

"A very good idea, Priestley," said Moffatt. "Quite a
possible one, too."

"Doesn't appeal to me," Kidd said frankly. "Whose
pistol was it, to begin with? Miss Winslow says Winslow
doesn't own one."

"*She* may have had one," suggested Priestley, "and
wanted him to load it for her, or clean it for her. . . . I
don't profess to be an expert on firearms. I've never
handled one in my life; but it might have been done that
way. . . ."

"What's your notion, Kidd?" Moffatt asked.
"Whichever one sounds the best for Winslow is the one I
shall adopt—as far as Ursula is concerned. Personally, of
course, I think he's gone into hiding, and that mine is to
be the ungrateful task of digging him out—to reap his
and Ursula's combined thanks later!" he finished
gloomily.

"I think he's in hiding, too," Kidd said. "Now, listen!
Say he has an enemy who shot her in order to fasten this
on Winslow. Winslow lent her his key for some reason or
other—or Winslow, she, and this other chap all met here
yesterday evening for some important talk. I think the
other way more likely, for I can't see any important talk
at which both poor little Fay and Winslow would be
wanted together. Say she's in trouble about something.
Asks him to lend her his key so that she can have a

private talk; but instead of the person she expects, comes a man who's Winslow's enemy, and who shoots her, then slips out, and Winslow finds her dead—knows what will be thought, and knows why it was done in his rooms. He rushes into hiding, yes—but in order to bring the crime home to the man who did it! He's working for proofs which he can only get in that way."

"Sounds a bit Edgar Wallace to me," muttered Moffatt. "Do you think Ursula would swallow it? " he asked Priestley.

"Very far-fetched," Priestley said, shaking his head. "Mine is simple and—forgive me, Kidd—possible. Yours—" He shook his head again.

"But mine answers every difficulty," Kidd protested. "Just give it a fair hearing. Winslow hadn't a pistol, we're told, and probably poor little Fay hadn't one, either. None's wanted in my theory. The murderer brings his own pistol and takes it away with him again."

"And why should Winslow have such a savage enemy that he's willing to kill a girl in order to harm him?" Moffatt asked. "Ursula won't accept that, I'm afraid."

"You must grant something, of course," Kidd said; "in this case we must assume a bitter enemy. Winslow was on the Stock Exchange . . . of course, I know that's the difficulty," he tapped his pipe against the mantel. "I grant that we must find someone with a sufficient reason to want him out of the way—but granted that, the rest all falls into line. Winslow sees the danger at once. . . ."

"But why should he be supposed to kill Miss Starr?" asked Priestley. "I don't mean the real murderer; I mean why should the murderer think that the jury would think that Winslow killed Miss Starr?"

"I see your point—" Kidd had not thought of that objection before. "That's to find out," he said finally. "There would have to exist—you're quite right, Priestley—some hidden reason known to the murderer which, when known, would look as if Winslow had shot her; a reason known to Winslow, too—which is why he would at once see that he had no earthly chance of getting off if he were found. Yes, your objection only strengthens the idea; which rather proves there's something in it."

"At any rate, it whitewashes Winslow for the time being," Moffatt said after thinking it over several times. "I'll adopt it as mine. I'll take it as the foundation of my investigation, for the worst of it is, Ursula expects me to start in and produce her cousin. If he's in hiding, it won't matter much whether your or my theory is the right one," he went on, "and yours sounds better. Meanwhile, Priestley, I'll tell Ursula yours, too; as a matter of fact, she is already at work on the hospitals."

"I can't quite see Winslow with a deadly enemy," Priestley said, getting up, "nor a secret link between himself and Miss Starr. Two absolute necessities to your theory, Kidd. However, it does justice to your inventive powers. I should never have thought of it in a month of Sundays! Are you going to lay it before that interesting-looking chap who's in charge of the investigation?"

"Rather! Nothing like being in with the police. If you want to hear what they think, you must be matey, and tell 'em what you think."

"If you want them to suspect you, tell them you want to work in with them," Moffatt said in his driest tone. "My dear Kidd, don't you ever read detective fiction? It's what the criminal invariably does. When a gent or lady comes forward and offers to be of use, you've got the villain ticketed."

"Oh? Well, perhaps we had better work it by ourselves," Kidd said to that.

"Especially as if by any chance Moffatt's idea of Winslow being in genuine hiding should be true, it might be awkward to have the Yard at one's elbow," Priestley suggested.

"Quite so!" Kidd looked a trifle appalled. "One has to think of everything in detective work," he confessed. "Personally I've always thought I would like to solve a stiff problem. And in spite of the difficulties which I allow my theory will have to meet, I still think it's a very good, workable hypothesis, and psychologically possible. I wonder what Lightfoot will say to it. He always struck me as being rather clever."

"Any chap who played bridge as he does is clever," Priestley agreed, and Moffatt nodded assent. "But," Priestley went on, "so often, when not playing bridge, he struck me as though woolgathering."

"An absent-minded detective would be a bit cramping," Kidd said. "Leave his notes behind him, or forget that his toes were sticking out under the screen . . . yes, perhaps we'll leave Lightfoot out of the club." And it was decided not to include him.

"I presume you won't mind my assuming charge of our work." Moffatt spoke as though that were a foregone conclusion. "One person must do the arranging and directing, or we shall get nowhere."

The chief inspector meanwhile had gone back to the Yard. For the moment he had to pause. Being a Saturday evening slowed up many inquiries, but taxi-cab drivers would shortly be reporting who had taken up Miss Starr or Winslow at Victoria. A great deal would depend on what they had to tell.

He had a first brief interview with the assistant commissioner, who listened with close attention to Pointer's brief summary of the little that, so far, was known.

"I see no signs of a struggle; the telephone hadn't been tampered with," Pointer wound up. "Nothing to suggest that Mr. Winslow as well as Miss Starr was killed last night, and that his body, has been taken away; but, of course, that's possible."

"That would mean a link between him and the dead girl," Major Pelham said promptly—"I mean a real link. Jealousy, for instance?"

"Just so, sir. That's a possibility one keeps at the back of one's mind."

"How do the people connected with the case strike you?

"Mrs. Clarke, the owner of the house—a very ordinary type, I fancy, fairly straightforward; but I shouldn't bank on her being truthful if she thought a lie would whitewash anything she wanted whitewashed. Unlike Miss Winslow, whom I would expect to find truthful no matter how much a lie might be to her advantage."

"And the men?"

"Mr. Priestley seems a very pleasant, kind-hearted type. Very keen on his work, which seems to be a genuine labour of love with him. He has a face that's almost Chinese, it's so inscrutable. Looks as if nothing would ever move him to anger. . . . Mr. Moffatt . . . looks a selfish type. Shouldn't be surprised if Miss Winslow found him a bit hard under his rather superior airs. A bit grasping, even; but so long as you don't have to face up to him I daresay he's very agreeable. Captain Kidd . . . strikes a hail-fellow-well-met note which may or may not go deep. A certain look about his jowl suggests that he might be reckless and passionate. I haven't met Mr. Lightfoot yet."

"Any theory of what happened? "Pelham asked, pushing his cigars across the table.

"Not yet, sir. Too many possibles. I wish—" Pointer stopped and looked at his shoe tips.

"Yes?"

"I wish it had been some outsider who had seen Mr. Winslow leaving—not only Mrs. Clarke."

"Why should she lie about it, unless she's in the crime in some way. And apparently you don't think either of the women is that."

"No, sir, I don't—so far. As to why she may be telling an untruth, well, I have an idea that she would grasp at anything that would take attention off the house—especially the attention of the police. She sets us the riddle of finding Winslow outside—not of what became of him inside. Where he's gone to now, rather than of why the girl came here, and why he did it, if he did it."

"Yes," the A.C. murmured, "yes, I see the idea. It does exist. One's mind does run on to where he is now, rather than to what he did before he went. By the way, I've met the Priestley you're talking about. F. C. Priestley. Clever chap."

"Is he?" Pointer was interested.

"You can get nearly to the end of one of his letters before you suspect it's a begging one," Pelham continued. "Distinctly brainy. Personally, I rather distrust philanthropists. But that's by the way. What about the servants?"

"The Capsticks seem to run the house. They're the modern type of servant. Take as much as they can and give as little as possible. Lazy, both of them. I never saw a man whom it would be easier to bribe than Capstick, and probably the same is true of his wife. My own landlady would burst into tears if she looked into the bedrooms, and into loud sobs if she inspected the cupboards. They have a couple of maids in to help them daily, and now and then a man to help wait at a dinner party."

There was a short silence.

"So far, from what's told you, do you think there was any real entanglement between the dead girl and the missing man?"

"I can't say, sir. Miss Winslow thinks there was nothing but a flirtation, if that, on both sides. Mr. Moffatt doesn't think she cared two pins for him, really. Mr. Priestley thinks they were very much in love with each other. Captain Kidd suggests that Winslow cared for her, but that she didn't reciprocate. They all seem to feel sure that Winslow's not the type to have shot her— intentionally. The accident theory and a dash on his part to safety is very possible indeed. Only, I can't quite see why he took the revolver with him, and went through his papers so carefully."

"May have been looking for money," suggested Pelham prosaically. Pointer agreed that that was possible—barely possible. Being Saturday, he could not get into touch with Winslow's bank manager until Monday morning, as all efforts to reach him over the telephone at his private address had so far failed.

"The trouble is," Pointer went on, "that it's not Mr. Winslow's dead body we've found, or he would open up. But as it's Winslow who's missing—however, we may get something out of him. Unless Winslow has sent him word to say nothing."

A knock came on the door. It was the enlarged photograph of Winslow which Pointer had had made from a group portrait. He laid it before his superior.

"That's Mr. Winslow, sir. Taken about twelve years ago, unfortunately."

"Nice looking lad." The A.C. studied the features. "Not the shooting type, eh?"

"Nor the head-losing type, either," Pointer added. "I should expect a boy with that face to grow calmer the greater the trouble. That boy's danger would come from too great a reliance on himself, not from his nerves."

"He may have changed," came doubtfully from the A.C.

"A man quoted an Arabic saying to me the other day, sir, to the effect: 'Tell me that a mountain has changed its place and I will believe it. Tell me that a man has changed his nature and I will not believe."

Pelham nodded as though he rather agreed with the Arabs.

"There is one possibility, sir," Pointer went on. "As I say, I haven't any theory yet—that Mr. Winslow saw someone shoot the girl by accident, and rushed away so as not to have to appear as a witness."

"Humph," came from the A.C. "He's on the Stock Exchange, you say. I don't see any sane person doing anything so madly altruistic, except to save a girl he loved. Apparently Winslow has no known attachment.

And you think his cousin hasn't a hand in the business. How about the girl having been shot after he left the flat? Mrs. Clarke, supposing she is telling the truth, may have seen him after he returned for something. This is what I have in mind—" Pelham started a fresh cigar. "Just the merest possibility, of course. Say Winslow lent his flat to Miss Starr to have an interview with some chap of whom she's—rightly—afraid. Blackmailer or jealous lover; husband, perhaps. Say Winslow has forgotten something in his bedroom, which has its own door into his lobby, lets himself into his suite early this morning, only goes in to his bedroom, takes whatever he came for, and hurries out."

"Yes, sir, I—"

"Thought of that and rejected it, eh? Why?"

"No, sir. It's possible. But why were his papers searched?"

"Money," again suggested Pelham. "Her handbag is missing for the same reason. She may have had quite a good deal of money with her."

"Each possibility is a lottery ticket," Pointer said with a smile. "Only time can tell which one will win. There is another possibility which would suit his face better than any other so far, but it's farfetched—fantastic—"

"Let's have it!"

"Well, sir, that he and Miss Starr were linked in some common danger. That she was killed, as the next best thing to killing him, by someone who expected to find Winslow in his rooms and found her instead. That Winslow at once guessed what had happened, and, since he could no longer help her, got away to carry out something vital . . . finish some job which the murderer hoped to prevent. Her handbag gone, his papers looked over, might fit in here."

"And it fits his face as a lad," agreed Pelham. "But, as you say, a bit fantastic."

"Especially as she looks the last kind of a young woman to have been chosen by any man as a helper in anything dangerous. Not that she's a coward's face; far from it. But it looks—well—somehow it doesn't suggest the helpmeet. She may, of course, have gone to his rooms for safety . . . but she seems to've taken no precautions— back to the door. . . ." He picked up Winslow's photograph, looking once more at the resolute, self-reliant young face that said that Winslow would feel himself eminently capable of looking after himself and his own affairs.

"Jealousy, of course, is what leaps to the mind," Pelham murmured. "Pretty girl . . . young man's rooms at night . . . nothing found out yet about the girl?"

"No. The women detectives feel sure that her clothes are all English. She hadn't changed them since her journey, say the others. Miss Winslow guesses her position as that of a shop girl or cashier, even possibly a servant, who had learnt how to carry herself and what clothes to wear at certain hours."

"She seems definitely to dislike her?" said Pelham thoughtfully.

"She does; but it would take remarkable evidence to make me think she shot her. The curious thing," Pointer said, after a pause and eyeing his shoe tips closely, "is why the affair took place in Town—in Winslow's rooms— when both the people concerned seemed linked with Vipiteno. Out there a murder would be easy. Roll anyone in the snow and hold them there, and you've a corpse very quickly. Drop them over a bergschrund; twist a toboggan runner and send them off on a nasty ice run; or merely hit them on the head with a lump of ice and claim a tobogganing accident. Nothing would be easier. Yet it's done—whatever was done—here in Town."

"Any theory to fit that?" Pelham asked with a smile.

Pointer was thinking aloud. "It isn't as though any length of time had gone by after they arrived here. In which case one could think that something was to be carried out for which the murderer waited. She's killed the same night as she gets here."

"Looks to me like jealousy," said Pelham. "Some old flame. She may even be married; her husband, in that case."

"Then where's Mr. Winslow?" asked Pointer. "Unless, as may prove to be the case, he was followed as he rushed out of the house, and was sandbagged, hoisted into a car and has been taken off somewhere. But why did he rush? That face doesn't suggest cowardice."

"So you come back to your theory of his vanishing in order to strike harder?" Pelham was interested, very, but he laid down his cigar—a sign that the interview was drawing to a close.

"Oh, don't call it a theory, sir!" Pointer begged. "I don't own such a thing yet. At present it looks, however, as though Vipiteno was in some way the link—unless, as you suggest, Mr. Winslow is a coward, and bolted when he saw what had happened to Miss Starr in his rooms." And, rising, Pointer made for the door.

CHAPTER EIGHT

POINTER had hardly got back to his rooms before a message reached him. Priestley's telephone was being rung. One of Pointer's men was listening in and telephoned the conversation on immediately. Lightfoot said that he had just met the telegraph boy on his doorstep, and what was wrong? Priestley only repeated that he couldn't explain over the 'phone. Would Lightfoot mind coming round to the house as soon as possible? Lightfoot said that he would be there within ten minutes.

Pointer was there within eight. When Lightfoot arrived and asked for Priestley, by arrangement with that accommodating person, he was shown at once into the room where the chief inspector stood waiting for him. It was Mrs. Clarke's dining-room.

A dead white room with jade green carpet, hangings and chair seats. Admirable for showing up clearly any change of expression on the faces of those to whom he talked, the chief inspector thought, but rather apt to make people look pale.

Lightfoot, however, looked almost black as he faced the other. The tan of many hours in the sun and wind and snow had turned him into almost a Hindu. Pointer thought that he had an uncommon face. He would expect the man who owned those features to pursue undeviatingly any line on which he had started, blind to all other things. He could be, the chief inspector thought, like a receiving set tuned to but one wave length. Not a criminal type, as a rule, but if the something on which this type has set his or her mind is outside the law, or morality, it would not make the slightest difference. Utterly ruthless, often clever and cunning in gaining the end determined on . . . not a good lover, as a rule, but if jealousy be roused, then no bounds need be looked for.

Pointer repeated to him the ambiguous words that he had used before.

"A dead body has been found in Mr. Winslow's suite, and as you were at Vipiteno recently, I should be much obliged if you can confirm its identity for us."

Lightfoot stood quite still. His eyes were so firmly fastened on the chief inspector that it looked as though he were trying to read what lay behind the words.

Pointer stepped aside at the door, and signed to the other to precede him up the stairs, talking as he did so. Lightfoot hurried up them without waiting for any directions, and pushed the door of the suite open. He stepped towards the sitting-room at once. Then he seemed to stop himself.

"Eh—which room? Where is he?" he asked. And he drew a deep breath as though steadying himself.

"The body's in here," Pointer said, stepping forward, and again uncovering the face that had been so gay in life, and was so quiet now. There was absolute silence from the man who stood looking at her. Then Lightfoot said calmly:

"How dreadful! That's a Miss Starr, with whom Winslow was very much in love. How did she come to be here in his flat? She intended staying on another fortnight when I saw her last at Vipiteno. Poor girl! What a ghastly thing to have happened! Was it an accident? How did she die?"

"She was found shot through the heart from the back."

"Here, in this flat?"

"Here in the sitting-room."

"Dreadful!" Lightfoot was pale under his tan. "Shall we go downstairs?"

"In a minute. Sorry, but I'm wanted upstairs." Pointer left him alone with the knob on the table. After three minutes by his watch, Lightfoot was asked to come

downstairs. Ursula had insisted on coming back with
Moffatt for a word with Kidd, which meant with
Priestley, and as soon as they heard that Lightfoot was
here they had gone to the morning-room again with the
uneasy, hard feeling that people have at such times; a
feeling that when there are two or three together some
bright illuminating idea will come. Ursula did not
pretend to be convinced by Moffatt's and Kidd's theory of
the events of last night. She shook her head when asked
about any enemy. Hugh had none, she maintained, could
have none. And as for any link between himself and Fay
Starr, was it likely? Didn't they all know that they were
the merest of strangers, chance met for the first time at
Vipiteno? But she agreed that it offered an explanation
which left Hugh—as she knew, she said, that he would
prove to be—innocent of Fay Starr's death, and that was
what really mattered. In working along it she thought
that a more likely solution might come. Or Winslow
himself come forward. She very much preferred Mr.
Priestley's idea of an accident to Hugh as he had rushed
out for help.

Lightfoot was shown into the room where they had
assembled afresh. He seemed to take it all very calmly,
they thought, though he said the correct words of
amazement and horror.

Upstairs Pointer asked one of his men, who had been
stationed in the bathroom, as to how Lightfoot had
occupied himself during the three minutes in which he
had been alone in the sitting-room. He had not glanced at
the little knob, said the man, but after waiting a few
seconds, apparently listening attentively to the chief
inspector's footfalls dying, away up the stairs, had flung
himself on the writing-table. He opened each one of the
three top drawers and searched it swiftly and carefully,
as though looking for something in the nature of a paper.
He was at work on the middle drawer when he heard
steps, and shut it, to stand again in the middle of the
room looking at nothing in particular. No, he had not

taken anything out of any drawer; but he had hunted like
a man tremendously keen on finding something.

Pointer reflected on Lightfoot's silence. If ever a
mouth looked like that of a talkative man, Lightfoot's
mobile lips did, yet he had said very little. The chief
inspector decided to ask him further questions before the
others. In cases of this kind one listener sometimes
checked the other.

He came in with his note-book in his hand. He had
already asked the others their names and addresses. He
now did so of Lightfoot.

"I'm a drifter," the latter said easily, "of no fixed
occupation—artist,   photographer,   etcher,   designer
sometimes of modern furniture. . ."

Photography and etching might explain the stains on
Lightfoot's nails. As to where he had been last night, he
had spent it driving half over England, he said. He had
wanted to have a word with a scientist on a book which
the latter was writing, found his house in Cambridge
shut up, had decided to go on to a friend who lived at Ely,
and got lost on the fens. "Through trying to drive by the
stars," he added with a laugh. "Rather a hobby-of mine,
finding my way by them."

Lightfoot claimed to have finally driven back to Town,
arriving at his house somewhere around half-past five.
He had no servant, he said, mentioning that he was
thinking of going in for Chinese servants, as he had no
luck with British domestics.

"And when did you see Mr. Winslow last?" Pointer
asked.

"Did he do as he said he was going to," Ursula broke
in, "and take you back that elbow pad you lent him?"

Lightfoot looked at her for a second. "Yes," he said,
"he dropped in yesterday evening. On the way here from
Victoria, I think he said anyway, he returned it all right."

"What was it exactly?" asked the chief inspector as
though he had no idea what was meant.

Lightfoot explained that on the day of the race Winslow had scraped the leather off his pad so badly that the stuffing came out, and that when he, Lightfoot, left Vipiteno he lent Winslow one of his own pads.

"There certainly was no rush about returning it last night," he said with a faint smile. "It will hardly be used for another year, I'm afraid."

"About what time was this?"

Lightfoot said it was about a quarter past nine. "Did he stay long?"

"A bare ten minutes. Just for a chat, and a cocktail, and then off, back to his rooms."

"Did he refer to Miss Starr in any way?"

"No."

"Did he seem as usual in his manner?".

"Just as usual; but—" Lightfoot repeated that Winslow had only stayed a very short time.

"Did he come in a taxi?"

"Yes. He kept it while he ran in."

So that call and its duration would be easy to trace.

"Did your cousin have an umbrella with him?" Pointer asked Ursula. He had not wanted the question to seem important, and had reframed from including it with his previous ones to her.

"He had one when we got off the boat. It was raining hard. He wouldn't be likely to put it away before seeing what the weather was like at Victoria," she said.

"Miss Starr?"

She thought that Miss Starr had none.

"Could you describe his umbrella?" Pointer asked.

"A stout crook, light brown, polished wood. Quite plain. No band or initials on it."

"Carved?"

"No. Quite plain." Ursula had given it to her cousin, it seemed, and was certain about it. She repeated that in colour it was light ash.

One of Pointer's men came in to say that he was wanted on the telephone. It was an arranged

interruption. Pointer hoped that the fair-haired young
man who began to jot down the points of the interview
would be able to detain the others in talk for twenty
minutes. At any rate, Jackson could be trusted to do his
best.

Just around a corner was a cul-de-sac where cars
were parked. One of Pointer's men, looking like a street
loafer, was "minding" them just now. The chief inspector
had keys that would open any of the usual makes. He
looked inside each. Moffatt's was a hired car from a smart
garage. It was as spick and span as Moffatt himself. It
would look like that Pointer thought, if Moffatt had
committed a murder in it. Moffatt was of the careful type.
Captain Kidd's was his own and, as one would expect,
bore the marks of many joyous encounters on the road;
but they were all external. Priestley's car was kept in a
garage nearby. Pointer's man had already seen it, and
vouched for its innocence. It bore marks of hard and fast
travelling. Had been driven at top speed for hours on end,
but it bore no marks that could be connected directly with
last night.

Pointer was interested in all these cars, for he
thought it possible that Winslow, rushing off—for
whatever reason—had been followed. Possibly
sandbagged. Priestley's car he was told was very
efficiently engined. Pointer would expect this to be the
case. He now stepped up to Lightfoot's. Its carpet was
extremely muddy. The weather last night had been vile.
It looked as though the car must have been stuffed with
people with muddy boots; and the mud was unusually
black—blacker than the ordinary London mud. As for the
car itself, it was old and worn, but its engines were good,
and not more than two years old. The tyres were good,
too, and a couple of spares were carried. The mileage
indicator was out of order.

Pointer scraped some of the black mud from the floor
into an envelope. Running his hand carefully over every
inch, into every fold, as he had done with the others, he

felt something solid between the driver's seat and the back. He pulled out an umbrella. A man's quite good silk umbrella. It was of dark wood with a crook handle. On the top of the crook was a tiny projecting peg. The crook was so bent that the actual end was barely noticeable. But there had undoubtedly been a small knob there. He took out his copy. It fitted perfectly. Even to the mark of the rasped place which continued down the crook itself for about an inch.

The question was, whose umbrella was it? It was too important a matter to tackle lightly. He put it back again where he had found it, gave his man instructions to watch it very carefully, and went on to the garage where Priestley's car was housed. He showed his official card and was allowed to look over the charity letter-writer's run-about. He found that his man had reported its blamelessness correctly, and went on to a nearby telephone. He wanted a witness when that umbrella should be officially found. A dependable, unshakeable witness. He rang up a solicitor in Lincoln's Inn Fields to whose granddaughter he had once done a signal service— if saving her life might be called one. Mr. Dorset-Steele had a reputation which would ensure any testimony of his being received with the utmost respect in any court of law. Dorset-Steele listened with apparently mingled impatience and amusement to what was asked of him.

"Regular comedy you want me to play!" he growled: "Well, I don't say I won't allow myself to be used. Yes, I'll be coming down the steps of the house at the hour agreed on, and be on the look out for you. An umbrella, eh? Oh, of course, routine work, that's understood. All right, I'll come in as your accomplice." And Dorset-Steele hung up.

Pointer went back to the house. He wasted no time in speculating as to how that knob could have got into Winslow's rooms; but he did allow himself to feel tolerably certain that Winslow had not borrowed the umbrella, lost the knob and returned it to Lightfoot last night. They had not travelled home together.

As Lightfoot stepped into the hall, he found the chief inspector just coming out of a room. Pointer asked him if he would be kind enough to drop him at a house in South Kensington not far from his own home in Cromwell Road. Lightfoot said that he would be delighted to be of any help, and the two walked on to his car and got in.

Just before the place where Pointer had asked to be set down, an elderly man walked briskly out of a front door. Pointer hailed him, Lightfoot pulled in, and, leaning out, Pointer handed Mr. Dorset-Steele an open letter from his pocket, or rather tried apparently to do so, but he dropped from it whatever its contents were, which he seemed to think important, for he fumbled on the seat beside him, drew out an umbrella, handed it to Mr. Dorset-Steele with a worried, "Just hold this a moment, will you, sir? I can't have lost it!" and fumbled on. On the floor he seemed to find what he had lost, and putting it into the envelope, handed the letter to the solicitor. Then he seemed to realise that Mr. Dorset-Steele was still holding the umbrella. Pointer, with an apology, took it, seemed to see it for the first time, and again looked around him. "Where's its knob? Dear me, I seem to be very awkward. Why, but surely!" He stared at it attentively. "Surely I've seen the knob which belongs on this! This had a knob!"

Mr. Dorset-Steele in his turn examined what he had held for a moment. He examined it closely and carefully. "Yes, undoubtedly it had a knob. A fine Malacca cane this. Came from abroad, I fancy."

Lightfoot sat watching the two with a faint smile on his thin lips.

"Had it a knob?" Pointer asked. "Is it yours, sir?"

"Yes, it's mine. But I don't know if it had a knob or not." And Lightfoot stretched out his hand for the article in question, but Dorset-Steele was still looking it over, spectacles on nose.

"Dear, dear, Chief Inspector! I think a claim could be made against the Yard for rough usage, if these scratches are your doing."

Pointer shook his head. Dorset-Steele now relinquished the umbrella to Lightfoot, who dropped it carelessly at his feet; but looking at him, the chief inspector met the dark intent eyes of his companion staring at him as though trying to read his very soul. A vain effort, as far as the chief inspector's soul was concerned.

Pointer glanced down at the umbrella and again picked it up. Drawing from his pocket a little knob, he fitted it in silence to its end. Then he looked at Lightfoot inquiringly.

"This seems to be the missing knob."

"Seems to be. Is this gentleman an umbrella merchant?" Lightfoot asked.

"No," Pointer said to that. "But I must ask you to let me keep this umbrella for the time being, Mr. Lightfoot. And I wonder if you, sir "—he spoke to Dorset-Steele who, judging by the grim humour of his glance, was enjoying the scene—" would be so good as to take it back to your office. I shall call for it in a few minutes." And with that Pointer bowed and drew up the window. The solicitor walked off, the umbrella dangling from his arm.

In the car there was absolute silence for a full minute.

"Why are you keeping that gamp of mine?" Lightfoot asked, thrusting forward his chin. He had ugly eyes at the moment.

"Because the knob I had in my possession which fitted it was found on the floor of the room where Miss Starr was shot, Mr. Lightfoot," Pointer said to that.

"Impossible."

The chief inspector made no reply to that foolish exclamation.

"I may have lent the umbrella to Winslow—or, I know! He probably took it out of my stand last night. It was pouring, you know. At any rate, I know nothing about it, chief inspector. And no amount of talking will alter facts. However much you police would like to implicate me in the murder of that poor child." Lightfoot spoke contemptuously, and yet with a sort of inner heat. "You can't do it!" The words and tone were quietly exultant. "As I say, Winslow, when he came to see me, probably took the thing out of the stand to borrow it, the knob dropped off into his coat pocket, he decided against the umbrella, put it back, and the knob got carried to his rooms. Now where can I put you down?"

It was an unanswerable explanation, especially in its latter garb. Even without the suppressed fury with which it was given, however, Pointer would not have believed it. But for the moment it must pass, and it might pass later on with a jury, for the same reason—that one could not disprove it.

CHAPTER NINE

POINTER thanked Lightfoot for the lift, and got out near the Yard. There he learnt within ten minutes that Lightfoot had made for his club. A message, in code, was sent to one of Pointer's men asking him to try to detain Mr. Lightfoot by any means short of downright coercion until a telephone inquiry should reach him, asking, "Are you Smith?", that would mean that he could let up on his efforts, and permit Mr. Lightfoot to take his departure.

Pointer himself drove at once to Lightfoot's house. There he got out and looked about him. Just around the corner were several small shops of the kind that any householder would probably patronise through his servants, if not in person. A tobacconist, as the nearest, seemed the best chance for inquiries. He stepped in and bought some tobacco. While it was being weighed he began his questions. He explained that he himself was a shopkeeper, none too certain of Mr. Lightfoot's credit. Did the tobacconist know any gentleman of that name at such and such an address?

The tobacconist was prepared to hold forth on the gentleman for several minutes. Mr. Lightfoot, according to him, ran a sort of boarding-house.

"This is only my private idea, mind you!" he added, "but I don't think I'm far out. Foreigners mostly," he added contemptuously. "And a cheap lot. They come in here for their smokes, and you never heard such rum things as they ask for!" He went on to say that Mr. Lightfoot employed no regular staff of servants. He had a charwoman who came in occasionally, she was the one the tobacconist employed, too, and from her he learnt that the boarders did the cleaning. Apparently taking it in turns to do the cooking and the rooms. They never stayed long, and no wonder! He couldn't remember any face that came to his shop for more than a fortnight. Over here to learn enough English to get a job, probably, which was one thing the shopkeeper didn't hold with. "If I were you, I shouldn't give Mr. Lightfoot any extended credit. He can't make much out of them. Can't. This is between ourselves, of course." Pointer thanked him and left the shop. He tried a telephone from nearby. There was no reply from the house. Apparently there was no one at home. So much the better. He tried ringing the front door bell, and there was no answer. He decided to reconnoitre. Two houses farther down the road was a house to let. Pointer whirled off to the house agent in his car, showed his card, and borrowed the key for "observation purposes." The obliging agent was able to add a seven-foot ladder from a builder's next door, and a long tape-measure. Pointer meanwhile quietly annexed some of the firm's cards. He rang at the house next to the empty one, between it and Lightfoot's, showed the house agent's card to the servant, and asked if he might be allowed to take some measurements of the back garden. No, he did not want to come into the house, except to pass through it. It was merely a question of walls and surveys. She retired for a moment, and brought back a message to say that he could cross the yard and take any measurements needed; and that the tenant hoped that at last something would be done about the dog in number nineteen and the gramophone at forty-two. Pointer said that he hoped so, too, and went through with his ladder. He did some quick measuring, put the ladder against the wall, and was over into Lightfoot's garden. A square of gravel and what had once been flower-beds, neglected and evidently used as a supplementary dust bin. One solitary plane tree managed to survive in the centre. As he expected to find, the door at the back was locked, but with a lock which he opened in a minute. He stepped inside. He was in the usual narrow back passage which in this case, from its smell, might have been a tunnel through cheese and garlic. The first room off it was a windowless sort of scullery between a kitchen and a larder. It had a boiler in it, once intended for washing clothes, a small supplementary range and a sink. What arrested Pointer was that all four walls had just been colour washed—a deep orange. The stuff was still wet. Even the sink had been enamelled to match in bath enamel which lay in thick ridges and waves.

Apparently the work had not been done from any love of cleanliness, nor, to satisfy any love of beauty, for the ceiling had been left as black as soot and London grime could make it. In the centre of it was a wavy outline where some central light had been recently detached. A large affair of several circles, it had apparently been fastened there with a thick flex, to which now hung one ten-watt lamp; a new one. The floor of uneven stone was very clean. It, too, was still wet in places. Odd, this interest in an apparently unused room. There was a cupboard in it. Opening it, Pointer saw the piles of old household gear—strips of dirty carpet, worn-out matting, cardboard, papers . . . Hungarian and two Spanish papers of some months ago. Judging by marks on the walls, a couple of big cases or trunks had recently been stored here. As recently, Pointer thought, as the washed floor and the painted walls and the new bulb in the ceiling. He could not spare the time to go through the cupboard. At any moment someone might return and discover him. But he glanced at the upper shelf, where lay a sort of large four-leaved clover of white painted wood. It was a holder for a set of five electric bulbs. On top of it were lying the five bulbs, ground glass, each of sixty watt. Three hundred watt light in this little room. This room, whose walls had been recently painted, and whose floor was still wet from scrubbing. By the door Pointer found a piece of wood carelessly nailed over what had been a number of switches. Counting the one left for use, there had been five switches in all—one to each lamp. A curiously intricate arrangement. A windowless room. Pointer flashed his torch very carefully along the floor. It showed no splashes of metal which the chief inspector was prepared to find. But it had been scrubbed with tremendously strong ammonia. Well, judging by the look of the ceiling, it might have been necessary. Still, it was odd. Pointer passed on. The kitchen was filthy with what looked like the accumulation of months. The stove was a mass of rust and grease. On it a battered coffee pot with very good coffee in it. The larder was a little cleaner, and housed an unusual amount of cheap tinned food. There was a big dish of macaroni and cheese and tomatoes. Admirable, even when cold. It had been made some time last night, he fancied, from its solidity. Apparently last night had been a busy time. That painting in the other room must have been started about then. Those trunks, or cases, moved. Lightfoot's car used. . . . Apparently the owners of the trunks had been the users of the lights, He went upstairs. A shabby little sitting-room by the front door looked as though it were intended for the use of many people. Out of it opened a dreary little study. The desk, a roll-top affair, had a special lock and was closed. Locked, too, were the couple of fitted cupboards by the fireplace. Pointer soon had them open. They were absolutely empty. The floor above was one big L-shaped room—the drawing-room. The main room held no furniture now except two rows of mattresses on the floor, while the smaller end was fitted with four washstands of the cheapest quality. There were eight beds in all. Above was the single bathroom and a small bedroom, spotless and tidy. A huge and once beautiful wardrobe occupied the whole of one end. Inside it were complete outfits of clothing of various sizes and kinds. There were three priests' soutanes, collars and hats, a couple of scoutmaster's rigs, nonconformist clergymen's outfits filled several pegs. And the remainder were such as any workman or small tradesman might use. On two pegs were waiters' things, and on two were really good suits complete in every detail. One small end of the wardrobe held women's clothes of a nondescript dress and long coat and felt hat type. This wardrobe, too, had been locked. Pointer left it as he found it. The two top rooms were bare and apparently could be used as additional dormitories.

Pointer returned to the windowless little room in the basement whose walls, alone of all the rooms in the house, had been colour-washed, at some time last night or early this morning, whose stone floor was so recently scrubbed. There was one particular spot where the thick distemper had been put on apparently with a shovel. With a knife from the kitchen Pointer flaked off a bit of colour that dropped in brittle hail to the floor. Under it was a surface which made him wonder whether the room had been used as a coal cellar. He carefully detached a flake of the black wall below. What he got away he put into one of his wax-paper envelopes. He tried two other places, but the distemper was too soft for him to get the under dirt off in one piece. He tried the sink next. There, also, scrapings in two places showed that underneath each had been a thick black deposit. Apparently the same as on the wall. He tried other spots, and though he occasionally struck a grey whitewash, he several times found the same black surface. Going into the kitchen for a rag, he managed to wash some of the distemper back over the scrapings which he had flaked away. It was plastered on nearly a quarter of an inch thick in some spots. The one aim had evidently been speed, and to hide the black marks. Pointer looked up again at the outline of the big electric lights. If he was right in his guess, those smears of black would turn out to be a mixture of boiled linseed oil and lamp black. It is a mixture which may serve various innocent purposes, as every gardener knows who paints his conservatory pipes with it; but Pointer did not think pipes had been its object here.

He found the coal cellar, and flashed his torch about. The small garden outside had not been disturbed for at least a year, but a coal cellar has possibilities. At present perhaps half a ton of coke lay piled in it. It had been recently disturbed, for there was anthracite dust on the floor, and some of it on the top of the coke. The scrape marks on the floor were either made to-day or very recently. Pointer found some overalls behind the cellar door. They were stiff with more than coal dust, stiff with the same black liquid, apparently, as he had found splashed on the wall and the sink. The overalls which he tried on first were much too small for him; the others might have fitted Lightfoot, or some man of his slender build. Pointer found a spade leaning against the wall, also behind the door, and examined it very carefully, after first putting gloves on. He had no time to test it for finger-prints. It might be that beneath that heap of coke lay . . . He did not finish the sentence even to himself, but he set to work with a will, careless as to whether he were discovered or not. He had nearly got to the bottom of the coke when his careful spade struck something different from the coke. He worked like lightning, but it turned out to be only a box about a foot square, tied in a newspaper and with a long loop of cord attached to it, so that if one knew of its presence, it would have been possible to find it and retrieve it in a minute. It was securely locked. Pointer opened it and stared at the contents. They were not unexpected. They were tools, and tools that he knew how to use, for he himself was extremely fond of etching.

Here was a burin, set in a much-used handle. Here were needles for dry-point etching in varying sizes. Old dabbers, and scrapers, and all the paraphernalia of the engraver's art. Pointer stared at them thoughtfully as he retied and carefully placed the box to one side, to be buried again when he had finished with the cellar. Pointer found a second box in another moment. It was not tied up in any way, and only contained bottles with their labels soaked off. A sniff told him the contents. They had held various acids and the protecting gum solutions used for plates. There were no plates and no paper. Pointer discovered nothing else. And the floor beneath was of untouched concrete. He left everything as he had found it and had a wash at the kitchen sink. He expected to be back shortly with a search warrant. There are not many etchings or many books which have to be made and printed in secret, This house did not suggest indecent literature or pictures. What it suggested, and very strongly, were counterfeit bank-notes. Those powerful overhead lights in that otherwise safe dark room, that would explain, too, why no paper had been left, why the all-important plates had been taken away, too. As for the tools which had been left behind, that looked as though the engraver, or etcher, thought, or knew himself suspected, and dared not risk having his tools found on him. It all looked to Pointer, as he drove away, as though, supposing he were right, the plates and the paper were in the charge of one member of the gang whose luggage would be considered safe from investigation. Plates and paper go into a very small attaché case. That the owner of the tools felt himself insecure was shown by the fact that he had not dared yet to throw away the bottles, even without the labels on them.

Pointer thought of the etching stains on Lightfoot's fingers, of the man himself, of all that seemed to have happened in the house since last night or during last night—of what had happened in Lowndes Square last night or this morning. Those flakes of black would be analysed at once, and by an expert, but he expected to find that in addition to linseed oil and lamp black would be rosin, and possibly soap. In other words, he expected to find that the black splashes had been made by good permanent printing ink; for he could think of nothing else which would fit that house which he had just left behind him. Probably one of the innumerable small presses worked by a power-plug in the corner would lie dismantled in the cupboard, or had been taken away in pieces in the trunks or cases. And the owner of this house had just been to Italy, as had Winslow, who was missing—as had Miss Starr, who was now dead. A thrill ran through the chief inspector. It was as if he watched on the blank wall something being drawn or painted for him which would yet explain that murder and that disappearance. Counterfeit banknotes.

Lightfoot had left Vipiteno a few days before Winslow and Miss Starr. . . . He would have paid his bill a few days before, therefore, just a couple of days before. . . . Suppose he had passed off there some of the work which might well have been done in that little middle room. . . . Was Miss Starr an accomplice, or had she blundered innocently into this affair? Women are skilful in passing off bad notes.

She seemed—according to what was told him by the others—to have no firm social background. Supposing she had changed a false note at a time when Winslow was with her? He might have detected it. Would he be likely to? And on that came the answer that Pointer had just been told by Ursula Winslow that Hugh was the nephew of Joliffe and Joliffe, the men who made paper for the Bank of England.

Winslow, of all men, save an actual bank clerk, might be expected to know a good note from a bad one.

Leaving him on one side for the moment, there had lately been some remarkable forgeries of Bank of England notes. In strict confidence—for the Old Lady of Threadneedle Street has her own detectives—the Yard had been told that the notes were all but perfect. Yes, the painting on the wall of what might have happened was growing clearer. And if so, Pointer's fantasy—it was no more—that Winslow might have rushed from the house, leaving a dead girl in his rooms, because he felt that he must at all costs live to catch the murderer—who would be the forger in this case—might prove to be not so wild as it had seemed. Say that Miss Starr and he had alone known the truth except for the gang of criminals . . . say that he did not know who the forger was, only suspected, perhaps strongly, one of the small band of English people who had been with him at Vipiteno. . . . In the light of that thought, the fact that it was to Lightfoot that Winslow had first rushed when he got back to Town acquired a new significance. It might have been from him that the note had come, this hypothetical forged note which would explain so much. Even so, Winslow might have gone to Lightfoot without any suspicion of the man, just to find out where Lightfoot in his turn had got it, and been put off with some excuse—or did the knob of the umbrella belong here? Had Winslow given Lightfoot an appointment? Lightfoot would probably have to say that he could not remember where he had got the note . . . that would be the only way to gain time at once. . . That Miss Starr should be at Winslow's rooms, too, looked as though she were concerned in that note. She could hardly be one of the gang, one would think, if she had indicated Lightfoot as the person from whom she had originally got the note . . . it looked as though the forger Lightfoot might have decided to get rid of the only two people in the world who knew him for what he was. The question was, and had been from the beginning, for Pointer:

Was this a single or a double murder? If Winslow had escaped, it was odd that he had not sent in any word of what had happened to the police. And odd, too, how Miss Starr had reached Winslow. Or had they driven off together from Victoria to have a word with Lightfoot? Lightfoot might well have refused to acknowledge that; though the fact that he had not done so made Pointer think it had not happened like that. He believed Lightfoot to be too clever not to tell the absolute truth—when it could be found out by the police, and very shortly the taxi drivers would be telling their tale.

The news came within half an hour. Two separate taxicabs had been hailed and had driven off. The first drove Winslow to Lightfoot's house and then on to his own rooms. There he had just got down, said the man, and was ringing the bell and saying that if the servants were out would he, the taxi driver, take up his two suitcases for him, when another taxi had driven up, out of it had jumped a very pretty girl in a red dress and coat with yellow fur around the neck. She had kissed the young gentleman and they had gone in and up to the flat together. The driver had set the suitcases down inside the door in the lobby, and been well paid for his trouble.

The second driver amplified this. A young lady had engaged him at the Victoria boat-train platform, and had told him to follow a certain taxicab which she pointed out to him. He had followed, first to a house off Cromwell Road, then on to Lowndes Square. Near the latter, when the first cab drew up and the fare got out, the young lady had shoved a note in his hand—a pound note—told him to keep the change, and had rushed up the steps and kissed the young man. Both drivers agreed that Winslow—for it seemed he by description—had appeared very surprised. He had not kissed her in return, but had merely held the door open for her to pass on in and up the stairs.

So they had not gone together from Victoria.

Did this mean that Miss Starr was not connected with the notes? If not, why her interest in where Winslow was going? It looked very much to the chief inspector as though she were more deeply connected with them than Winslow had thought. It seemed likely that he had let her see—or that her guilty knowledge had shown her—that he suspected the genuineness of some note which had been passed by her, or where she was present. It looked as though she did not intend to lose sight of Winslow. She had not come forward openly and gone with him to see Lightfoot. She had not gone in at all, but waited in her taxi, said her driver, and sitting well back out of sight, too.

Then, when Winslow was going up to his rooms, she had jumped out and rushed the position—apparently. This version made the mystery of her murder all the deeper. For it looked as though she were an accomplice of the forger, and in enmity to Winslow.

Pointer decided that he would see what her luggage could yield. Two cases and a large wardrobe trunk labelled with her name had been acknowledged by the Customs as waiting at Victoria. They were handed over to the Yard now. Pointer and two women detectives went through them carefully. They told nothing, except that Miss Starr had no letters or papers of any kind whatever in them. They were packed simply and solely for use in a winter sports resort, and shed no light whatever on her past circumstances or business. They had all been bought at various smart London shops, all the frocks and coats were "off the peg"; the shoes and gloves and hats told the same tale. Such of her things as had been washed had been laundered at home. Gone, as far as women are concerned, are the old days of laundry marks.

CHAPTER TEN

THE report on the black stains was hurried in to the chief inspector. It was printing ink, pure and simple, of a well-known proprietary make. The mud off the carpet in Lightfoot's car was the same, with dust and pavement mud added. So the chief inspector's guess was a certainty, and his reconstruction of how that little room without a window, but with such powerful overhead lights, had looked before last night seemed the true one. Remained to prove what had been printed there, or etched there. Winslow had visited the house around nine, said Lightfoot, and around five next morning was seen— according to Mrs. Clarke—hurrying out of her house and round a corner. Was it possible that here was one of those damnable coincidences which almost invariably turn up to test a detective's theory? Had the printing press nothing to do with Winslow's absence, with Miss Starr's murder? Then how did that knob off Lightfoot's umbrella come to be in the room where she had been found dead? Was it possible that she had been murdered and Winslow carried off? Had he a forged note in his possession which they wanted back?

Was there, for instance, some writing on it which would bring it home to one of the gang? Was Winslow being kept until he would hand it over, or tell them where he had put it? He got up. He had sent in word to Superintendent Horrocks, who dealt in forged notes— officially—all the particulars' of the case as so far known, and had now received a summons to meet the superintendent in the room of the A.C.

Pointer amplified what little his notes left obscure. The two listened very closely.

"It certainly provides a good motive for a murder," Pelham said. "Well played, Pointer! Good work."

"Thank you, sir. It would explain a lot, as you say—"

"You mean this girl's murder? She's not a member of any gang known to us. Neither is any of your lot—Lightfoot included." The chief inspector had taken snapshots of everyone connected with the case so far, and they had been immediately enlarged and were now in circulation.

"She may have been a member of the gang whom they thought trustworthy, but who lost her heart to Winslow," Pelham suggested thoughtfully, "and gave the show away to him."

"The charm of this case is, you can turn it in a hundred directions, and each one seems possible—though improbable," Pointer said grimly.

"You say that the idea of the others, on the whole, is that she was not in love with Winslow," Horrocks said; "that looks to me as though she may have been playing a game. Or, as you say, this case is the devil for ifs and ors—on the other hand, she may have rushed in to his flat to warn him of some danger, he hurrying off with the incriminating note or notes; was stopped under some pretext, or sandbagged, and carried away, and is being detained to tell them. Where he put the note, or has been disposed of. Have you communicated with the uncles in any way?"

"Miss Winslow and Mr. Moffatt are going on down there this evening," Pointer said. "All we did was to send them a guarded inquiry as to where Mr. Hugh Winslow is, and received a very cool and vague reply to the effect that the last the speaker heard of him he was off for Italy for a holiday. His partner seems unreachable. He's evidently gone up north by car, not by train, or he would have got our telegrams and messages."

Horrocks rose. As one of the Big Five, he had twenty jobs for every second of the day. "We'll see if any of our special men can link up that house off Cromwell Road with forgery dens. It's often easier to link a house than a person. So far, we've nothing in that respectable locality on our books. In my opinion, you can't do better than carry on as you're doing at present, Pointer," and Horrocks hurried away. Pointer followed. He was fuming at the week-end delay. Not till Monday could the case really hurry on. And when on a case the chief inspector was like a terrier at a rat hole—unable to leave it till he had finished his investigations, however deep they went. This question which so worried him, of a double or a single tragedy, seemed unanswerable at the moment. Of whether Winslow was the criminal and in hiding, or being hunted by criminals and working for the law; or in their hands; or already dead. What had happened to Winslow after he dashed out of the house this morning— according to Mrs. Clarke—dressed as for a journey, suitcase possibly in hand. She could not be sure about that, she said. And to Pointer it seemed an odd uncertainty.

Pointer next had an interview with a constable whose duty brought him at intervals past the house in Lowndes Square. He had passed there about nine in the evening, and again, at half-past eleven. The man himself had nothing to report. Did he know the neighbourhood? Thoroughly. Was there anyone likely to be standing about near the house around ten, and past it? Any servants coming home last night opposite, or on either side of, the house in question?

The constable's eyes sparkled.

"Yes, sir. There's a young milkman courting a young woman in service in a house nearly opposite; and last night was her evening off. Her mistress often lets her go with him to the pictures and stay out till eleven. Other times she has to be in at ten. Either way might suit the inquiries." The man would, of course, be off duty now, for milkmen have early hours. But the constable had an idea where he could be found. As he glanced at the clock, Pointer rightly inferred that the question of the young

man's whereabouts was not unconnected with opening
and closing hours. Within ten minutes the constable had
brought the man along in a taxi, very much excited at
being taken to the Yard.

He was a bright-faced young fellow, and seemed only
too delighted to be of use. And what he had to say
promised to be of great use. He said that last night
Aggie—she was now, Miss Blackmore, and now Agnes,
and again just Aggie had had leave to be-out till eleven,
but that he and she had had a bit of a tiff, and that she
had insisted on returning sharp on ten. He had tried to
make his peace with her before she went in, but that she
refused to listen to him. The damsel, it seemed, had
accused him of carrying on with another maid; and,
judging by some incoherences, just here, Miss Agnes
Blackmore had reason on her side. At any rate, she had
gone in, and refused to listen to his protestations. He had
waited about, hoping that she would relent and take a
saunter with him. He had stayed till past eleven o'clock
before finally going home. Part of the time he had walked
about, part he had spent leaning against a lamp-post
reading a newspaper, and part sending in messages by a
sympathetic between-maid to his obdurate fiancée. He
had had plenty of time to watch the street, and had been
only too thankful for any little diversions which it had
offered. At close on eleven last night he had seen a man
come out of Mrs. Clarke's house and walk around the
nearest corner to the right. His description added nothing
to the one they already had of Winslow. Dark overcoat
and black bowler hat. The man had not noticed his face.
But he could only say that it had not struck him as
unusual in anyway.

Pointer had him accompany him to the spot himself,
and stand as he stood last night. Then Pointer took his
place, and the young milkman acted the part of the man
coming out of the house and closing the door very quietly,
as he now remembered. Then the milkman walked
around a corner, and after a second, grinning, returned in

his own person to say that if a film had been taken last night and another just now, he didn't think there'd be an inch out, or a foot's difference. "Though the chap was taller than me," he wound up. Now Pointer had very carefully not mentioned Winslow's height, or lack of it. The milkman was around five-foot ten. Winslow was only five-foot six, or a shade less, said Ursula, and his clothes in the wardrobe bore that out. Was he quite sure that the man had gone to the right— into the cul-de-sac. He was, absolutely.

Pointer thanked him, tipped him, and thought it over. That the milkman should see someone going to the right at eleven, and Mrs. Clarke watch Winslow leaving around five this morning turning to the left, seemed to show that more than Winslow and Miss Starr had been in his rooms. The first one had probably gone to where he had left his car. But Winslow? Pointer had described Lightfoot casually, and the milkman had thought it sounded very like him. It would be no use asking him to identify anyone. He frankly acknowledged that he had paid no attention to face or figure or gait. Was it possible that Winslow had been in the flat from the time the taxi man dropped him there around half-past nine until this morning at five—alone with that murdered girl—and had not tried to get into touch with a doctor or the police? Unless he had left the flat before ten, he had not left till well after eleven, when the milkman had finally gone home; and during that time he had not tried to reach the police in any way. . . . If Mrs. Clarke's story was true, the facts were even more difficult to explain. Pointer determined to test that tale. He asked for Mrs. Clarke now. She sent down word that she was feeling too disturbed at the dreadful thing that had happened in her house to be able to talk about it any more. But Pointer was insistent, and she finally came into the drawing-room looking very stiff, and as though she thought that common decency, to say nothing of higher feelings, should have kept her from this.

Pointer asked her if she were quite sure of the direction which Winslow had taken when she saw him leaving the house this morning.

She stiffened. Certainly she was. Her mouth shut firmly.

"I ask," he said pleasantly, "because we have another witness who saw him leave here earlier, but he turned to the right—not to the left. There's no doubt about it. If you're quite certain, then it looks as though the house held something very important which had brought Mr. Winslow back. We haven't thought the house—as such— important. But, of course, this shows us to be wrong. The house must play a very important part in the crime—"

"But how can it!" she exposulated.

"Why did he return, then?" Pointer asked. "Our other witness saw him leave here at an earlier hour than you. Saw him go towards the mews as though to try to drive away. But you—well—obviously he came back here for something so valuable that it had to be fetched or found. If he didn't find it, we must. I think the press can help us best here—" He got no further. Mrs. Clarke, with a sound between a snort and a gasp, held out a hand.

"Chief Inspector, I've a dreadful confession to make! I don't know what you'll think of me! I'm not untruthful as a rule, but in this case, knowing as I did that *of course* Mr. Winslow had left the house, I wanted to make it quite certain that you wouldn't waste time looking the place over and over for him, and I said what I knew to be true, though actually I hadn't seen it happen with my own eyes. I mean his leaving the house. I didn't see him at all, chief inspector. That's the real truth. And, as I say, I very much regret having stated the other thing. Only, you see, I was right! He *had* left here! Only I was wrong in the direction I said he took, which I really thought of no importance, provided you knew that he had gone right away—absolutely away."

Pointer questioned her about this retraction, and she stuck to it, stuck to it, moreover, with a thankful look and an almost babbling relief which showed that, though she could lie when she thought it useful, she did not like the practice.

Pointer was very grave and very official, and very doubtful as to whether she would not be summoned at the inquest on her previous tale, but on her signing a complete retraction of every former word, he promised not to rake it up, if it could be avoided. The words were Mrs. Clarke's own.

So she had not seen Winslow at all. And the other man had not seen Winslow, either. He had got to his girl's house opposite before ten . . . and the taxi had brought Winslow to the house after half-past nine.

Had Winslow gone straight off to some other place? Back to Lightfoot's, with some information supplied him by Miss Starr, who, waiting for his return, let in someone whom she evidently did not distrust, and was she then shot? And had Winslow met his fate outside the house? This seemed feasible. There, were no signs of struggle in the house which the chief inspector had searched, but with so many inmates as it suggested, it would be an easy matter to overpower him. Was he driven away in the car with the many marks of feet on the carpet? The car where the umbrella had been found?

Pointer felt he was one step further into the fog. At least he knew that a man—not Winslow—tall as Lightfoot, had left the house around eleven. That careful closing of the front door . . . it suggested that the girl already sat there cold and stiff by the table upstairs.

That dismantled printing press, that odd house off the Cromwell Road. . . . And then Pointer thought of the flat above Winslow's own. He had gone over Priestley's handsome rooms and found nothing. But was it possible that a crime had taken place there? Priestley. . . . A thought of all the money that passes through a charity appealer's hands sent a faint flush for a second over Pointer's high cheekbones. Had the man who might be Lightfoot come back later, and had two men carried a third down the stairs and into a car which the first would have brought to the door? Yes, it was possible. An accomplice actually in the house, able to be summoned by a sharp cough, or a tap on the radiator, would be a great help when it came to getting the better quickly and neatly of an active young man. Priestley did not look the part, but that counted for little. It was an odd coincidence that he should have changed his rooms just before this crime, even though he had a perfectly good excuse. The house where he had stayed gave him an exemplary character. He could have stayed on undisturbed for another six to eight weeks, had he chosen. And then came an urgent summons from Superintendent Horrocks. That good man had had a talk with higher powers, and was no too pleased at the outcome.

"We're muzzled," he said briefly, "and tied by the leg, too. Nothing is to leak out publicly, here or abroad, as to any forged Bank of England notes. That's a distinct, direct, not-to-be-evaded order, Pointer. It's to do with the state of the exchange just now. For a fortnight yet we must not let it be known that there is any question as to the goodness or not of any English note. After a fortnight we may take what steps are necessary. I've had the Home Secretary himself talking to me. That's all. But be very careful. It's very important, I was told."

Pointer said that he would bear it carefully in mind, and left.

That same evening he had a talk with Winslow's bank manager at the latter's Kensington house. As Pointer had thought would be the case, the manager was not disposed to be very communicative, but he could and did assure the chief inspector that a better customer than Hugh Winslow was not on the bank's registers.

This only fitted in with the accounts so far gleaned from his school, where he had been a prefect. Straightforward, reserved, and honourable. Not in the least brilliant, but anything but a fool. Very tenacious, very self-reliant. More or less the same had been swiftly

learnt at his college, where he took a pass only, but had
not intended going in for Honours. And with that, for the
moment, Pointer had to consider his day finished. He had
set his baited lines near and far, and must now wait for
the hours to work with him. Among other things, he
wanted to know whether any chauffeurs had been
waiting near the house in Lowndes Square; they, if so,
might have seen something. No mention of Winslow was
made, but the entire hunt centred around the dead Fay
Starr.

Her picture was thrown on the screen in as many
picture halls as possible The B.B.C. contributed its help
by asking for anyone to come forward who had ever
known her, or who had seen anyone going or coming from
the Lowndes Square house that night.

Meanwhile Captain Kidd met Moffatt and Ursula on
their return from the country, where Ursula had broken
the news about Hugh's disappearance to her uncles. He
was full of something that he had learnt about Miss
Starr.

"It's only a trifle," he began apologetically, "but I
asked them to let me know as soon as you would be back.
She once spoke of a garage in Brixton—Lavender Hill—
something about its being the only garage which were
never late in sending a car round. She spoke as though
she kept it there by the month."

"Oh, but," came impatiently from Ursula, "it couldn't
have been at Brixton, Captain Kidd. I don't want to jeer
at the poor girl, now she's dead, but surely it was
somewhere in the purlieus of St. James's Palace?" Kidd
gave a fleeting grin.

"We were talking of funny names," he said, "and she
said the man there was called Lord Earl, which she
thought exceedingly quaint. Now I've looked up the name
in the telephone directory, and it's there. Lavender Hill.
Suppose we look into it?" He addressed Moffatt, who

nodded and told Ursula that there might be something in it.

"But only about Fay Starr," she expostulated.

"How will that help you to get into touch with Hugh? Frankly, I fancy Miss Starr's past would be very commonplace. Brixton very likely, and an assistant at a hairdresser's establishment there, then some"—she hesitated—"rich man's darling," she had been about to say, but remembering Kidd's liking for the girl, which at one time had seemed very genuine, and not so shallow as, or passing as he now would have it appear, she changed to, "some lucky chance gave her a little money, and she blued it in a winter sports place on the chance of making interesting friends."

Ursula was feeling very depressed. The uncles had been rather trying. They refused to think it anything but sinister that the murder should have taken place in Hugh's rooms. In vain she pleaded that if one left one's suite it might happen to anybody. Both the men had shaken their heads and agreed that you were known by your friends, and that sensible people saw to it that they lent their houses —or flats—to people like themselves. Moffatt had done better than she, with his very temperate but, on the whole, kindly stand for the absent nephew. Christopher, the elder brother, spoke of some inquiries of his made over the telephone, which had seemed difficult to understand, but which were now explained. He only hoped that the relationship of the missing young man with himself and his brother could be kept dark. Ursula had not stayed long, but she was glad that she had persuaded Moffatt to come with her. As for Kidd and his transparent paper, that would have to wait a while, she now said deprecatingly. Later on, a letter of introduction.

"Don't trouble," Kidd said promptly. "Winslow gave me one in Vipiteno. Said you might be too busy to remember, or the uncles might be out the day we intended to blow down all together. No end kind of him.

I'll wait, of course, till things have calmed down and he's back, and then take it myself down to them. Well, Moffatt, coming down to Lavender Hill?" Moffatt rose with a sigh, and with another sigh took a seat beside Kidd in the latter's little car.

"I see nothing but trouble for myself, whichever way things go," Moffatt began as they bounced along. "In a way, it's not a bad idea to work away on Miss Starr's past. It'll look like doing something, and give Winslow time to come to his senses—literally or figuratively. Unless he's out of England. Anyway, it gives an idea of doing one's best."

"I want to do mine," Kidd said shortly. "Winslow comes second to my mind. He's a man, after all, and can, or should be able to, look after himself; but that poor little girl, shot through the back like—like—" He paused for a comparison.

"Like an old house-dog," Moffatt said very gravely. "Yes, Kidd, in a way if I weren't engaged to Ursula, and if she did not make it a condition of our engagement that I find Hugh, I should agree with you. But, of course, as things are—" He gave his faint smile, and Kidd responded instantly.

"Besides," Moffatt went on, "I don't think Miss Starr would thank us for what we're doing. She very much wanted her background kept shaded. Focusing the spotlight on it is the last thing that she would want—at least, that's how I see it."

Kidd frowned. "Yes, but she wasn't murdered then," he said. "I mean, facts alter feelings. She was quite a bit of a spitfire, you know. I can't see her sitting down under this, and not wanting to have the chap who did it hung."

"Oh, quite," Moffatt agreed promptly. "I should feel that way. But, then, I don't pretend to come from the heart of the aristocracy, and to be related to quite such high-born dames as Miss Starr liked people to think she did. However . . ." And Moffatt looked resigned to whatever might come of their inquiries. It was not much, and yet it was a step forward.

For they learnt that Miss Starr had a little Ford runabout which she kept at Lord Earl's garage in summer, selling it in the winter, and buying another next spring. Her address was a boarding-house in Brixton. Kidd learnt that she had lived there for a month some two years ago, leaving when she found a small flat to suit her. The woman of the house seemed to have a pleasant memory of the girl—but not of that hunchback who came to see her now and then. "Horrid face, he had! You felt he had a grouch against all the world." She had no idea where Miss Starr had moved to, nor had she seen her or the hunchback again.

"I call that a big step forward," Kidd said in some elation as they drove back again, this time to his own pleasant rooms in Westminster.

"Towards finding where Hugh Winslow is?" Moffatt asked; and Kidd had to laugh.

"I suppose not. Frankly I don't see what one can do about that. It's not a bad thing to find out how deuced difficult these things are for private people to work. I mean—how does one find anyone who isn't there?" Kidd spoke rather helplessly. Moffatt only laughed a short laugh and added, "Especially when he may not want to be found. I still—when alone with you, Kidd—think the truth will be an accident, and a most ill-considered flight. But having flown—well, in his shoes I think I should stay fled until things are a bit cleared up. At the inquest on Monday something may turn up."

"This hunchback may come forward and give us some idea as to where Miss Starr comes from, who she is, what she does or did for a living . . ." Kidd suggested.

Moffatt looked uninterested. "I don't want to be brutal, dear boy, but who cares?" Moffatt asked. "What we want to do is to have some idea of what happened in Winslow's rooms last night."

CHAPTER ELEVEN

POINTER was most flatteringly appreciative of Captain Kidd's efforts to find out something about Miss Starr's past. That lucky recollection of her words about the name of the garage keeper had been a real help in starting to unwind her past. But, like Moffatt, he regretted that it brought them no nearer to finding out what had become of Winslow. Unless he, as well as she, had been a consummate liar and actor, the two had never met before Vipiteno. And now that he had what seemed so straight a lead as to the possible motive for her murder, it was Winslow, much more than the murdered girl, who engaged the attention of the Scotland Yard man. And, quite to his surprise, he was to learn an interesting new fact about him on the following day. He was lunching on the Sunday at his rooms in Bayswater when the telephone rang. Making a long arm, he drew it to him and heard the voice of the bank manager to whom he had gone last evening about Hugh Winslow's account. He had something to say which, under the circumstances, "the odd circumstances, he really thought that he might call them—" Pointer assured Mr. Merryweather that he thought he might, without any exaggeration. "—he believed should be told the chief inspector in strictest confidence." Could he see Mr. Pointer to-day? He understood that the chief inspector was very keen on learning anything that would help him to get into touch with Mr. Hugh Winslow.

Pointer again assured him that he had understood quite rightly.

"I don't know that this will help towards that," Mr. Merryweather hedged, "but it's an odd fact. And—well,

I'll call and explain more fully in person, and in the very strictest confidence. My son-in-law happens to be in town, and he and I will come on at once, if we may. Where shall we find you?"

Pointer asked if Bayswater would be out of the way for the manager, and learnt that he was speaking from that quarter himself, and could be in Pointer's rooms within a few minutes.

It was within the quarter of an hour when the bell rang, and Pointer's landlady showed up Mr. Merryweather and a young boyish-looking man, whom he introduced as his son, who was also in the same bank as his father, but in the Dover branch, and one of the paying-out clerks there.

Their joint tale was that the Dover branch had had a cable from Winslow on the day he left Vipiteno stating that he would want to cash a cheque there for five hundred pounds and would want the money in one-pound notes. He would like the packets to be made up in fifties and be ready for him when the boat should get in. This demand had gone to the head office, where Winslow's firm banked, and where Winslow kept a current account and securities which would always enable him to draw up to a thousand pounds at a moment's notice.

Mr. Merryweather had had no notion of this communication, and would, in the ordinary course of things not have heard about it, but when the Sunday papers came out as they had with the news of the accident in a Mr. Hugh Winslow's flat, the owner being, it was believed, still away on his holiday in Italy, the son had come up to see his father, who had brought him along to the chief inspector. Pointer promised that, unless absolutely necessary, the information would not be labelled as coming from the bank clerk. This particular young Merryweather knew Winslow by sight, for he had been for a time a clerk in his father's bank, and had only been lent to Dover to cope with some additional accounts down there. He and Winslow had both recognised each other. Winslow was looking very brown and fit, the young man said. He took the notes in the packages and stacked them in his small suitcase, which he was carrying. No, Winslow had not slipped in in any secretive way. But he had been in a great hurry. A young girl had looked through the glass door once, and she, the clerk was prepared to swear, was the dead girl—Miss Starr. Whether she was with Winslow or not, he could not say, but he had at the time the notion that she was waiting outside for him.

He did not know whether Winslow was walking or driving, nor whether the girl was. There was no commissionaire at the bank who might be able to tell. He only saw her glance in the once. He thought she seemed very haggard, though very much made-up. Perhaps it was the look in the eyes—somehow he thought of her as unhappy. Young Merryweather could give no further information; but what he had brought was very important, Pointer thought. He asked him to keep it to himself, unless asked by the police to come forward. Alone, for the friend who shared the rooms with him was away, Pointer walked up and down his long room thinking hard. If anyone else knew of the five hundred untraceable pound notes in Winslow's possession from Dover on to Town, then another fresh motive for his murder was to hand. Why had Winslow wanted the money in that particular, unusual way? This first answer that leapt to the eye was blackmail, of course. But did it fit here? Pointer held no card for blackmailers, but they, do punish criminals which the law cannot touch. Yet Winslow? Everything that they had learnt about him negatived the idea of some secret plague spot in his life. Also, he was in a position to snap his fingers at most sorts of blackmail—unmarried—his own master—not especially marked for a large fortune in anybody's will, as far as the chief inspector could find out—so that he might be supposed to be afraid of losing his inheritance. But the money taken in that untraceable way did fit in with the theory—the possibility, rather—that Hugh Winslow had in some way come upon a forged note, and had rushed home to try to trace it. He might well feel that he wanted to be in possession of ample funds of just that kind of currency, something which the taker could not fear would be traced to him—or her. It looked as though he thought that he might want to bribe his way. It bore out the evening's visit to Lightfoot at a time when the banks would long have been closed.

What was the position of Miss Starr in all this? The girl who had looked through the window at Winslow when he took the notes in Dover; the girl shot dead that night in his rooms in Town; Miss Starr, who had lived a very short time at a Brixton boarding-house, and said that she was going on to a flat of her own; the hunchback, her only visitor, disliked by the landlady, who seemed to have liked Fay Starr.

Pointer walked to the mantelshelf and took down a Chinese puzzle. Hollow globes, one within the other, they turned, and he had never found the secret which would get them out. He had a feeling that, in its own way, this puzzle was going to be as difficult. The missing young man, the dead girl, the five hundred pounds in one-pound notes, the printing ink on the walls of that room in Lightfoot's house—they all seemed to turn within the other; but could he find the key?

That man who had been seen by the milkman walking down the steps of the house in Lowndes Square was the key. Pointer thought he was the murderer. But where was Winslow and his five hundred pounds? If Miss Starr had been killed in connection with those forged notes, would the forger let Winslow, infinitely the more dangerous antagonist, escape? And if he had not escaped? Pointer could learn of no one who had seen anything suspicious last night or this morning, or anything that could—in the light of what the police suspected—be twisted even by them into anything suspicious. Pointer put back the Chinese puzzle and decided that he must go to Vipiteno at once. Everything, to him, looked as though Winslow had come on a forged note there. True, his rush home was caused by his partner's own need to leave town, a need which had been looked into and which seemed genuine, but his actions on arriving in England were those of a man following a plan. Lightfoot's house was not to be searched yet. Superintendent Horrocks wanted more proof; and the stringent orders to make no arrests still held. Lightfoot could claim that he always dismantled his printing press over the week-end, and liked to keep his engraving tools under his coke. Even the finding of Winslow's body, for Pointer thought that Hugh Winslow was probably dead, and probably well hidden somewhere, must wait, he thought, until he had found on the Brenner what he believed lay there—the end of this tangle. The search for Winslow alive or dead, the watching of Lightfoot's house, the effort to trace Miss Starr's past, would go on as intensively as though he were in Town. He had an interview with the A.C. at the latter's own home, and it was agreed that he should go to Vipiteno and see what he could find on the spot. Even while they were talking it over some news about Miss Starr came in. She had been identified, from her picture shown last night on the screens all over England, as the daughter of a small tradesman in Manchester who had got a place in London as a manicurist, first in the suburbs, then in Kensington, then in Knightsbridge. She had lived first near the Crystal Palace for some time at a boarding house, and then for a short stay at Brixton. The former; like the latter place, had only vaguely pleasant memories of her as always cheery and full of fun. There, too, the hunchback caller had come—but, only once, and just before she left.

To-day was only Sunday. Both men felt sure that they would learn a good deal more on the Monday, some of it false, but possibly some of it true, and therefore helpful.

So Pointer left next morning by the 8:15 Imperial Airways 'plane for Cologne, and on to Munich and

Merano, which he reached at six. He had overshot
Vipiteno, but a car rushed him away from the pretty little
mountain resort, windless and sunny, to his goal on the
Brenner Pass itself. He put up at Winslow's hotel, and
had a private talk with the proprietor after dinner.

He told him that he was a detective—private was
inferred—and that Mr. Winslow was missing from his flat
in London. Lost memory, his family thought. He wanted
to learn as much as possible about him and his friends
during his stay here in Upper Italy. One swift expression
that flitted across Signor Landsmann's face puzzled the
astute chief inspector. It was so swiftly gone, that it was
difficult to be sure of just what it meant, but it did not
indicate mere amazement. Startled though it was, it was
rather as though the man were struck with some sudden
thought—possibility—fear. And he suppressed it almost
instantly. Beginning to speak at once of Lady Browne,
who had left the day after Miss Winslow, finding herself
sometimes without a soul with whom to play even double
dummy, and who, he believed, was making for London in
a leisurely way. He spoke of each of the group of men who
had been linked with Winslow while at Vipiteno.
Lightfoot came last, and of him he only said that Mr.
Lightfoot was well known throughout all the region as an
artist and photographer of merit, with a real love of
nature. Pointer let him gracefully glide away from
Lightfoot, and then brought him back to him, to find each
time that, after some respectful but quite formal remark,
as of one who was in reality a complete stranger, mine
host was off again at a tangent. For some reason the man
did not want to discuss Lightfoot. Was it fear of him? It
seemed a quaint notion, for Pointer could not see how the
hotel proprietor could possibly be afraid of the
Englishman, but Pointer was sure that at least, or at
best, some fear was associated with it. As for what Mr.
Landsmann said, it amounted to nothing new, except for
one thing. He believed that Mr. Winslow had saved Miss
Starr's life at a neighbouring ice run when the girl had

tried to toboggan down it for the first time without any irons on her shoes or the faintest idea of how to steer the skeleton. Mr. Landsmann was called away just then, and Pointer sat looking around him at the typical Tiroler room with its brown painted and varnished pine dado shoulder high, its distempered cream wall, above with the chamois heads on it, its photographs of pretty scenes around. In the corner a big china stove gave out a delightful warmth. It was a dark room—Tirol rooms are dark as a rule—but it was very charming. Pointer's eyes were hardly conscious of it as he mused on what he had just learnt. So Winslow had saved Fay Starr's life. If verified, that fact meant a great deal. There was that in the dead girl's face that said that it would have meant a great deal to her, too. A good turn would always be paid back, unless he were much mistaken, and a bad turn also.

Then, if this were true, she had not come as an enemy to that suite of rooms which she was not to leave alive. Did she know her danger? And like a flash came the reply, probably not, since she was caught unawares; but very likely she knew of Winslow's danger, and was there to help him. If so, it explained her following him from Victoria. It explained her running up the steps to him when he was about to enter the house where his rooms were. Did it explain her death? It might. If whoever wanted to silence Hugh Winslow knew her well enough to know that he must silence her first. In that case her death was not pivotal to the real crime, but almost outside it. Yes, Pointer thought, he knew of nothing to disprove this idea. She stood for nothing in the real struggle which was between the forgers and the man who had found them out. But how would the forger know that she knew of the notes? Even supposing that Winslow had spoken to her of them, as was possible, though not likely, Pointer thought, how would the band know of it? Winslow did not know where to locate them, he felt sure of that. Winslow evidently, or possibly, suspected Lightfoot, but Pointer did not think that he would have left the house in

Cromwell Road as quickly as he seemed to have done,
unless he had merely had his doubts, or possibly not even
that. He might have had reason to connect Lightfoot with
the notes, and yet never suspected him of more than a
chance connection with them. But Fay Starr and the
gang? Winslow was hardly likely to have mentioned to
Lightfoot, in the few minutes that he talked to him, that
he had passed on his doubts about a note or notes to Miss
Starr. If the gang knew that she knew—as seemed
evident—then she must have been in the gang's
confidence beforehand. And what more likely? Women are
always much used by forgers to help pass on their wares,
and this place Vipiteno was not badly chosen. All around
it were winter sports. A note could be changed in a fresh
place almost daily. And the way to and from it lay
through Innsbruck-Basle-Paris.

No, not at all ill chosen.

When Mr. Landsmann came back, he asked him if he
could change a twenty-pound note into some smaller
English notes. Say three fives, and the rest in lire.

The proprietor looked surprised. "I would with
pleasure, but I'm afraid Mr. Winslow took all our English
notes. He asked us to do the same thing."

Pointer felt his pulse quicken. Oh, he was on the trail
all right, and Pointer felt as though he could race along it
without rest. Winslow had taken three notes. One or
more were probably in the possession of the murderer. He
even learnt, over a chat, that Winslow had wanted the
notes initialled, had said it was the custom in England.
Pointer upheld this, and said certainly—a fixed rule. And
by a little further talk he learnt that one of the notes had
been paid in by Miss Starr, and one by Lightfoot. More, as
the chat with Mr. Landsmann went on, he learnt that
Miss Starr and Winslow had gone off together, to initial
the note probably, as they had turned into the writing-
room. Pointer made great play of tracing Winslow by the
notes. He might lose his memory, but his money, this
money, would in time help to locate him.

Of the porter Pointer inquired as to pleasant excursions, and in so doing learnt of those taken by the *Speedwell's* team, with which Miss Winslow and Miss Starr were bracketed, but from which, as a rule, Pointer found that Lightfoot was omitted. He preferred lonely expeditions, the porter said. As was natural with a gentleman who knows all the neighbourhood so well. And liked to find fresh bits for his camera or brush.

Your Tiroler is not suspicious—except of a Blackshirt—and Pointer's good German was an open sesame here. As the porter said with a naïve smile, "One rejoiced whenever one hears it spoken!"

Pointer noted down in his own room every expedition of which he learnt, from the porter or the Boots. One thing struck him as he looked the list over. Neither of them had referred to Bressanone, which was on Miss Winslow's list of expeditions. She had made a very careful daily one for Pointer at his request, and had sent it to him by hand on Sunday morning. Pointer wondered whether this omission were but chance. The two men were hardly likely not to have omitted anything. But Miss Winslow's notes said:

"In afternoon, drove in sleigh to Bressanone and back from hotel. Bobtailed behind on home journey, after practice on ice run there."

He rang for the Boots. Where could he get a good skeleton toboggan. What about driving with it over to Bressanone; there was a good run there, and he, Pointer, was fond of ice runs.

The Boots said it was often done.

The *Speedwell* bob was taken there once, wasn't she?" Pointer asked casually. Instantly the Boots whipped about and said he had no idea, and if the *gnädiger Herr* didn't need him at once he would look out a good toboggan, and fled—quite frankly rushed from the room.

Pointer took the train early next morning to Brixen, or Bressanone, as his ticket called it, and walked to the ice run. It was outside the little town proper, and began in some grounds belonging to a small inn. The Stella d'Oro its sign called it.

Pointer tramped on to the verandah and ordered coffee and rolls and some of the much overrated Vipiteno butter. To the waitress he mentioned that he was a friend of some English people who had been here ten days ago with their bob. It was the bob that had won the Giovo Pass Cup. He gave the date as an afterthought.

"On that day!" She looked as though about to cross herself. "On that day!" she repeated under her breath.

"How did it happen?" Pointer asked, for evidently something had happened.

She looked about her—they were quite alone—and if there was one thing *das Mariele* loved, it was to talk. "The poor young man! Engaged to Fräulein Anna of the confectionery shop over there. He must have made a mistake in the darkness of the counter. They found him quite dead with the bottle beside him, lying among his beloved films. Sad, wasn't it!"

"It must have been a fearful shock to you," Pointer said sympathetically. "The young man was a photographer, wasn't he?"

"A wonderful man at the work. But it was really because of Fräulein Anna that he came here. To be near her he took on the job of looking after the hotel now, when no one stays here overnight. They used to be together every afternoon. She's going into a convent."

"Yet the ladies of the party had no idea anything was wrong. They haven't any idea to this day," Pointer said, greatly puzzled, though he did not look it.

"No. We hurried them out to the sleigh. The gentlemen and we. Why should they have such a shock? Two such nice ladies; one of them was quite a girl—no older than Fräulein Anna."

"It was Herr Lightfoot who found the man, wasn't it?" Pointer said in the tones of an avid gossip, and as all the Tirolese are gossips to an extent undreamt of in places where there are other interests beyond one's neighbours' affairs, the waitress thought this talk was only natural. "No." So she evidently knew Lightfoot by name. "Another of the party. Very tall and young, blond, laughing all the time—until we found poor Herr Seiler. He couldn't speak German. Nor Italian either. He *was* funny!" But Pointer was told that it was Herr Lightfoot who had arranged with the Boots that there was no need to mention anything about any guests being in the hotel at the time. It wasn't even as though they were staying here, the waitress went on, who evidently sympathised perfectly with the feeling. "Who wants to have anything to do with the Carabinieri?" she finished up.

Pointer had a word with the Boots, apparently apropos of taking a sleigh back to Merano; he did not speak as though he were staying in Vipiteno. The Boots, a hard-faced, silent, embittered Tiroler, was brief and laconic, and dried up still more at any mention of that day—the day when the Swiss had been found dead. Oh, yes, he knew Herr Lightfoot; but Pointer's assertion that he was an acquaintance of his met with no loosening of the man's speech. The talk about the sleigh came to nothing definite, and Pointer strolled over to the confectionery, towards which *das Mariele* had glanced when she spoke of Fräulein Anna.

And behind the counter Pointer saw a tragic-faced young girl with eyes hollowed by grief and sleeplessness, and a mouth tight closed and, as it were, sealed. He would get nothing from her. No one would. Yet that face told of some dreadful knowledge kept battened down. Fritz Seiler's death was no accident to Fräulein Anna, of that Pointer was sure. But he was as sure that no word on the matter would he get from her. She eyed him, she eyed another customer with the same cold hostility. This young girl had put a barrier between herself and the world.

But though that was his conviction, nevertheless he must try his luck. When they were alone together, and he had ordered another cup of *kaffee mit obers,* wondering where he was going to put it, he leant forward sympathetically.

"I am a friend of Herr Lightfoot's—" he began. On the instant her face, pale already from grief, flamed, and then turned livid. She gave him one look of such burning fury that he knew that had she been able to she would have struck him dead; and, turning on her heel, left him. A middle-aged woman bustled in looking half-frightened, half-indignant. Pointer at once explained.

"I'm afraid I was tactless," he said. "I spoke of Herr Seiler; I meant no harm."

The woman's face softened. She sighed. "You mustn't refer to him. None of us may. She won't mention his name, nor hear it spoken before her. Even the Franciscans can do nothing with her. They tell her it's the will of God, but she won't answer them; just shuts her face and refuses to answer. Yes, yes, if you spoke of dead Fritz Seiler, her young fiancé, she would go up to her room and lock herself in as she has done. She's going into a convent next month. She was such a happy young thing, laughing and singing all day long! It was hard on her. They were to have been married in the spring."

"Herr Lightfoot was a friend of young Herr Seiler's, wasn't he?" Pointer went on. "He's an acquaintance of mine." But the woman did not seem to know the name. But Fräulein Anna had, and it had acted on her like vitriol. He went to the local newspaper office and asked to see the files of the day when the bob had been here, and the following days. He read the few lines about the occurrence; but, as the Cup was shortly to be won, and as the place was full of winter sports guests, it was dealt with as briefly as possible. Pointer found no reference to any visitors being at the little hotel at the time.

He went on to the police station, the *sotto prefectura.* He had all the necessary papers with him, and sent them in. In a moment he was taken into the room of the under prefect's first secretary, who was anxious to give him any help possible. His superior was away for the day in a neighbouring town.

Pointer explained that a young Englishman was missing from his home in London, and as he had just returned from some winter sports at Vipiteno, he, the chief inspector, wanted to trace all his activities during his stay here. It was no question of any foreign complications, he added with a smile, but of merely—as a matter of routine—following him up day by day during his holiday. They talked a little of the Giovo Pass race—the secretary himself had been on one of the bobs—and then of the accidents peculiar to winter sports, and then to accidents in general.

Finally Pointer heard about the mishap to the young Swiss at the hotel here. One of those fatalities which can only happen from too great a familiarity with danger. "He must have been surrounded with his poisons so often," the secretary went on, "that he had grown accustomed to them. He must have put drinking water, or cold tea, into one of them, and forgotten which one . . . or some brandy . . . or a cocktail of some kind. A most respectable young man, apparently. At any rate, quite a newcomer to this place. He was engaged to a pretty little Austrian girl, the daughter of a wealthy wholesale confectioner of Schönbrunn. She had come here for the winter air and to have some idea of how confectionery shops were conducted. A sad affair. She took it very hard. A lovely young thing, too, who talked of going into a convent—and meant it, according to rumour." Pointer seemed to grow interested in the human tragedy. He asked various questions which arose out of the account just given him. The secretary, on whom the affair had made a great impression, pointed to a cupboard.

"There are the exhibits. It was a clear case of accident, I think. Of course, one always suspects suicide in these cases. But here I really think it must have been sheer mischance." He unlocked the cupboard.

Pointer saw some bottles and films and photographs, also a cardboard box with money.

"From the till," the secretary explained. "We are going to send it to the hotel in due course; but we have been so busy with some of the everlasting smuggling that goes on along this frontier—"

"The till doesn't seem to have amounted to much," Pointer said.

"Ah!" The secretary looked wise. "An open till, hotel servants . . . what would you? As a matter of fact, a five-pound note is missing; that's why the money is still here. The hotel claims the sum entered in their books, and the young man's books showed that he had just changed an English five-pound note for someone. Well, the note is missing. A very easy thing to pick up is a five-pound note," the man said with a wink, "and can be changed anywhere at sight."

"Didn't the cashier make a note of the number?"

"He did. That's what we're waiting for. That's why no mention was made of its being missing. The person who annexed it will very soon feel bold enough to change it, and then—one thief the less for a while!"

Pointer was looking at the dead man's books. He made a careful, mental note of the number in question before the talk turned to London. The chief inspector told a thrilling tale, of a recent crime there, and then turned to the still open cupboard.

"That was the bottle found beside him, I suppose." He looked towards one standing by itself. "His finger-prints on it, I suppose?"

The secretary waggled a forefinger portentously. "No finger-prints whatever on it! Most amazing, eh? Perfectly clean. So are all the other bottles. It seems young Seller every now and then would wipe everything off and tidy up preparatory to going off and having an hour or two with his girl. A habit of his that speaks of a careful nature. But it is odd that he could drink from it and yet leave not a smudge on the surface, eh? Perhaps he had a rag in his hand and held it by it, and the rag was kicked to one side by the hotel Boots who found him. We have our eye on that Boots, of course. And for other reasons; too, with which this has nothing to do—political ones. But I think he will be the one to try and cash that note, eh?"

There was nothing more to be learnt, Pointer found, and, after paying for his entertainment with still another good yarn, he took his leave, and went on to Merano by train. He looked very grave. The cashier was found dead after cashing an English five-pound note, and the note itself was missing. Pointer did not suspect the Boots of its theft. He suspected the man or woman who had changed it. As he saw the probabilities, they were strongly suggestive that young Seiler had changed the note, and then detected something wrong with it. Either at once, or when whoever had changed it had passed by counter again. The latter probably; as he had entered it in his cash-book. And then? Pointer's inquiries just now had told him that the dead man's mouth was badly burnt, almost as though bruised. As Pointer saw it, Seiler had been clutched suddenly from the back, the contents of the bottle held by a gloved hand had been poured into his mouth, opened to call for help, and the deed was done. The horrible deed which had left the young man dying in agony, unable to call for assistance, and a young girl with a broken heart and no further use for a world where such things could happen. Her attitude, when the name of Lightfoot came up, suggested that she certainly connected him with Fritz Seiler's death, and did not consider that death an Act of God. Evidently she had no proof, and knew that she never could get any. Pointer could only fancy that Seiler had, spoken before about some note given him by Lightfoot, or traced by him back to Lightfoot, with which he had not been quite satisfied. It must have been but a vague suspicion, or he would not have cashed this one. Or had the note been presented, not by Lightfoot himself, but by someone else—by Miss Starr, say? Pointer did not yet know of the way in which she had taken the news of the young Swiss's death. But it seemed very possible to him that it was she who had paid over that note which was now missing.

He took the Luft Hansa 'plane next morning back to Interlaken. Seiler came from Interlaken. His body had been sent on there. His father was head cashier at one of the big banks there. Pointer had a talk with him.

It is to be feared that he represented himself as an acquaintance of Miss Anna's, who had been so touched by the tragedy, that he had stopped over to express his sympathy.

The father was a typical Swiss, brusque in manner, heartbroken in the depths. Fritz had been his only child. He was immensely proud of him. Out of grief he talked to Mr. Pointer of his boy's gifts. He was no mere photographer, said the father scornfully—he was a most promising young chemist. A great future in that direction lay before him. Why, he had devised a re-agent for testing bank notes which he, the father, found simply invaluable, even though Fritz considered it but a beginning. It detected the wrong papers with uncanny precision, perforating forgeries, but leaving the genuine notes unharmed. It was made up, of course, into different formula for the notes of different countries, and was by no means complete yet. But the father used it for English and French notes. Of course Fritz intended to extend it to other countries. And, of course, in time he would have passed on to finding some re-agent which would detect the various inks used. So far, his discovery only concerned the paper. Italian notes? No, it did not help there, unfortunately, for after all there were more forgeries of them than of English bank notes. Oh, yes, his son had a bottle of it in daily use, of course. He had not been able to test it much, because he had had no bad notes. But he had lived in hopes . . . the father gave a sad smile and fell into grieving silence. Pointer did not try to solve the puzzle of the elder Seiler, as to how it was possible for his son to have drunk from that bottle by mistake. He was more interested in learning how often the father had heard from his son. Not often. The young man had taken the post for six months so as to be near his fiancée, and he loathed writing. He would unpack all that had happened on his return to his father in the spring, but letters—a card now and then, of course; but Fritz was notoriously unwilling to sit down and write his thoughts. He, the father, suffered from the same complaint—it was a family one. And he had not expected letters. Did he speak English? Perfectly. He had been three years in England; and, besides, English was compulsory in their schools at Interlaken. Pointer left Interlaken with a face still graver, if possible. There had been no bottle of this re-agent among the bottles in the *sotto prefectura*, nor any mention of it in the list which lay in the cupboard, and at which Pointer had glanced with a seemingly incurious eye. Bottle and bank-note were both gone. And both had been taken by the murderer, he felt sure. Or had, Miss Starr seen to them, while a stronger hand and arm settled the young Swiss?

It was a tragic story indeed. That note had caused the death of young Seiler, and probably stood for something in the murder of Miss Starr herself, in the very probable murder of Winslow, which to the chief inspector was more and more an accomplished fact, in the broken hearts of Seiler's father and fiancé, and ultimately, so hoped the chief inspector, in the death of the murderer himself. The double, and probably the treble, murderer.

CHAPTER TWELVE

POINTER had no longer any doubt but that Winslow, too, was dead. This was now Wednesday, the day of his return to England by 'plane from Merano, and there was still no word from him. For Pointer, the question was where his murder had taken place. As far as he could see into the case, Winslow's own rooms would have been a good place to choose. He could quite understand why the murderer or murderers had wanted to hide his body, hide the fact that he was dead, to make it look as though he had killed Fay Starr, to divert suspicion of this being anything more than a *crime passionel*. But, granted that there had been some means of hiding the body or getting it out of the house, then he thought that Winslow was killed immediately after Fay Starr had been shot. But where was the body? He had left word some time ago that the coal cellar of the house was to be quietly searched. It had been. Nothing was found in it. Mrs. Clarke used gas and electricity entirely, and the cellar housed nothing more than a few odds and ends of boards and boxes.

The state of them; and of it, showed that it had not been disturbed for over a year. Priestley's rooms were equally innocent looking, and as he had had his halls and margins freshly painted while he was away, they would certainly have shown any rough usage. Capstick, with the slackness which Pointer had read in his face, had put off the work until the Saturday morning, when it had been hastily done, so that by Saturday night the boards would have been barely dry. And though one might avoid the margins his lobby was too tiny not to step on the paint when crossing it.

There were no marks of a struggle in the flat. He would have been either sandbagged or shot, Pointer thought. Probably the latter. The murderer apparently had a revolver with him, though it might have belonged to Winslow, in spite of his cousin's ignorance that he owned one, or it might even have belonged to Miss Starr and have been carried by her for her own protection—or taken with her for the protection of Hugh Winslow. Now that Pointer believed her presence in his rooms, her presence throughout his journey to have been in requital of the service which he had rendered her, he thought it quite possible that she had brought one with her. All this was of little importance compared to the one vital question as to where his body now lay. Not that Pointer let his ideas assume the position of theories. All this was but an idea of how things might have gone, but it was an idea which fitted the facts as so far known to him. It was barely possible that Winslow had himself come on—or been given by Miss Starr—a clue so straight and direct that he had thought it would only be a question of hours before he would land his fish—and had instead been landed in his turn. As for kidnapping, Pointer could not see any possibility of it; nor, as he had told himself many times, could he visualise Winslow leaving his flat with Miss Starr in it.

Pointer did not think that Capstick was in the crime. A very clever man of his had been at work, and, so far from having money to spend, the butler was being hard pressed for some payments due on a new suit of clothes. Capstick gambled on horses, as well as dogs and football matches, and a suggestion of the detective's that it might be possible to let him in on a syndicate which expected to mop the board had only brought sighs from Capstick, and tales of bad luck. Yet the detective knew that he himself had not been suspected as such. No, Capstick and his wife both seemed outside the crime.

Effingham, the missing man's partner, had been to the Yard. He was most emphatic in his certainty that

Winslow had met with an accident. He even feared lest some uninsured brute of a driver had run him down, and, afraid of the consequences, had dumped the body into the river, or buried it in his back garden.

Pointer, after reporting at the Yard, drove at once to see Miss Winslow. No one but the police knew of his trip abroad. She thought that he was working at Miss Starr's past, and he had some minor facts to give her. In reality the Yard had cleared up a good deal of her past, but not the all-essential part of the most recent years. They knew now that, under the name of Mrs. Kershaw, she had taken a furnished flat at Knightsbridge, giving as a reference a solicitor's address in a country town, who seemed to have moved away a week after giving it, and moved in a week before. Her other reference was a lady now untraceable, but at a most exclusive club.

The club in question felt sure that she must have been a member of the staff who had access to the letters. Mrs. Kershaw, however, had proved a most satisfactory tenant, and had only given up the flat on the return of the owners a month ago. As far as could be learnt, she had lived very quietly. She had gone to her manicure post daily, giving out there that she was the companion of this Mrs. Kershaw. She seemed to have had few, if any, visitors, but have lived in very great comfort, denying herself nothing from the restaurant below, and using a car almost every evening, a car which she drove herself. Here again the figure of a hunchback appeared. Only a few times was he noticed coming and going, but he linked her definitely to Brixton.

She had no personal servants. The flats were service, flats, and Mrs. Kershaw was hardly known by sight to most of them, as she left around half-past nine on week-days, and on Sundays was often in the country.

Pointer only mentioned a few of the most uninteresting and unimportant facts as an excuse for his call on Miss Winslow. Ursula was not feeling her best to-day. She and Moffatt had quarrelled; or, rather, she had quarrelled, and Moffatt had tried to pacify her. But she considered that nothing was being done to get into touch with her cousin.

"Of course she's right," Moffatt said ruefully to Kidd, to whom he related the whole thing. "We haven't got one inch nearer his hiding-place. I'm beginning to think he flitted at once from England —that same night."

"Where would he make for?" Kidd inquired.

"How about Iceland?" suggested Moffatt. "I heard him and Miss Starr talking of Reykjavik in the compartment one day. She thought it would be a complete change."

"Sounds as if it would be," Kidd agreed with one of his old grins. He, too, was feeling rather blue. He explained this as due to disappointment at getting no further along in the inquiry.

"When we struck that trail at Brixton I thought it would lead us home in no time. It hasn't me. Has it you?"

Moffatt disclaimed any special good fortune in the discovery line. He still maintained that Winslow was avoiding them, and, though he could not say so to Ursula—perhaps wisely so—until they, knew the result of the inquest which had been altered from Monday to to-day, Wednesday. It was a purely formal affair, but even so, the papers were full of theories and surmises in none of which was Winslow spared. They were his rooms. Where was he? The girl had been an acquaintance, if nothing more, of his. Where was he? The identification was not satisfactory, according to the coroner, who wanted members of the dead girl's family. Where were they? The police seemed to have no theory of what had happened. In short, where were they, too, demanded one of the cheaper papers. Pointer had not been present, but he had been at the Yard should he have to put in an appearance. The inquest was adjourned for a fortnight, and the coroner earnestly hoped that something more definite would be learnt by that time—a hope in which the police most cordially joined.

Ursula had been one of those who gave her evidence. It had been a dreadful ordeal, and in her gratitude at Moffatt's unobtrusive appearance and help, she felt more than ever that she had been too hasty. After all, if the police were baffled, how could she expect him to succeed? He was going down with Kidd to her uncles. They had come up for the inquest, and Moffatt had found an opportunity, at Kidd's urgent request, to introduce him. Kidd's charm and pleasant manners did the rest. The uncles, glad to be distracted from the dreadful suspicions hovering around their nephew, had asked the two men to come down for the night, so that Kidd next morning could have an interview with their manager. Moffatt, in spite of Ursula's coldness, they considered as one of the family now, and a welcome addition. They had no illusions as to the possibility of finding Hugh, supposing that he did not want to be found. And on the whole they hoped that he would remain unlocated; which was really why they wanted a talk with Moffatt. Should he come upon Hugh, or any traces of him, he was to let them know, but turn a blind eye, and, above all, not communicate his discovery to their niece. But it was Mr. Priestley who made the greatest conquest of the two elderly men. They had not met him before. He introduced himself at the inquest, and insisted on carrying them off to his rooms for tea, which he declared the younger generation had forgotten how to make. Ursula, who went, too, even though she dreaded entering the house where the tragedy had happened, felt cheered by the kindliness he showed in face and voice, by his gentle yet charming manners. He was a good story-teller, too, and deftly kept the talk on distant places to which the two elderly men had been in their youth, and of whose changes he could give them amusing accounts.

When Ursula returned home Moffatt had only put her into her car. She expected to find Lady Browne just arrived, but it was the chief inspector who rose from a chair by the window.

Ursula felt a thrill at sight of him. He looked very impressive standing there with his bronzed face and steady eyes. And, oddly enough, though he did not show it, she felt sure that the case had taken a great step forward. This was not a man casting about in his mind, but a man with a theory that could now stand by itself and be tested. What he had come for, he told her, was to get a better idea of Miss Starr than he had yet obtained. He wanted her to go through the days they spent together and give him, as carefully as possible, anything said or done by the dead girl. He hoped in that way to arrive at some picture of her character, or, failing that, of the sort of circle in which to look for traces of her.

There was not much to tell. "She and I didn't get on at all well," Ursula said frankly. "She quite misunderstood the relationship between myself and my cousin; or, if not understood, then there were times when she disliked it. She was of a very jealous nature evidently; and just because she felt like that, and showed it almost against her will, I think she cared for Hugh more than he, or anyone else, realised. I always shall think so."

She was as carefully exact as possible, but really she and Fay Starr had hardly ever talked together. The longest interval which they had spent alone together was on the drive to and from Bressanone. She told the chief inspector of the tragedy there, of which she had only learnt from the local paper the day after. He on his part seemed to hear it now for the first time.

"Now, leaving the poor chap's fatal mistake entirely on one side," he said finally, "do you feel quite sure that Miss Starr hadn't met him before?"

She stared at him a second. "Do you know, that's what Mr. Moffatt asked her later. So Mr. Priestley told me. She seemed so overcome by the death. And she assured him and the rest standing around that she had never been to Switzerland in her life. I wonder if she spoke the truth. She didn't often when it was a question of where she had been or what she had done."

Pointer decided to ask Priestley, or Kidd, or Moffatt, for an account of how Fay Starr had spoken when she learnt of the "accident." Just now he wanted to find out whether she had talked alone with the young Swiss. Ursula said she hadn't the faintest idea. All of the party strolled in and out, buying photographs which he had taken, and mounted, or getting stamps, or seeing to something or other connected with the bob. But she had been with Fay Starr when they entered the little boarded-off part of the verandah where he had his portier's counter. He had a lot of German postcards of something or other that had just taken place there, and Miss Starr made fun of them. He didn't like it. So when he passed through the verandah later she called out, '*Heil Hitler!*' and saluted in the way they do. He looked very angry. And Miss Starr said he was a German, and she loved chaffing Germans. "Well chief inspector, as we know he was a Swiss, that doesn't look to me as though she knew him before. Also, she seemed too casual. And so did he."

Pointer seemed to think Miss Winslow might be right, but he tried to find out whether Fay had talked alone with the young man for all that. For instance, did she change any money as an excuse? No. Ursula said Fay Starr had found out in the sleigh while going that she had left her purse behind her, and she was very vexed at it. They had only a twenty-lire note between them—Miss Winslow's note —and Fay had had to borrow from her for the few cards she bought at Bressanone.

Ursula had been quite certain about this; and about Fay Starr's irritation at finding that she had left her money behind her. A few more questions, and Pointer left her. Moffatt was out at the moment, but learnt from Mr. Priestley about Fay Starr's horror when she heard of the accident to the young Swiss. Captain Kidd, with whom Pointer had another few words later, told the same story. Both agreed on the haste with which she had assured them that she had never been to Switzerland.

"Rather as though she were a bit frightened at what she had said," Kidd said, "or not frightened, perhaps, but the sort of way one speaks if one has let a cat out of a bag and wants to cover it up again. That sort of thing. Do you know, chief inspector, I don't think I'll try and cut you out of your job. It's not so easy as one thinks. I mean detecting isn't. I think I'll stick to my transparent paper." And Kidd gave one of his hearty boyish laughs at nothing in particular, that so suggested a merry heart. "I rather hoped I should meet you on the trail of that poor girl. We haven't seen anything of you for the last twenty-four hours, so I hoped you were really getting to grips with the murderer," Kidd went on, his face very grave. Just then, his partner came in, and after a word with them opened the safe behind Kidd. The chief inspector was at the latter's offices in the City. As the newcomer rummaged for some paper which he wanted, Pointer sat facing into the small steel affair. On a shelf on the top, thrust far back, was a small bottle. The light happened to shine full on it. There was a label on it with some writing, but printed in bold black letters on the bottom of the label were the letters AKEN. The rest of the word was turned into the shadow. It was a smallish two-ounce bottle, and on the top was the Swiss white cross on a red field.

When they were alone again Pointer returned for a second to Miss Starr and her denial of ever having been to Switzerland. Did Captain Kidd know Switzerland at all? The Berneese Oberland? Interlaken? No, he had never been to that part, Kidd said, but he knew St. Moritz quite well.

Pointer did not ask to see the bottle. It might be too direct a clue as to the course of the investigations. But he told himself that he would have a good look at it later— much later—some time past midnight, probably.

"Speaking of that sad affair at Bressanone," Pointer seemed to hark back, "Miss Starr felt it very much, didn't she?"

"Rather! Completely bowled her over. But Lightfoot dealt with her quite splendidly." He related just how Lightfoot had calmed Fay Starr when she seemed overwhelmed by the news in the paper.

"Yes, that's why we're so interested in it, too," Pointer went on; "undoubtedly there was some connection—however remote—between her and his country, if not himself. Besides, his whole death was extraordinary. I think you're a quick observer. Did you notice anything odd about the people around the body? Say it had been a murder, you were summoned to give evidence at the inquest; would you have had anything to tell the coroner?"

Kidd hesitated. "Well, there was one odd thing. But—well—it was odd."

"Who was it?" Pointer asked; "I mean whom did the oddity connect with?"

"Lightfoot," came the reply. "He took something off that chap, chief inspector. He was bending down staring at him like this." Kidd illustrated the attitude. "I happened to be looking at them, and I saw his arm go out like this "—he made a motion—"and then his hand slip something into his pocket a second later. I'll tell you who else saw it, and that was Winslow. I saw him eyeing Lightfoot afterwards."

"And you haven't said anything about this? Why not?"

"Why should I? Or Moffatt?" demanded Kidd. "It's none of our pidgeon. Might have been a pin he took from the other chap's lapel. But he took something."

"Could it have been a letter? A paper?" Pointer asked.

"Could have been, yes, provided it wasn't tucked away deeply anywhere. Whatever he took away, came away, or out quickly."

"Ah, he didn't take anything out of the dead man's pocket?" Pointer persisted.

"Well, he certainly just touched the man's waistcoat pocket, as though he ran a thumb along inside it. He took nothing out; I'll swear to that. My idea was that something raked his hand, and that he was feeling for whatever it was that had done it—found the pin, and stuck it in his own coat—we were in topcoats—and felt to see if there was another. Acting as one does sometimes automatically."

"Mr. Lightfoot . . ." murmured Pointer as though recalling something told him. "He had got the man to change a note for him, hadn't he? He might have had a chat with the Swiss, and learnt something from him, which—supposing Miss Starr had been to Switzerland after all—might let us link up with her. It's a roundabout way of getting facts."

"Very roundabout," Kidd agreed, looking impressed. "I don't know if he changed a note. Yes, I think Lightfoot did. I seem to remember . . . yes, he did! I saw him counting the Italian notes over to himself as I went through the hall. He was always changing notes, that chap, whenever I happened to see him."

"Oh?" Pointer looked amused. "Lucky fellow!"

"Perfect mania of his. Got me to give him some English notes I had one day, and the next time I saw him he was changing them all back again for lire. I suppose he makes a bit out of the exchanges. Fact is, I taxed him with it and he confessed I was right. Can't think how he works it."

Kidd seemed to have no more to tell. Pointer asked if he might telephone to Mr. Moffatt and ask that gentleman for an interview as soon as possible. Moffatt was in his rooms and suggested an immediate call. Hurrying round to Hill Street, the chief inspector asked some questions about Miss Starr's manner when she learnt of the death of young Seller. Moffatt said that he thought she only showed a natural amount of shock. He considered that Miss Winslow was much the more startled of the two; but, then, Miss Winslow had a very gentle and deep nature. Taking him back to Miss Starr, he agreed that his question about Switzerland had seemed to silence her at the time. Pointer next asked him about the actual finding of the young man's body. Moffatt seemed to have nothing fresh to add to what was already known.

"None of your party took anything from him, you feel sure? There has been a suggestion that one of you felt something rake his hand, and took whatever it was that scratched him out of this young Seiler's coat, and felt for the cause of it. Did you see anything of that sort?"

Moffatt said that he had not, but added that he was often quite blind to what was going on in front of his eyes if his mind was on something else; and of course his mind was very much on what could have caused that sudden end to a young fellow with whom they had all talked and laughed not five minutes before.

"So Captain Kidd's interesting story of Lightfoot's action stands by itself?" Major Pelham said a little later to the chief Inspector. They were in the A.C.'s room at the Yard. "And was related after the safe was opened and the bottle could have been seen, that bottle would interest you." The A.C. looked at the other, seemed about to say something, and stopped himself. "That may lead to more routine work on your part, I fear," he finally said, and Pointer, with a grin, only said, "Very possibly, sir."

"By the way, you know we've tested Effingham's alibi and found it indisputable," Pelham asked.

Pointer nodded. He had never suspected Winslow's partner.

"And that there's no doing anything with the fingerprints in Winslow's rooms? All are only blurs."

Pointer had learnt that too.

A message was brought to the Assistant Commissioner. Superintendent Horrocks wanted a word. He had it, seated in a comfortable arm-chair and with one of Major Pelham's cigars alight.

"Of course, sir," began Horrocks to his chief, "this embargo of the Home Secretary's has been most strictly kept."

"I should hope so!" came stiffly from Pelham. But his eye was searching.

"But I happen to have a young friend in the Sweizer Bankverein at Basle who—quite privately, sir—quite unofficially sent me over a Bank of England note which struck him as not being quite all right. He substituted another of his own for this; so that there's no question of any inquiry or trouble."

Major Pelham knew Superintendent Horrocks' carefulness and nodded.

"But it's interesting, none the less, for it's the very finest counterfeit I've ever seen." And the superintendent took out with great care a note from an envelope in his letter-case. He laid it on the table and then he laid another note beside it. "To look at they're identical. But there is just something about the crackle . . . almost undetectable unless you're listening just for it. . . ." The two men tried the two notes several times. Yes, if you were listening for it, you could detect a something less stiff—a different note in the rustle that one of them made, when flipped between the fingers.

"Marvellous!" said Major Pelham; and his two subordinates agreed.

"It's photographed," Pointer said as though in a dream. "I mean, it's not engraved at all!"

"Well done, Pointer!" Superintendent Horrocks applauded. "That's quick work, to detect that. You're right. It's a marvellous photographic reproduction. Done by some entirely new method; and devilish difficult to detect; in fact, almost undetectable. But what's gone wrong?" For the chief inspector stood quite still, staring down at the forged note which he had laid down again on the table.

"But—then—the dismantled printing press . . . the engravers' tools . . . they don't mean anything, sir!"

"Evidently Lightfoot has bettered his process."

"No, sir," Pointer spoke firmly, "there wasn't any camera of a kind that could do this work at the house; no decent dark room; no tanks; no chemicals. . . no lanterns or suitable lights. . ."

"Just so," agreed Horrocks while disagreeing; "the old things stayed, the better process was taken along by his band when they separated. He's a crack photographer, you told us. Well, then! There you are!" And he pointed to the precious note.

Pointer stared at his shoes while the superintendent talked on to the A.C.

Those recent ink splashes which had been just painted over the night of Winslow's disappearance . . . the night of Miss Starr's murder . . . the absence of any room which could have been used as a dark room, for there were no hypo stains, nor any of the signs that photography leaves behind it in that dark little middle room in the basement. No film cuttings in the dustbin or passages, no lines for hanging prints, no frames. . . . Pointer was certain that his theory had caved in, entirely and absolutely. Yet what other explanation than the one which he had unearthed could there be for those printers' ink splashes, that house, the knob of the umbrella found in the room where the dead girl's body had been discovered? Or, for that matter, for Fay Starr's murder and Winslow's disappearance?

"I suppose there's no history to the note itself?" he asked the superintendent.

"None, unfortunately; except that it's not been in circulation long, and was handed in at Basle itself. But exactly when, or by whom—" Horrocks shook a rueful head.

Pointer left the two still talking it over. He himself felt as though a stone wall faced him, and he could not see over it. He was vexed at this. Facts seemed against Lightfoot; but were they? Could not the thief inspector see through them to reality; or were they reality? Unless Lightfoot was guilty, there must be some explanation which would explain every one of them, and yet clear him. Could the chief inspector not find it? Or did it not exist? Was the superintendent right in maintaining that Lightfoot had another house somewhere else where the photographic part was carried out?

Pointer thought again of the house off Cromwell Road. It was too recently and hurriedly altered for that theory to be his. Step by step he traversed it as he had before, from the time he clambered over the wall by means of the step ladder. The wall . . . the gravel courtyard . . . the plane tree had had some letters cut into the trunk quite recently. J. E. L. Lightfoot's name was Edward. As for the J—. A light seemed to snap on in the chief inspector's mind. . . . Lightfoot, who seemed to command such attention in Bressanone and around it that no one would mention the fact that he had been at Bressanone the day of the tragedy. Lightfoot taking something from the dead body . . . often changing bank-notes, and changing them back . . . keeping the odd house filled with foreigners in Town, poor foreigners, too . . . yes, a light had snapped on in Pointer's mind. Yes, he saw a possibility of another theory than the one which he had held of forged bank-notes, saw that it would cover the J. E. L. which no longer stood for any man's initials . . . cover the dismantled printing press, the hidden engraving tools . . cover everything which he had so far learnt.

CHAPTER THIRTEEN

POINTER decided to go over the house again, beginning at the top this time. He had a search warrant now. But he hoped not to have to use it. He knew from the men watching the house that Lightfoot had gone to London Bridge Station. There had been no more guests lately. Lightfoot seemed to live by himself, doing his own work with the help of the same charwoman who now came in daily.

Pointer borrowed the ladder again, and again made his way across the back of the next house. Again he stood in the little courtyard and glanced at the carved initials. J. E. L.; yes, it might be.

He lifted the latch of the back door and stepped inside. Up to the top he went and slowly started looking under all the pillows and mattresses of the beds.

He found something under a blanket of the third bed which he tried. It was a picture cut from a newspaper. A young man's head craning forward with something eager and birdlike in the poise; with it was a book of poetry in paper covers. The poems were in Italian, and on the cover was the words: *Luce*, and below, *Lauro de Bosis*. Pointer held the little volume for a second before replacing it. Yes, *Lauro de Bosis* and J. E. L. might well go together.

He had just neatened the coverings when he heard the front door being opened. Running noiselessly down to the first landing, he looked over. He knew that long stride that came in first. It was Lightfoot. But after him stumbled a thick-set man who seemed hardly able to stand. He stood a moment inside as Lightfoot shut the door. He was dressed in such clothes as a coasting seaman might choose for his Sunday spree. But from beneath the dreadful bowler hat showed a pallid intellectual face, a Jew for certain. He staggered. His hands, thin to emaciation, clutched at his heart even as the door closed. He swayed. Lightfoot tried to support him, but he was awkwardly placed. On the instant, out of nowhere as it seemed, Pointer was there. He gathered the man up in his arms and looked at the other. "To the kitchen?" he asked. "He's starving."

"This way," Lightfoot said, after one start. He spoke in a hostile voice, but as though he would accept the other's presence in his house—for the moment.

Pointer carried the thin figure, whose ribs he could count under his fingers, down the narrow dark stairs and placed him at the table. Another moment, and Lightfoot was holding some broth, which he took from the stove, to the thin lips. It smelled like good chicken broth. After a second's gulp, claw-like hands reached out, and the man took a long drink. Then Lightfoot swung the cup away, and the man nodded with a patient half-smile. Then he had another drink, and another wait. Finally the bowl was drained. Lightfoot stood watching him the while. Pointer knew that his own presence was quite forgotten, or put on one side as temporarily unimportant.

"Can you walk up the stairs?" Lightfoot asked his guest in German. "If so, there's a bed waiting for you. We're empty just now. I couldn't reach you to warn you. However . . ." Lightfoot shrugged his shoulders before he swung one thin arm over his neck and hoisted the man to his feet. He supported him up the stairs. Pointer came behind to help at the turnings, but Lightfoot did not need assistance. He was unexpectedly strong. In the bedroom, however, the one tidy, single one, he let the man slip on to the bed; and now again Lightfoot accepted Pointer's help without a word.

The clothes, none of which fitted, were taken off. A clean but worn nightshirt was slipped over the man, who was tucked up in bed with a hot water bottle, also standing ready.

"May the God of Israel—" began the Jew, but he fell asleep before he had finished his sentence.

Lightfoot stood a moment before he turned away, and his eyes were the eyes of the man on the bob who had called to Winslow, "On! On! Straight on!" Then he motioned to the chief inspector to come with him, and they left the sleeping man alone.

Pointer followed him down the stairs into a room on the ground floor. There, in answer to a curt wave of the hand, he stepped in. Lightfoot followed and turned the key in the door. He put it in his pocket, then he strode to a roll-top desk and unlocked it. Pulling a drawer open, he sat down by it, his back to the window.

"Don't shoot!" Pointer said with a faint smile. There was no answering smile.

"That depends," was the reply, and the chief inspector felt that it really did hang in the balance.

"Don't shoot!" he repeated again. "Not because it's naughty to shoot unarmed people, Mr. Lightfoot, but because it might slow up the inquiry into the murder of Miss Starr."

"Slow it up long enough to hang me, you mean?" was the indifferent retort. "That's all right. Don't trouble to continue wearing that cloak of hunting for her murderer. You and I know he'll never be caught."

Pointer looked at the cold eyes and the jaw which now showed very ruthless. Dislike of him bulged almost visibly from Lightfoot.

"I think there's a misunderstanding," he said slowly, "yet in case there isn't, I ought to warn you that anything you say—" he gave the caution.

"I thought that was only done in murder cases," Lightfoot replied. His lips curled contemptuously.

"And what else was the shooting of Miss Starr?" Pointer replied with an edge to his voice. "Come, Mr. Lightfoot, I'm not interested in your—shall we call it?—philanthropic work—"

"What do you mean by my philanthropic work?"

"That poor chap upstairs and what he stands for."

"And what does he stand for?" came curtly.

"Oranienburg, very likely," was the reply, and Lightfoot again gave a start. But he nodded as though he had expected this.

"Exactly. And yet you say you're not here on that account."

"I'm not—any more than on account of J. E. L."

"My initials," came warily from Lightfoot.

"Edward Paley Lightfoot?" asked Pointer with a smile. "J. E. L. stands for—I don't know the Basque, but it's usually translated, *God and the Ancient Law*. The war-cry of the young Basques, who are having a thin time lately. Just as those poems of de Bosis . . ." Pointer's tone grew warm as he said the name.

"And what of him, pray?" But Lightfoot's hand was no longer in the drawer, which he now closed.

"No more gallant gentleman ever went to certain death than he," Pointer said to that challenge, "when he flew from Marseilles with his 'plane full of leaflets to drop over Italy against the Fascisti, his own old party. He got as far as he could, and then, as he knew would happen, was shot down. I think you're probably actively connected with the Edelweiss league, or at any rate transmit funds for it. The league which tries to protect the Germans of the Trentino."

Lightfoot was leaning forward now, his lips parted, his eyes looked as though lamps had been lit behind them. He was staring at Pointer as though life and death depended on his not making a mistake in reading this man.

"In short, Mr. Lightfoot," the chief inspector went on in his quiet way, "I think you're a helper of under-dogs. Isn't that about it? The politically oppressed under-dogs? And I assure you that if that dismantled printing press downstairs and those buried etching tools have to do with propaganda work only, they interest me no more than they interested Winslow. But you must be frank, and explain them—and this house—and why on the night that Winslow disappeared everything was cleared away so swiftly. The downstairs room where the printing press stood, freshly distempered, the sink enamelled . . . and so on."

"Winslow!" repeated Lightfoot, and his face was wary and hostile again. "Winslow was an agent of the British Secret Service, as you very well know, chief inspector. He came here to make his inquiries, threatened to have the house searched. Of course we separated; and I took what measures were necessary for the safety of the men who came here for shelter."

"I hope those measures didn't include shooting Miss Starr."

Lightfoot looked at him coldly. "Hardly! We're not murderers. But an agent's life is always in his hand."

"You think she was a Secret Service agent?"

"Winslow was; so she was, probably," was the reply.

"I can assure you, Mr. Lightfoot, on my word of honour, that our Secret Service absolutely repudiates any knowledge of Mr. Winslow—or of her. I put that question to them very early in this case."

"Quite the right thing for them to do," Lightfoot said to that. "Of course they repudiated Winslow and that little Fay Starr. They had failed."

"Do you mind telling me just what happened when Mr. Winslow called here?" Pointer asked. Lightfoot was a man who, once he got an idea into his mind, could not see past it. Pointer thought that he really had believed—and still did believe—that Winslow had come on some inquiry linked with his work. Pointer knew from the Special Branch that there was a great deal of ill-feeling abroad because England acted as a refuge for some of those unfortunates who, often from no fault of their own, are savagely ill treated.

"This is what happened . . ." and Lightfoot proceeded to give Pointer an absolutely misleading account of Winslow's call. He put no words into his mouth that were not said, he omitted none, but he cast the whole in a mould of his own imagining, a mould where Winslow, under but the flimsiest of pretexts, had come to the house and wanted to have it searched.

"We had been notified that someone would come —in just that way—with some pretext or other as a cloak," Lightfoot went on, "so we were all ready with our plans. Of course, we separated at once—as agreed on—and, for the rest, well, we spent a hectic night clearing away traces of the printing press, which is one of our best weapons to break down the stranglehold of tyrants over their victims, and the engravings which, if I may say so without conceit, have done a great deal to cast ridicule on some of the laws recently passed." He smiled a little, a sardonic smile.

Pointer would have liked to tell him that Winslow's pretext was only the sober truth, but for the fact that the forged notes were not to be referred to. They were the closely-kept secret of the police investigations still.

"I want you to tell me very exactly, please, just what happened when you went to his rooms. You were seen coming out of them, by the way. I know you carried your umbrella, and lost the knob there in the sitting-room."

"I never went inside his rooms," Lightfoot said unexpectedly and very earnestly. "This is exactly what happened: Winslow said he would wait until half-past ten. I knew that he would be better than his word. I knew—for up to this moment I thought I knew—that he was giving me time to get the coast clear. The Secret Service men of all countries generally work it that way when it's against one of their own nationalities.

"Obviously—I thought—they had received some word they couldn't disregard, word to break up this house and stop its work. So we did our bit; cleared away everything, and I went on to see him. My visit to be a tacit signal that all was in order, and that the house was searchable. I got there just as the clock was striking eleven; and it was a rush! The front door was ajar. I went on up without ringing. He had told me that his rooms were on the second floor. As I reached his door I heard his voice talking in rather a clear, sharp, excited way. No, not angry, but excited sounding. I tried to hear better, and to do so pried open the letter-box flap—or endeavoured to do so. That was when the knob of my umbrella came off. I didn't notice it at the time, but the lobby has a thick carpet, I saw later; and also, it could have rolled into the sitting-room if the door was open. As it was, I think, or I shouldn't have heard his voice so clearly. Perhaps, though, someone kicked it without noticing it. Anyway, there's no other way it could have got where you found it, but as I'm telling you." He looked very straight at the chief inspector, who only nodded.

"What else did you hear, Mr. Lightfoot?" Pointer asked, for something in the man's face, a tautening of its muscles, told him that he had heard something of importance.

"Of what he said, nothing except 'No trouble, at all. The whisky is here.' He was bending down and had his back to the door evidently. But the next instant a revolver shot rang out."

"And you?" For Lightfoot had paused and was slowly snapping his fingers one after the other. A trick of his.

"I hurried home as fast as I could make it. Something was wrong. Evidently. My duty was to my guests."

"You heard no other voice?" Pointer pressed him.

"No. If the gasp which came so quickly after the shot was Winslow's—as I think it was, though of course, I can't be sure—I heard only Winslow. But—"

"Yes? But?"

"Miss Starr was in there."

"What makes you so sure?"

"The perfume she used. As I lifted the flap of the letter-box the whole place reeked of it. When the shot came I expected to see her come flying out. One of the reasons I jumped the stairs six steps at a time, and hared off here, to get here first and clear my people out.

"But she wasn't the person to whom Winslow was speaking. His tone—apart from what we now know—told it was another man. Rather perfunctory . . . a trifle preoccupied . . . it was unmistakable."

Pointer took him backwards and forwards, but Lightfoot did not contradict himself or falter.

"And, when you heard of the murder of Miss Starr, what then?"

"My dear chief inspector, apart from other reasons, there are in London at this moment at least four men— one from each of four countries—who would murder a roomful of babes to get the papers which they hoped that Winslow—or Miss Starr as his subordinate—had got from this house. Why, that man upstairs now—there's a price on his head that I was going to say would surprise you; but you probably know all about it. On the Friday night of which we're talking we had a young Spaniard—" Lightfoot gave a whimsical twist to his smile. "I never thought he'd live to get here! Of course I thought up till now that Fay Starr's death was political, and that Winslow's disappearance proved it, if proof was needed after his visit here. It was the only thing he could do. That any of us would have had to do—carry on; don't be turned aside; don't slow up for the sake of those who fall by the wayside, are mottoes which we have to learn early in this work. Obviously Winslow was after bigger fish, or on some other mission. But you tell me it's not political. . . . You really mean that? I assure you I'm amazed! Amazed!"

He sat silent for a full moment, frowning as he readjusted his thoughts.

"You didn't go through his papers to find out whether your suspicions were right?" Pointer asked.

"Didn't get the chance!" was the reply. "I was able to glance at a few when you left me alone in his suite that one and only time. But, of course, I knew that he would have his own on him. I was looking—merely as a matter of duty—to see if there were any notes about the house here. Not political!" he repeated as though still unable to believe it.

"And that elbow pad, Mr. Lightfoot? The one you said he brought you back?"

Lightfoot seemed unable to recollect it for a moment. "Oh, that! I suppose it's with his things still. Certainly he didn't bring it back to me."

"And how about the young Swiss at Bressanone?" Pointer asked next. A dark look came over the face of the man talking to him.

"Fritz Seiler's death was a political murder, chief inspector. Even you can't deny that. He belonged to the Edelweiss League, and was one of its honorary secretaries. He had just helped two unfortunate lads to get out of the country, one of them on a stretcher! Oh, the Fascisti had been trying to get him for some time."

"Tell me: Did the proprietor of the Orso know of your interest in this League?" Pointer thought of Mr. Landsmann's expression when he had made his inquiries about Winslow. He felt sure of the answer. It came.

"Naturally! Naturally! Every Tiroler wishes us Godspeed! If ever it has been a case of *vae victis*! Why, they even refused to let a bob race for the Coppa because its name *Edelweiss* made them certain there was some political reason for its being there." Lightfoot pulled himself up. "You don't want a political tract, I know," he said a little bitterly.

Pointer nodded. That was not his purpose, nor did he think Lightfoot was a good man to follow. He was too one-sided; incapable of seeing the whole.

"You took this young man's pin, didn't you—his Edelweiss badge? I have been told you all wear one."

Lightfoot's eyes opened.

"You seem very well-informed," he said shortly. "Yes, I did. We try not to let them fall into the Blackshirts' hands. Sort of regimental colours. I also felt in his secret pocket for his papers. But his fiancée told me later that he had left them with her, and that she had flung them into the fire when she heard of his assassination. Poor girl! She feels very bitter against me. I had to give him his orders—pass them on to him—and she . . ." Lightfoot sighed and looked suddenly tired.

"I suspected Winslow of having something to do with Seiler's death. Oh, not directly. No, I never thought that. But we knew that spies were about; and I had rather suspected Miss Starr from the first. She seemed so out of place at Vipiteno—so determined to be 'in' with us all."

"Was that why you told her Seiler had always suffered from fits?" Pointer asked.

Lightfoot nodded. "Just to see how she would take it. She seemed to swallow it all right, but she wrote and posted a letter immediately afterwards. Oh, it was a letter to the local supply shop only but addresses mean nothing in our game."

"Do you mind explaining why you so often changed Italian money for English notes, and back again?"

"So as to confuse the trail of where the funds came from, of course. You've no idea how keen the various governments are on finding that out."

There was a short silence.

"Mr. Winslow was not connected with any secret service investigation as far as I know or can learn," Pointer said slowly. "Can you assure me that he is not being detained somewhere by some member of your organisation, owing to the same misunderstanding under which you seem to've been up till now?"

"That's quite impossible, chief inspector." Lightfoot spoke with evident conviction. "We're not an offensive league. We offer sanctuary to all who need it. Nothing more. But I don't mind saying that you've simply amazed me—about Winslow, I mean. Of course when Miss Starr was found shot in that inexplicable way—otherwise inexplicable—it seemed to prove our suspicions. He watched me, I thought, at Vipiteno."

Lightfoot fell into a reverie.

"It was you who arranged to have your names kept out of the paper, I suppose," Pointer said, "that day at Brixen."

Lightfoot nodded. "Of course. It would have been a joy to the others to link me with him. They had tried to catch me out so often. I got Winslow to hand on some funds to one of our secretaries just to test him. But he was suspicious. At least we thought that was why he carried out my request. But according to what you say—" A keen glance swept the other.

"—Believe—am certain of—feel convinced of," Pointer amended.

"Then, of course, we have been suspecting the wrong man. But there's someone after us" Lightfoot fell again into deep thought.

"And that poor fellow upstairs has just got through from Esterweege," he went on. "He has been in one of the cells there, where a man can neither lie nor stand, and—well, they don't exactly overfeed them." For a second Lightfoot's face contracted with a spasm. "However . . . as he was wicked enough to be born and live a Jew and a rabbi, like his father and grandfather before him, doubtless they were quite justified!"

"And, by the way, from whom did you get that five-pound note that you say served as the excuse for Winslow to come here?" Pointer asked carelessly.

"From the Bar Hotel cashier, I think; but I'm not sure. But what was Winslow's real object, then?"

"Ah," Pointer said to that, "I can't tell you yet, Mr. Lightfoot. But I think you'll learn one day." And with that he rose to go. He was by no means certain that Lightfoot was innocent. A man might keep this house for just the purpose he acknowledged, and yet have another, as Superintendent Horrocks thought, where the notes were being forged. But Pointer did not show any suspicions.

"We are told that one of the bottles belonging to young Mr. Seiler was missing. Do you know anything about it?"

Apparently Lightfoot did not. His reconstruction of the young man's death was that he had blundered in some way, and that one of the secret letters which he was supposed to hand on had gone wrong, that a Fascist had come in and questioned him, seized him by the throat and poured the contents of the bottle of corrosive poison down his throat. According to him, the grip of a hand was distinctly visible on the throat when he first saw it.

Lightfoot shook himself. "I try not to think of his end," he said simply. "Fräulein Anna Meyerhof knew that he was in danger. He had been warned more than once. She curses me and our work. It's natural, I suppose." Again he fell into a reverie with the chief inspector standing ready to go. Then he looked up, and something like a twinkle came into his deep-set eyes.

"Pity you can't wait. There's a chap coming this evening—getting here at the rate of eighty miles an hour—who can tell one of the few funny tales that come our way. You may have heard the story—it's going the round even of the Embassies. But he's the chap it really happened to. He's a North Italian silk manufacturer, and his car broke down in some small town of North Italy a few days ago. While it was being mended at the local garage he stepped into the nearest cinema to pass the time out of the wind and sleet. By an odd chance the Duce's car was also being repaired in the same town, and he, too, had wandered into the same cinema. At the end, of course, Mussolini's portrait was flashed on the film and everyone stood—except Mussolini himself, who sat on. What does our silk manufacturer do but lean forward, tap him on the shoulder and whisper:

'I quite agree with you, my friend; but, believe me, it's safer to stand!' Mussolini turned his head, and Signor Blank nearly fainted. He staggered to the door, found his car ready, and made straight for the frontier and us. Fortunately his mother lives in Switzerland, and he's not married. You bet he's going all out to get here."

Pointer laughed; too. But he looked very grave as he left the house behind him. He still had nothing to prove that that man in there was not leading a double life. Philanthropist and forger. If he were innocent, then who was guilty? The notes were certainly the motive, of that Pointer had no doubt whatever. It was possible that their only connection with the *Speedwell* bob party was through Fay Starr —that she was the only guilty person at Vipiteno; but Pointer thought she could hardly alone have been of much use to the gang of forgers, or to the forger, if there were only one. Two people can treble the work of one. . . . Certainly none of the men connected with the crime had tried to change any doubtful notes over here in England. . . . Fay Starr's life was being fine-combed and might yet lead to the forger. That hunchback who appeared now and then on the scene. . . . Pointer decided that he must concentrate now on what had become of Winslow. He believed that much of Lightfoot's story, at any rate, that the young man was not being detained by him or any of his associates. It was a possibility that had always been present. Now there was no hope of finding Hugh Winslow alive—for Pointer did not think that he had left the house of his own free will. But if killed in his rooms, there still remained the conundrum of how the body had been taken away or hidden.

Pointer went there now and, locking himself in the suite, stood staring about him. What had he missed? By his orders the rooms had not been cleaned. There was one thing which had struck him at the time, and that was the amount of thick fluff that lay against the skirting board. He picked up a roll, and it came to pieces in his fingers. It was just a roll of fluff and dust such as any carpet when swept makes. Something was stirring in the chief inspector's mind. He had it! There was an electric vaccuum cleaner downstairs, and in every room were power plugs for its use. Then why had these rugs, in here been cleaned by some laborious old-fashioned method?

And, even so, could these rugs have produced this amount of fluff? There were only two of them, short-piled and firm woven.

He took a letter from his pocket and picked up the paper shears from the writing-table to trim it into a scoop with which to lift intact one of the rolls. The shears refused to cut, and, looking closer at them, he saw that they were widely sprung apart at the central screw. Fine dust fell out as he opened them. He folded the paper with the dust, and, picking up some fluff into another envelope, put both away. He had already fished out two ends of stout cord from the waste-paper basket on his first arrival, they had not proved of any use whatever so far. Did they link with the sprung shears and the fluff? And could they in their turn be linked with Winslow's inexplicable disappearance? Pointer stared at the shears as he held them in his hand. The ornamental fluted handles precluded any idea of finger-prints. They were of a good and very strong make. They must have been used to cut something extremely thick or coarse . . . he looked around the room again and found nothing else that even he could fasten on. He stood deep in thought. Was he to learn from this slender clue where Winslow's dead body lay? That the man was alive seemed negatived by every reason so far known for the crime. Also, there was the fact that none of the "crew" had absented themselves from their rooms or offices. Each had been watched day and night, and not one had acted in any way differently from usual. There had been no time to see to the wants of a captive, even had there been the inclination.

He rang the bell. Capstick came. He asked him for the day's paper, and then, when that was brought, for some shears. Capstick instantly went to the writing table.

"Not far to go for these, sir." He handed them to the chief inspector. Pointer made as though to cut out a column; he sawed at the paper and looked at Capstick.

Capstick appeared amazed.

"Well, that's a new one on me, sir," he muttered, examining them. "Sharp as razors, they always have been. I saw Mr. Winslow cut stout cardboard with them just before he went away, and these shears went through it like as if it had been tissue paper. And that was the morning he left for Italy."

"Seems to have been their swan song," said Pointer. "Perhaps you have another pair downstairs?"

Capstick said no; there was only his wife's scissors from her work-basket, small scissors.

Pointer decided to take the paper as it was. He drove to the Yard and had the fluff and the specks that had fallen from the shears examined microscopically.

The fluff he was quickly told came from some material made of camel's hair, and with it were particles of embroidery silk in pink, blue and green; hand-twisted silk, vegetable dyed; Eastern all the lot. The specks were exactly the same.

Pointer copied out the list of components and made for the carpet warehouses of the Port of London. There, on great tiled floors, carpets are sluiced, and squeezed, and sluiced again, by the week if need be, till they assume the lovely mother-of-pearl or tortoiseshell tones which make them so valuable. A confrere at the Yard had told Pointer of one of the Port of London clerks at the warehouses, who would be able to help him if any man could. King was the name. Mr. King turned out to be a stout white-haired man with a florid face, pop-eyes and a small hat on the back of a. large bald head. He had a flower in his button-hole, and a gaily-patterned waistcoat. An umbrella stout as himself dangled from one arm. Mr. King was never seen without that umbrella. He took the paper with the fluff in it and sniffed thoughtfully at it like a cat presented with a new dish. Then he felt it carefully with the tips of his fingers. Then he stood a moment, his head thrown back, his eyes screwed up tight.

"*Namdah*," he pronounced at length, and in a tone of finality. "I'll show you some of the stuff. We don't have many of the kind I'm going to show you—the kind this fluff came from. No, I don't mean the felt used for under saddles, I mean the rugs that come down from Yarkand into Kashmir by the Road of Death, and which the Kashmiri embroider with leaves and lotuses so closely that you can't chop a pin on a plain spot. Come and see them. You won't find any like them in the shops, nor the kind that fluff came from."

He led the way through the stuffy paths of carpet-land to a shed which he unlocked. "Never have many," he repeated, and went to a small pile by a window. "Lovely, aren't they?"

They were, but Pointer was not interested in beauty just now.

"Woven in Thibet, and down the Caravan Road of Death they've come, every one," Mr. King went on, lost to the world, his hat on the back of his head, his eyes again screwed up. "'I've been up that road, and down that road, and there's not many can say as much. Turns you into a fatalist, does that road. Skeletons all around you—" He unscrewed his eyes in response to a question. "These rugs? They sell them chiefly in Srinagar. Lovely place that. When I die I'm going there. Straight to Srinagar. To Takht-i-Suliman. The floating gardens—the water lilies— the roses! I never smell a rose that I don't think of Srinagar. There was a girl I used to know—" Again the eyes were screwed shut. "Her father sold these in his shop. The designs are based on the windings of the Jhelum River—" He opened his eyes, smiled a little, sighed, and settled his hat on the back of his bald head, shifted his umbrella to his other arm, and humming under his breath what Pointer rightly guessed to be a Kashmiri love song, Mr. King led the way out again— from dreamland into the Port of London basin.

Pointer thanked him. Kashmir—Srinagar. . . In Mr. Priestley's rooms was a gay wall-hanging which Pointer had taken to be Chinese, and which Priestley had told him had come from a Thibetan monastery, though bought in Srinagar over the border. Mr. Priestley had a few other things from Kashmir, some of their peculiar copper and silver beaten work.

Pointer asked him now over the telephone if he might have a word with him. He was asked to come immediately if he could, as the other was just on the point of rushing out for a chat on the Nibelungenlied in aid of the blind ex-soldiers.

Priestley pushed back a big pile of papers and seemed genuinely pleased to see the chief inspector.

Pointer was covertly studying him. He had again the impression of a man most easy to meet and very difficult to know.

Pointer asked a question or two which were the ostensible cause for the visit, ostentatiously noted down the replies and rose.

"I suppose this rug, too, is Eastern," he said. "Excuse the question, but you interested me so much last time with that Kashmir hanging of yours—"

"This is Indian, and not bad," Priestley bent over to look at it afresh. "I had some namdahs, six beauties, but they didn't go with the covers in these rooms, somehow. Too light, I suppose. So I sent them into storage. Otherwise I could have shown you something really lovely."

Pointer glanced at—and into—the open safe beside him.

"I wonder you don't get robbed, sir." His eye indicated the pile of notes inside.

"Fortunately I'm rather a good-sized handful," Priestley said with a smile. "I used to box a lot in my young days. And, as Moffatt says, 'one loses one's hair, and one's teeth, and one's eyesight, but one never loses one's accomplishments.'" Priestley gave his chuckle.

"More to the point, not to lose one's revolver, I should think, sir," and the chief inspector made for the door.

"I'm not bad with a revolver," Priestley, spoke with an air of quiet confidence. Pointer let himself out and went down the stairs to look for Capstick.

To him he said that he wanted to go over again the dates on which Mr. Winslow had left, and when he had first spoken of taking a holiday, and when he had spoken of coming back. That done, and duly noted, he turned a fresh page.

"Now, then—Mr. Priestley—" Capstick went through the dates when Mr. Priestley had first written to Mrs. Clarke, when his things had arrived and when Mr. Priestley himself had first taken possession of the upper suite.

"Did he send any of his furniture away?" Pointer asked, eyes on his book—apparently.

"His rugs, sir. Sent them off the day after he got here. Pretty, I thought them."

"Where did he send them to?" Pointer asked in his most routine and dull tone of voice.

"Monday he got in. Tuesday he told me to have them sent off to Patterford's warehouse. They went off Wednesday morning. I gave him the receipt when he got back on Saturday."

Wednesday morning! And Winslow had been killed Friday night, so Pointer believed. Pointer asked some more questions, noted down the answers, and then left. Wednesday morning . . . Friday night.

Was this another stone wall? An inquiry immediately put through to Patterford's, the big carriers and warehousemen, confirmed the butler's statement. Their books recorded the arrival on Wednesday afternoon of a parcel of rugs from the house in question, which parcel had been collected on their van's first round; about nine in the morning, that would have been.

He went down to the warehouse himself. Privately and very confidentially he interviewed one of the managers. To him he explained that there was some talk of a theft of very valuable Eastern things from Mr.

Priestley's flat. Mr. Priestley himself was not quite sure as to whether these rugs—Namdah rugs—were or were not in the flat at the time.

The manager again consulted the books. Again he assured Pointer that the rugs had arrived at the warehouse . . . he gave the date and the hour. Pointer stopped on the way out for a word with the foreman. As the word opened with a half-crown the man, a keen-eyed, sharp-faced man of middle age, was quite willing to hear more. Pointer explained to him that he must see the rugs that had come from Mr. Priestley's rooms in Lowndes Square—he gave the number—on such and such a day. Mr. Hotchkiss, the foreman, scratched his thick hair. Fortunately they hadn't been long on the premises.

Three days' notice was usually asked for an inspection. Pointer told him that—privately—he would make it right with him and his men. Hotchkiss summoned two of his underlings, and with their help, cleared a way into a cubicle.

"Here we are, sir. There's more of Mr. Priestley's stuff in here. That long bundle there will be what you want. Now, then, my lads, handsomely does it! Handsomely!" And the big roll of rugs fell with a thud on the floor at the inspector's feet.

He bent over them. They had been well corded. And they had reached here on the Wednesday, before Mr. Winslow had arrived in England. Yet the cord was the same as the two cut pieces which he had fished from Winslow's paper basket. The ends were solid roll. There was no slackness. But if his theory was right as to what had blunted those shears, he would not expect to find any slackness.

He photographed the bundle first, and made a careful sketch of the knot as well. Had Hotchkiss sign the sketch and then cut the cord. The bundle was set rolling. Almost instantly it looked odd. The rugs seemed to protrude from the ends in the most extraordinary fashion. Another roll, and the cut tops and bottoms of two rugs fell away, leaving in the centre of the rugs the dead body of a young man.

It was Winslow, and he had been dead a week, by the look of him. Naphthalene was strewn thickly over him. It whitened the floor all about the men, who stood rooted to the spot in horror.

Stooping down, after photographing the body, Pointer saw that Winslow had been killed by a blow on the top of the head. A fearful blow. Meant to kill.

More photographs were taken. A police van was summoned. In a few minutes the carpets and the body were again rolled up and deposited in it. The men drove off. Pointer stayed behind to ask for the carman's name and address who had delivered that bundle—on Wednesday!

Hotchkiss had him fetched into his own small den; and strict orders were given to the fetcher not to breathe a word of what had happened.

"There's something wrong about those rugs you fetched from Mr. Priestley's new flat," Hotchkiss began shortly. "You didn't collect them on the Wednesday, so why did you hand in the slip marked with that date? Now, no more humbugging!"

"It was the butler there, sir." The carman's face had turned first red and then pale. He looked uneasy. He forgot to ring us up until Friday afternoon. I called for them on my first round on Saturday. He met me on the way down and asked me to enter the date as Wednesday the 21st. Which I did. I didn't think there was any harm in doing him a good turn."

"Didn't you!" snapped Mr. Hotchkiss caustically. "Well, a few more such good turns and you'll land yourself in jail, my lad. How did you get the rugs? Did he bring them down to you, this butler chap?"

"No, sir. I know the house; we often deliver and fetch from there, which was why I didn't mind obliging him. Anything big he always leaves in a recess on the second floor. He's none so young, and doesn't like stairs. So I don't ring at the door if he's not downstairs; I go up to the recess, fetch what's there, and leave the receipt on the hall table. It saves his legs and my time. Only this once he helped me down with the rugs and asked me to alter the date. I did. And you say something's missing from those rugs?" Smiley finished up anxiously. "They were all corded up for me to take away. I didn't touch them except to carry them."

"Nothing's been taken away!" snapped Hotchkiss. "Who said anything about anything being missing? But you put in another wrong date, and you'll be sorry, my lad! Now go. And not a word about this, mind, or you're fired. Understand? One question, one whisper, and you're off our books."

When a crushed and wilted carman had left, Hotchkiss turned to Pointer.

"Trouble with him is, he's good-natured. Honest as the day, but always trying to oblige people. That sort of thing doesn't do—not in business. However, now you know that you were right, sir, in thinking the date was wrong. 'Something taken away!' My eye! A deal too much added." And Hotchkiss rubbed the back of his head with a horny palm.

"I've been in a good many things," he went on. "Earthquake in Palestine, when a camel saved my life. Don't you believe what they tell you about camels, sir." He broke off to say earnestly, "They're fine beasts! And clever! You ask a Turk. And I've been in a fire. And in a swamped boat"—Mr. Hotchkiss seemed to be counting his blessings one by one—"but this is the first time that I've been mixed up in a murder." And it is to be regretted that Mr. Hotchkiss spoke in a tone of some pleasurable anticipation as one might whose daily round is just a thought monotonous—for a friend of camels.

Pointer drove back to the Yard deep in thought. He had won one round. At last he had the body of Hugh Winslow, who had been murdered just as certainly as Fay Starr had been murdered. And on the same night; and in the same place; and either Lightfoot, or another, had been the murderer.

If not Lightfoot, then the chief inspector thought that the facts clearly indicated who was the most likely to be guilty.

CHAPTER FOURTEEN

FEW things made more sensation than The Warehouse Murder, as Winslow's death was wrongly called. The Warehouse Grave might have had some truth in it. Capstick had proved easy to handle. He was not made of the stuff to withstand the cold steel of the chief inspector's facts. He broke down at the first thrust and acknowledged exactly what he had done. He maintained, truthfully, Pointer thought, that even after the discovery of the murder in the suite and the fact that Mr. Winslow was missing, he had not dreamt of connecting his disappearance with the bundle of rugs.

The autopsy and inquest established that Winslow had been killed by a blow on the head, and later rolled in the rugs in which he had been found. At the inquest the coroner went into details about the knots used, which were definitely not a sailor's, nor those of a man accustomed to tying parcels.

The place of his murder was taken back to his rooms by the scissors and the fluff, and therefore definitely linked with Fay Starr's death.

The police had by now found that she had secretly married a Mr. Kershaw, an actor, while still in her father's house, and before she came to Town. The question was—and the public fastened on it: Had she and he lived together again, at Knightsbridge, quarrelled again, and had the husband come upon her in Winslow's flat in Lowndes Square? According to the papers, this might explain everything—especially if Kershaw was a hunchback. He had not been one at the time of the marriage, but there were those who spoke of flying accidents and car smashes and lifelong maiming.

And then the coroner produced a tit-bit. In the pocket
of Winslow's coat was found a letter or summons made by
pasting cut-out capital letters from some printed page.
The note ran:

"The five hundred pounds must be in one-pound
notes. I will bring the letters. She can assure you that you
have them all."

What could be clearer, asked the coroner, than that
Winslow had obtained the money as directed, that Miss
Starr was at his rooms in order to verify the bundle of
notes, and that it was letters—Winslow's letters to her,
probably—which were being paid for. That some quarrel
broke out. Possibly Winslow had put the notes into safety
somewhere and refused to pay. That was for later
investigations, but, at any rate, he thought everything
went to show a quarrel over blackmail money, or over
Miss Starr.

The public finally became certain that here was a
crime passionel, and the coroner had the inquest
adjourned for a fortnight to give the police time to get into
touch with the husband. The police were not grateful,
except in so far as the name of Kershaw served as a
screen for what they held to be the real motive behind the
two deaths.

"You don't believe in that letter found in his pocket?"
Major Pelham asked Pointer after the adjournment.

"Mr. Winslow had a pot of Grip-fix on his writing-
table and a pair of shears, sir," was the reply; "and
evidently the murderer was not worried about time. I see
no reason why, finding the five hundred pounds in Mr.
Winslow's pocket-book, or bag, or having heard about it
beforehand, he might not have concocted just such a
letter."

"You think Miss Starr double-crossed him, as it's
called?"

"I think she may have told the murderer about Winslow's five hundred pounds—told him so as to put him on his guard. The murderer, to my mind, is undoubtedly the forger, and I rather think that Miss Starr was the forger's tool; which was why, I think, she was not frightened of him. It looks to me as though there might have been a love affair there, old or recent, and that she was afraid for Winslow's life, but not at all afraid for herself."

"Why didn't she warn Winslow? Or do you think she had done so?"

"I think very clearly she hadn't, sir, or Winslow wouldn't have gone to Lightfoot at once. Which is one of the reasons why I think Miss Starr may have been in love with the forger, or linked to him by some tie of old affection, if nothing more."

"Certainly he couldn't be the hunchback, one would think, or such a figure would have cropped up oftener. . ". Pelham was thinking aloud, ruminating as he smoked.

"I shouldn't be surprised if, the hunchback were the actual forger, sir, the photographer of genius, and the murderer the forger in the sense of the employer, the distributor. The hunchback not coming forward looks to me as though he were implicated in the forgery, and has to lie low. I don't think a stranger to Winslow would have found it so easy to do a double murder, as the man evidently did who killed those two in that charming little suite, and we cannot trace a hunchback among his acquaintances!"

"Perhaps the hunchback, too, has been murdered—if he was the actual producer of the banknotes," Pelham suggested.

"I doubt that, sir. He would be much too valuable. Miss Starr wasn't valuable; and Winslow, of course, was only a danger. But a forger—photographer of the kind that made those notes . . . If my theory of the criminal is right, he's in no danger whatever, but is being most carefully guarded and looked after. I don't say he's not a sort of prisoner, and won't spend the rest of his life in what is virtually a prison, working for his task-master. But he won't be injured in any way. At least, that's how I see it, sir."

"You don't think the papers are right, and that jealousy might be at the bottom of it?"

"I don't see how it would fit the facts, sir. Miss Starr's returning to England with Winslow might be held to be due to affection, but what about his five hundred pounds withdrawal at Dover?"

"Funds for their unofficial honeymoon, of course," said Pelham.

"But his current account would have seen them through any ordinary trip together," Pointer said. "He had dividends coming in in another fortnight which, with what he had on hand, would have been ample, one would think. And his visit to Lightfoot with his mention of the banknote? No, sir. The forged notes lie at the root of these two murders."

"And you think Lightfoot felt certain that Winslow was the Secret Service spy they had been told about? If so he's gone to a lot of trouble for nothing. Cleaned his house, sent his protégés off all over England . . . We know now that he covered eighty miles in an hour and a half that Friday night. Well, if he's genuine, it'll teach him not to jump to conclusions another time," Major Pelham said a trifle sarcastically. Then he looked sharply at Pointer. "You do believe his story, don't you?"

"I believe that part of it, certainly, sir. But as to whether there's more than that to Mr. Lightfoot —time only will tell. All we know for certain is that he was told about the forged banknote, had the time to get to Lowndes Square, and would have been admitted by Winslow, and that, if the forger, Miss Starr was his tool and therefore not afraid of him."

"Nothing prevents its being another aspect of Mr. Lightfoot the philanthropist, you think . . . humph . . . Superintendent Horrocks rather thinks so, too. Well,

Detective, time will tell," murmured the A.C. "What about the rugs?"

Pointer nodded as though to show that he, too, asked himself that question.

"Friend of Priestley's?" Pelham asked. Pointer thought that that was not necessary, though quite possible. As he saw it, the murderer was someone known to both Miss Starr and Winslow, who had followed them from Victoria or Lightfoot's house. He thought the former. Someone who had rung Winslow's bell or knocked, been admitted by Winslow, had a word with the doomed girl and his host, and while Winslow was busy with something—perhaps stooping to get out a whisky and soda which stood in the bottom cupboard of his writing-table, had shot her and instantly sprung on Winslow, bringing down on his head something heavy, probably the butt-end of the revolver wrapped in his handkerchief or his glove."

"His own revolver?"

"Either his own, or one brought by Miss Starr, for I think she was trying to repay him for having saved her life on the ice run. As I see it, I doubt if she wanted to be mixed up in all this at all. But she looks the kind to pay her debts. I can imagine her handing Mr. Winslow that revolver with very mixed feelings, as I rather think she may have had all through the journey back with him."

Pointer never knew it for certain, but he was quite right. Fay Starr had come to London, very much against her deepest inclinations, to save Winslow's life. She had handed him her revolver with a passionate anger at his proposed interference into something which need not have concerned him, something which was to land him into dangers at which, she knew, he did not even guess.

"I don't suppose he thought about moving Winslow," Pointer went on. "I think he went thoroughly through the papers in his table to make sure that he had left no note about the forged banknotes. Then he searched Winslow's pockets, took the five hundred pounds and all his papers,

concocted that letter from printed characters, left it
where it would be found, and went out. I think it's quite
likely that it was then he noticed the rugs in the alcove.
The curtain doesn't come down to the floor, and they
would show. It's possible that the curtain bulged a bit,
and that he got quite a shock thinking someone was
standing there. But the rugs with their naphthalene
smell suggested a brilliant idea, which he promptly
carried out, and finally left Winslow's body, carefully
wrapped around and around, behind the curtains, before
he let himself carefully out of the house with the two suitcases. Miss Star's bag was probably hidden in them, but
he certainly took that, too. Her suitcase and wardrobe
trunks were at Victoria, as we know, and might as well
have been in Timbuctoo, for all the help they've been to
us."

"Certainly his disposal of Winslow hung things up
magnificently," Pelham said, "and but for some good work
on your part, Pointer, might have led the hunt far astray.
You feel fairly sure of the end, eh?"

"As long as we can keep the banknote motive to
ourselves, I do, sir. Once let that leak out, and I think we
might well slip up on a conviction."

Which was why Pointer very much furthered the
journalists' idea of jealousy and a husband—hunchback
or straight—dashing in and executing summary justice.
Also the papers' efforts to find out the facts of Fay Starr's
life were so much to the good. Over and, over again, the
facts as known were re-established, some few ones added
but nothing of any value, so far. The papers, noticing this
themselves, went all out on the discovery of the
hunchback. As a rule such a marked man is not difficult
to find, but their best efforts only drew blank. Yet they
learnt interesting facts. He had been seen several times
slipping out of the house of flats very early in the
morning, or late in the evening, according to some
charwomen who worked near by. Opposite Mrs.
Kershaw's flat was another large building similarly used,

and from its landing a hunchback had several times been seen watching her house. All accounts agreed on his being a big man with a dark, forbidding, embittered face, a pair of long powerful arms, and strongly built. The last time he was noticed was about a week before Miss Starr turned up at Vipiteno. He had not been seen since.

Pointer meanwhile had sent around to all the photographic shows for details of any especially clever exhibitors. Amid the resulting lists that almost swamped Pointer's rooms, was one interesting fact. One of the best exhibitors in Town and the Midlands was a hunchback, a Charles Montgomery. He invariably got a prize, generally the first, prize or, a medal for the cleverest work. He was especially good at trick effects. A patent of his for photographing directly on to prepared silks or canvases was much in use for preparing women's woolwork. This clue led to a further one—a large shop in Chelsea, where Montgomery sent in specially-prepared lengths of various materials. There Pointer got his address—a small house in a quiet square off the Brompton Road. He had given it up on the Friday that Winslow had arrived in England from Vipiteno. He had received a cable, said his housekeeper, who liked what little she knew of him, offering him an important post abroad to which he had to go at once. He had packed up his photographic things, which were all over, the house, sent them off in packing-cases, and then, taking his few personal, belongings with him in his car, had left, paying her a month's full board and wages in advance, and putting the house in the hands of an estate agent. He had bought it freehold some years before, and seemed never to have lived anywhere else or to have gone away on a holiday. The agent, when questioned, had never met Mr. Montgomery. He did not expect to find any difficulty about selling the house, as the price asked, furnished, was most moderate; He was to get into touch with Mr. Montgomery through Cook's, the travel agents. The cable which had reached Montgomery had been sent off from Basle, and ran: "Better take holiday at once." It was unsigned, but the name on the back of the post-office form handed in was A. Swiss, with an address in Dulwich, England. A non-existent address.

So a warning had been sent the hunchback. Pointer, going over the house very carefully in the guise of a possible buyer, found nothing which could be considered suspicious. The man's work was done by the camera, and work of that kind had certainly been carried on here for years. The furniture—Pointer rightly guessed that Montgomery had bought it in the house, probably from an army man who was stationed somewhere else. Throughout, Montgomery had paid in full, avoiding the necessity for references. No persons visited him in the house, said the housekeeper, except on errands connected with his work, which was his one passion. She seemed a rather dull woman, and Pointer was very careful not to let her guess that the police had any interest in her master or his home. If free, Pointer thought that Mr. Montgomery would certainly send some of his work to photographic papers or exhibitions again in the near future, probably under another name, but he did not think he was—or would be—free. So that that chance of meeting him did not promise much. But there was the other end . . . the end of the murderer himself.

Ursula Winslow was present at the inquest. It had been a frightful shock to her. Her quest was now at an end. Winslow was found, and Moffatt need no longer expatiate in private to Kidd on his certainty that the finding would hardly advance his own position with Ursula. The inquest with its insistence on a guilty passion on the part of Hugh and its swift and terrible retribution had badly shaken her own conviction in her cousin. There seemed no other possible explanation of the fate which had overtaken him and Fay Starr.

It was a week later, Kidd, who was running down to see "the uncles" on the following day—they were giving his transparent paper a thorough testing—had asked her in to his office to hear a remarkable piano roll which was made from it, and which he also thought would interest her uncle's firm. He made quite a party of it, and Priestley and Moffat, came too.

Ursula was thankful of anything to distract her thoughts, and she was genuinely interested in the possibilities of mechanical music. The roll was much smaller than most, lighter, and, according to its proud parent, would not buckle. It played well, and she was looking at it now on the table.

The perforations seem much sharper edged than most. Is that because the paper is so thin? she asked.

Kidd gave a little smile. "Between ourselves, strictly, that's due to some wonderful stuff we use, a liquid preparation of our own making which cuts through it whenever brushed on just as a diamond would cut glass."

The safe was open, it was out of it that he had taken his precious single roll of music. She followed his glance by going to the safe, and to his annoyance putting her hand in and taking out a bottle which stood on the top shelf in a little square wooden box.

"Friederich Seiler . ... Jungfrau Apotheke. Interlaken. . . ." She read out and below Augentropfen. She turned in surprise "Seiler! That was the name of the man at Brixen who poisoned himself. Interlaken was his home."

They were alone at the moment, for the others had stepped out to speak to Lightfoot who had happened to drop in, so he said, for a word with Kidd.

"Those are eye-drops which the poor chap gave me that day, as my eyes were frightfully inflamed," Kidd said lightly, but he shut and locked the safe. "He said he knew of nothing to touch them. And they are wonderful. I use it sparingly, of course, as I can't get them over here." And with that, Lightfoot and the others came in again, and Kidd talked of the music roll, and of how he hoped to play it to her uncles next day. Ursula found her attention wandering. Now he put another, even longer roll into the piano. Her head ached. . . She had some shopping that must be done before she left Town again, this time for a long absence. She was screened by the piano, she thought. The others were all in an eager group on the other side.

She took out her purse. Yes, she still had a five-pound note left—one of the ones which she had taken to Vipiteno. She took it from its tight little compartment and opened it out. How oddly creased it looked. That crispness which a Bank of England note never loses under ordinary circumstances seemed lacking in its folds. The creases seemed so crumbly of edge. Ursula had just discovered a new, hitherto unsuspected, defect in the forged photographed notes. But all she knew was that it perplexed her. She, too, as a niece of Joliffe and Joliffe, paid almost unconsciously keen attention to a banknote's paper. She studied this one. She looked at the number. Struck by a thought, she pulled out the little ivory tablet from the same purse, on which she had marked the number of the notes handed to her. This was not one of them. For a second she fingered it, listened to its crackling, and the more she experimented with it, the less she liked it. How on earth had she come by it? She quite started when Kidd called her name—a second time.

Would she care to come with them to an upper room to hear how it played on a newer make of piano? Or did she prefer to sit there, gloating over her wealth?

With a rather forced smile she said that she felt a bit off-colour, and would wait here for them to come down again and tell her how wonderful it was. She sat on alone, still with the note in her hand. All of a sudden the puzzled look on her face gave way to the unmistakable look of someone who remembers something. Ursula felt sure that she knew how this came to be where it was. She looked about her, and stepped swiftly to a writing-table, where a brand-new, blotting pad invited correspondence. Sitting down, she dashed off a letter at top speed, folded the banknote, put both in an envelope, which she took from a case in front of her, sealed it, and hesitated. Finally she stepped into the outer room and asked the office boy to get a taxi, as she wanted to send a letter very urgently. The boy looked out of the window and said that a taxi was just turning away, and that he thought he could stop it. . . . Another second, and he told her that he had got it. Ursula went out on to the landing and handed him a letter addressed to Chief Inspector Pointer at New Scotland Yard. A couple of half-crowns accompanied the envelope. One was for the taxi driver who was to take the letter to its address, the other was for the boy, who assured her that the letter should go that "instant minute." She went back into the inner office, and when, a few minutes later, the others returned, they found her looking at a road map.

She and Moffatt were going down to the uncles on the morrow, and Ursula thought that a new route might be interesting.

The chief inspector had at last run the hunchback to earth, by means of a certain rare and expensive acid which the photographer used in some of his retouching. Pointer had quietly arranged with all vendors of the stuff to let him know instantly any was ordered; and he had just heard of an order for two ounces of it sent to the firm in question by a Mr. Mile, living in Brixton. The address was a small shop. There Mr. Mile had been found—and arrested—on the charge of being concerned in the shooting of Fay Starr and the killing of Hugh Winslow at the latter's flat in Lowndes Square. The man—a big powerful hunchback—had fought like the giant that he would have been had his back been straight. But Pointer's men were too much for him; and handcuffed, literally foaming at the mouth, he had been taken away. The shop in question was one that belonged to a Mr. Kershaw, it seemed, and had been run by various managers for some years. The present one, who had just taken it over, seemed quite ignorant of either the hunchback or, the owner's identity, but Pointer fancied his ignorance was not so complete as he swore it to be. He never read newspapers, he said, had no time for them, and as to supplying his lodger with all his food up in his room, well, why not? Mr. Mile wasn't feeling well, he had said, when he took the rooms and the cellar, and being a hard worker, he liked not to have to go out, but Pointer noticed the huge bolts on the outside of the doors . . . the manager himself was a great hulking looking navvy, with a brother the same size as himself. . . . They, too, were taken off to be questioned; and meantime their things were searched. But there was nothing to disprove their story that they had taken a liking to the shop in passing, and arranged with the departing manager to take over the business on trial. As to Mile, he had walked in on them and asked for them to let him board there. . . . Altogether their story would take time to pierce.

But meanwhile the search of the cellar used by Mile had brought a light of triumph to the quiet eyes of the chief inspector. All the photographic paraphernalia, necessary for the forgeries was there; and so was a stack of the paper on which the forgeries so far to hand had all been made. Also a wallet with genuine Bank of England notes of various amounts, the pinholes in the corners showing where they had been fastened to a board before being photographed.

Altogether, as far as Mile went, the haul was complete, and yet, thanks to the ideas spread by the press, he would only be charged on his arrival at the police station with being concerned in the two murders from the standpoint of a jealous lover or husband. Pointer for once was well pleased as he drove back to the Yard.

CHAPTER FIFTEEN

SUPERINTENDENT HORROCKS was already off on his way to the shop, but the A.C. had a few words with Pointer.

"Nothing found to link him to your master criminal?" he asked.

Pointer shook his head.

"One of the *Speedwell* crew, you still think?"

Pointer said that he certainly believed so.

"And how do you intend to catch him?" was the next question. Pointer said that Superintendent Horrocks and he were working out a very neat, promising sounding plot in which the part of the hunchback would be taken by a young C.I.D. man.

"Some more of your routine work, I suppose?" suggested Pelham, and the chief inspector, with a faint smile, only said, "Yes, sir."

"And that stuff in the bottle kept in Captain Kidd's safe, of which you brought us half by the same kind of methods," went on Pelham. "Is it what you thought?"

"Yes, sir. It's the testing liquid which the young Swiss invented. Our man is working out the ingredients. It certainly perforates that forged note the Super had sent him from Basle, and doesn't affect the real notes at all."

"That will take some explaining on the part of Captain Kidd," murmured Pelham. "Did he take the bottle from Seiler, do you think?"

"It looks like it, sir. It's possible that he took it from the counter after the discovery of the dead body. One of the things the Italians have is a piece of this transparent paper of Captain Kidd's, and it, too, has some holes on it. This stuff perforates it also. A large bottle of some similar liquid is in the partner's safe, and seems to be in use. It looks as though the firm might be using it for this new music roll Captain Kidd is trying out. I should fancy that he had shown some of his paper to Seiler, possibly discussing its possibilities for film cameras, and that Mr. Seiler, either from curiosity or by chance, tried his liquid on it, and that Captain Kidd saw the possibilities of the stuff. The bottle seems to be one supplied Mr. Seiler before he left his home with eye-drops in it. He may have kept to the label so as to put people off its real contents."

"Sounds feasible," said Pelham, cocking an interrogative eye at the other.

"Quite so, sir," was the noncommittal reply. Pelham saw that the chief inspector was not yet ready to come across. A tap came at the door. A letter had just been sent up for the chief inspector, marked "Urgent." A taxi driver had brought it. In the left-hand corner of the envelope were the initials: "U. W."

Pelham nodded permission, and Pointer tore it open. He had an impassive face, but it changed as he took out a five-pound note and read the letter.

"What's wrong?" demanded his chief.

"It's from Miss Winslow, sir," Pointer's voice was hoarse. "She encloses a banknote which she's just found in her purse. Look, sir! This hole in the corner was made by Seiler's re-agent, judging by its blistered edge. And this canary coloured smear! That's spirits of salts, or I'm all out. This must be the note taken from the Swiss at Bressanone.

"Please excuse me—"

And for once in his life the chief inspector had picked up the assistant commissioner's telephone without waiting for permission, and was asking for Miss Winslow's number. He listened a moment to some reply to his question.

"She's out," he said in a stifled voice. "Has been called for by a car, a strange one, the hall porter says, but which she seemed to be expecting, and is gone. Gone!"

Pelham had read the note, it ran: "Dear Chief Inspector Pointer,—Please do not trouble to reply to this, as it may not be of any importance, but I do not like the look of the enclosed note which has been lying folded in my purse for some days. At first I thought I was mistaken, and that it must be all right, but I see by my list that it is not one of those given me by my bank. And I should have no others. I believe that this note was substituted for one of my own by Miss Starr. It sounds a dreadful thing to say of her now, when she can't answer the charge. I only do so, because it may be of some use to you. Just before we got to Calais I stepped back quickly into my compartment and found her with my purse in her hand. She looked frightfully confused and guilty, and mumbled something about having seen it lying on the floor, and having just picked it up for me. I confess I thought she had helped herself to some of its contents, her face was so odd. But on counting over my money I found everything all right—apparently. And the incident has made me feel quite wretched ever since she was found dead. But now I feel sure that I was right after all, and that she then took out one of the Bank's notes and put this in its place. Is this of any importance—I mean to Hugh's dear memory? In great haste—Ursula Winslow. P.S. As I said above, do not trouble to acknowledge this if it is valueless.'"

"She's in danger?" Pelham asked.

Pointer looked at him for a fraction of a second before replying:

"If the forger—already a double murderer—thinks that she alone knows of the existence of these dud notes, I don't think there's that much between herself and certain death." He held up the thickness of the banknote which she had sent him.

"If she told him that she had sent us word I don't think that car would have called for her. Unfortunately most of our men have had to be called off keeping watch on the 'crew' in order to help us with that hunchback, and tracing his doings. Lightfoot alone is being followed, and he very likely has given the one man on his trail the slip." Pointer saluted and was gone.

Ursula was waiting to hear from Scotland Yard. She wished she did not miss Hugh so much. Her telephone rang. Mr. Priestley wanted to see her urgently. At one of his boy clubs in the suburbs. Very urgently indeed. Something to do with Miss Starr and her cousin. Good news. He was sending a car for her which was bringing him out some things for the boy's club; a wretched affair, but it would get her down by the shortest possible route. Meanwhile not a word to anyone. That was vital. Promised? Ursula promised instantly, and heard the receiver clicked down at the other end.

Mr. Priestley had been too excited to say where the club in question was. He had so many. She remembered one out by the Crystal Palace, one out in Bermondsey. The hall porter sent word that a car was waiting for her. She ran down. It was a closed car of some old-fashioned kind, but it was a cold night, and she bundled in, noticing that the seat opposite was piled with boxes like a traveller's samples. Indeed, the whole little coupé was just the kind of thing she had seen in the early mornings outside smart shops. . . How stuffy it was! And—the light in the cab went out. She tapped on the panes—there must be a fog outside, everything was black—and then the car began to go round and round, it seemed to her, while a horrid sickly smell—she knew chloroform—choked her . . . something was wrong . . . chemists' samples . . . she slumped back in her seat. Instantly the blinds were drawn up, the driver opened the door. He was in a deserted *cul de sac*. He tied a sponge over her mouth and then drew up a big travelling rug till it covered it, covered her nearly to her eyes. Then he sat her up neatly in her corner, tucked the rug around her in such a way that it held her in her place, wedged her in with some of the boxes from the opposite seat, and climbed into the driver's seat again. Then he set off once more.

Pointer drove all out. He knew where he was going: A swimming pool not far from Harrow. One of the members of the *Speedwell* was a member, and it was that especial one whom Pointer believed to be the murderer of Fay Starr and of Hugh Winslow. But in winter it was practically free to anyone who cared to drive in and use it. Hardly anyone did. You could drive up to the very edge and take a header off your running-board if you felt like it, or off the roof of your car.

As he saw it, nothing else would be so suitable for the disposal of Ursula Winslow. Blood must not be shed. A third murder would be too dangerous. Poison was barred, because it could be traced, and water must be found in her lungs to convincingly prove a suicide, by an overwrought girl, more in love with her cousin than anyone suspected . . . her body would not be found until spring, in all probability. He could think of no better scheme or place, and he had thought hard. He raced his car, and he was there first. He did not let panic tell him that he was mistaken. If he were, Ursula was beyond help; she was as good as dead. He backed his car once he saw that no other was there, left it hidden by the gate and raced on foot to the water. Nothing was to be seen. Pointer dragged two iron seats back to back with a space between. An old sailcloth was flapping over the door of a wooden shelter by the entrance. It sufficed to hide him, and yet did not suggest concealed danger. It looked merely as though the seats were to be given a little belated protection.

A wait of only some fifteen minutes, and he heard a car driving very quietly up to the entrance. Another minute or so, and the car crept noiselessly round the drive on to the cement platform by the tank. Another, and the driver got down and looked about him, standing on the running-board. Then he flung the door of the car open, and pulled out something long wrapped in a rug . . . he seemed fond of rugs, this man.

He himself pulled it off and the body of Ursula Winslow lay on the tiles.

Pointer sprang for him, and the most terrific fight which the chief inspector had ever engaged in began. To and fro; the man he tried to hold was like a conger eel. He was fighting for more than his life. So was Pointer.

There was another man with the chief inspector, but his instructions were to take Ursula Winslow at once to the nearest hospital. Pointer felt sure that the girl would be alive when flung into the water, but whether things would have gone so far that only a last flicker remained in her.

Inspector Watts did as ordered. He shut the door on Ursula's inanimate body, jumped into the driving seat, and raced her off to a hospital not far away. Then he tore back.

Meanwhile Pointer and the man whom he intended to take had the place to themselves. It seemed hardly big enough for the two of them. But in the end he lay panting, winded, done, and the chief inspector snapped the handcuffs on his wrists, saying in a whisper, for his own breath was gone, "Edward Moffatt, I arrest you for the murder . . . of . . . Fay Starr and Hugh Winslow . . . and the attempted—"

Inspector Watts got back just then, and finished the warning in proper form.

"Lucky for her you guessed her peril on the instant." Pelham said later that day when talking to a bruised and battered Pointer.

"Any one of the forged notes would have been bad enough, sir, but that especial one." Pointer drew a breath of relief that all was now safely over.

"Miss Winslow's danger was that he had no idea we suspected their existence. He would think that by suppressing her, all might yet be well. Let it leak out, and he wouldn't have much chance of getting into the uncles' paper mills."

"Why did I suspect Moffatt, sir? Why, the forger only needs the right paper to make his notes practically undetectable. The fact that one of the 'crew' wanted to marry the niece of the paper-makers, and so have—as he would have had in time—free access to their works, was the first thought, after Lightfoot did not seem to be a certain winner. Also there's the evidence wirelessed us by Lieutenant Charwood this morning, which, knowing as we do that Mr. Winslow saved Miss Starr's life, and that she was, presumably, therefore grateful to him, might suggest Moffat as the danger. He says here, as you know sir . . ."

"I haven't looked at what he says yet," Pelham threw in.

"Well, he says here, sir, that he travelled up from Dover, on the day Miss Starr was shot, in a compartment where the only other occupant was a grumpy young man whom he is prepared to swear was Winslow. And that he was asked by a charming girl, whom he says is Miss Starr, if he would change places with her. He did so, and within two minutes she was back in her old compartment saying that after all she preferred her own seat, there was such a draught in his. He wondered what had gone wrong. He says he didn't believe her reason for asking him to change, but was sure she wanted a word with the 'lad' in the corner with whom he tried, quite in vain, to get to talk. Winslow—he swears it was he—only gave the curtest of nods and closed his eyes."

"Thinking about what had best be done, I suppose," Pelham said, "poor chap! And you think her change of seat . . .?"

"I think the fact that she no longer took care to be in the same compartment with Mr. Winslow shows that after Dover, after Moffat, left the train in other words, she was not alarmed for his safety. When that wireless reached us I wanted to have Moffat carefully followed, but unfortunately he had left his rooms, and we couldn't catch up with him. Then too the character fits Moffatt, and none of the others. Ruthless, cool-headed, cold-hearted. I think, by the way, sir, that we shall find that it was he who paid for Miss Starr's—Mrs. Kershaw's—flat at Knightsbridge. I feel sure he was the man with whom she ran away from her husband, and that she was always in love with him. That antagonism of which Miss Ursula spoke, which she thought was due to mistaken jealousy of Mr. Winslow's affection for her, was a quite rational jealousy of Moffatt's feelings. I rather think that was why Miss Starr went to Vipiteno in the first place—to win him back again. I think she put that dud five-pound note in Miss Winslow's purse out of sheer spite, and—I feel certain, absolutely—against instructions. I think she hoped to land her in some difficult position.

"I think Miss Winslow was right, though, in maintaining that Fay Starr was not in love with Winslow. Evidently she told Moffatt of what had happened. She would have to do that, but she meant to see Winslow into safety, if possible. So as soon as he reaches Victoria she goes on guard again. What she did not realise in the least was that she herself was in danger. Moffatt probably slipped in at some moment when our young milkman was reading his paper, rang Winslow's bell and was admitted. I fancy he brought a sham message from Miss Winslow as his excuse. Once in the suite, he would stand chatting pleasantly, and then, when his chance came—we think it was as Winslow stooped to get out some whisky—he shot her, and instantly crashed the butt down on Winslow's bent head; probably first slipping his thick-lined glove over it. Then he calmly settled down to look through the papers in the desk, just in case Winslow had written a note, or stuffed the forged notes into a drawer. Next he went through his pockets and suit-cases, found the five hundred pounds of which Fay Starr had already told him, we may be sure, used some of the newspapers in the suitcase to cut out the letters which he used for his letter, to look as though Winslow were being blackmailed."

"Very likely," murmured Pelham, "and of no importance, either way."

"We know that he stood Winslow's body, well wrapped up, in the recess, went on down and around to the place where he had left his own car, the car in which he had followed Winslow and Fay Starr from Victoria."

"Had the girl ever been to Switzerland?" Pelham asked suddenly.

"No, sir. What stopped her flow of talk on that occasion was Moffatt's direct question as to whether she had known young Seiler. It was a hint that she was making too much fuss about his death. And it evidently did worry her—until Lightfoot spoke of fits, just to see what she would say or do. With all her faults, Fay Starr was no murderess. Poor girl! There was good stuff in her! Her panic when she heard of Seiler's body having been found as it was, was due to her knowledge that Moffatt intended to change a note there, and that Moffatt would stick at nothing. She was intensely thankful to have her fears disproved by Lightfoot's newspaper reading, I think."

"Moffatt must have thought that he had a special brand of guardian angel when no mention was made of the *Speedwell*'s crew having been at the little hotel that day," Pelham said.

"Yes, sir," Pointer agreed, "it must have puzzled him. But he was careful not to probe. The less said about Seiler, the safer for him!"

Pelham nodded. He took a photograph from some papers and held it out.

"Look at this, Pointer. Inspector Horrocks has a picture of the hunchback and another boy taken as children. I shouldn't be surprised if Moffatt is the man's brother. He has found that there were originally two of them. The hunchback, Montgomery, as he calls himself, was fond of Fay Starr, and had no idea that she had been murdered by Moffatt. He believes, still, he says, that Winslow did it—Winslow, of whose death he seems to have no idea yet; which may have been an additional reason for Moffatt disposing of the young man's body as he did."

At the trial, it was proved that the forged note which Ursula had found in her purse was linked directly with Moffatt, and with the unfortunate Fritz Seiler—through Lightfoot.

Lightfoot could prove that he had received it only a few days previously from Moffatt. He had its number duly noted down. Moffatt was aware of this habit of his. When the Swiss, while talking with him, had idly dabbed the note with his re-agent and found that it made a hole, he had called out excitedly "It's false! The paper's not right! I can prove it by that hole. Where's Mr. Lightfoot."

Those were his last words, for unfortunately if Lightfoot had gone on, Moffatt was still standing beside him, and Moffatt, gripping his neck, had poured that down his throat which for ever silenced him. The note with its curiously edged perforation and canary coloured smear had been given by Moffatt to Fay Starr to get rid of on the journey home, but she had preferred to land Ursula with it and chance the consequence. She had no idea that it was linked with Bressanone's tragedy in any way.

Directly Moffatt saw Ursula with it in her hand, watched her, as he had, listen to its rustle, stare at its creases, sit frowning with it in her fingers, he knew his danger. And believing that she had not yet spoken of it to anyone, had determined that she too must be silenced—like the others.

He had gone too far to let any whisper of forged notes get about, he thought, little dreaming that the chief inspector had so quickly reasoned out the motive for the three deaths which lay at Moffatt's door.

When the trial was over, and Moffatt duly executed, Pelham and the chief inspector sat one day talking over the case.

"Of course the judge stopped it, but I think the prosecution was right in hinting that these weren't his only murders," Major Pelham was lighting a cigar—as usual. "That gunsmith swearing that he had sold a hunchback last spring a Colt's revolver of the .3 type, which had been paid by a dud note, was a good witness. The permit was in the name of Kershaw, he believed. They seemed to have used that, any of them, as a sort of standing alias."

"Yet I think what counted as much as anything with the jury was finding that bit of Namdah fluff still in Moffatt's penknife," Pointer said. "He had evidently sawed at the rugs with that, when the shears gave out."

"Finest rugs of their kind I ever saw, and the largest." Pelham spoke with retrospective admiration. "Priestley is selling them on behalf of some fund or other. I hear he has had incredible bids for them already—because of Winslow. Funny world! And a funny case."

"It certainly was a curious one," Pointer agreed, "that I should have been right about forgery being the motive and yet wrong about that house in Cromwell Road, where I apparently came on the clue! Right, and yet wrong!" Pointer gave a little smile.

"Wrong, and yet right, Pointer," was the A.C.'s reply; "and very well played throughout, in my opinion—and that of the rest of the Yard."

THE END

Other Resurrected Press Books in *The Chief Inspector Pointer Mystery* Series

MYSTERIES BY ANNE AUSTIN

Murder at Bridge

When an afternoon bridge party attended by some of Hamilton's leading citizens ends with the hostess being murdered in her boudoir, Special Investigator Dundee of the District Attorney's office is called in. But one of the attendees is guilty? There are plenty of suspects: the victim's former lover, her current suitor, the retired judge who is being blackmailed, the victim's maid who had been horribly disfigured accidentally by the murdered woman, or any of the women who's husbands had flirted with the victim. Or was she murdered by an outsider whose motive had nothing to do with the town of Hamilton. Find the answer in... **Murder at Bridge**

One Drop of Blood

When Dr. Koenig, head of Mayfield Sanitarium is murdered, the District Attorney's Special Investigator, "Bonnie" Dundee must go undercover to find the killer. Were any of the inmates of the asylum insane enough to have committed the crime? Or, was it one of the staff, motivated by jealousy? And what was is the secret in the murdered man's past. Find the answer in... **One Drop of Blood**

AVAILABLE FROM RESURRECTED PRESS!

GEMS OF MYSTERY
LOST JEWELS FROM A MORE
ELEGANT AGE

Three wonderful tales of mystery from some of the best known writers of the period before the First World War -

A foggy London night, a Russian princess who steals jewels, a corpse; a mysterious murder, an opera singer, and stolen pearls; two young people who crash a masked ball only to find themselves caught up in a daring theft of jewels; these are the subjects of this collection of entertaining tales of love, jewels, and mystery. This collection includes:

- **In the Fog - by Richard Harding Davis's**

- **The Affair at the Hotel Semiramis - by A.E.W. Mason**

- **Hearts and Masks - Harold MacGrath**

AVAILABLE FROM RESURRECTED PRESS!

THE EDWARDIAN DETECTIVES
LITERARY SLEUTHS OF THE EDWARDIAN ERA

The exploits of the great Victorian Detectives, Poe's C. Auguste Dupin, Gaboriau's Lecoq, and most famously, Arthur Conan Doyle's Sherlock Holmes, are well known. But what of those fictional detectives that came after, those of the Edwardian Age? The period between the death of Queen Victoria and the First World War had been called the Golden Age of the detective short story, but how familiar is the modern reader with the sleuths of this era? And such an extraordinary group they were, including in their numbers an unassuming English priest, a blind man, a master of disguises, a lecturer in medical jurisprudence, a noble woman working for Scotland Yard, and a savant so brilliant he was known as "The Thinking Machine."

To introduce readers to these detectives, Resurrected Press has assembled a collection of stories featuring these and other remarkable sleuths in The Edwardian Detectives.

- The Case of Laker, Absconded by Arthur Morrison
- The Fenchurch Street Mystery by Baroness Orczy
- The Crime of the French Café by Nick Carter
- The Man with Nailed Shoes by R Austin Freeman
- The Blue Cross by G. K. Chesterton
- The Case of the Pocket Diary Found in the Snow by Augusta Groner
- The Ninescore Mystery by Baroness Orczy
- The Riddle of the Ninth Finger by Thomas W. Hanshew
- The Knight's Cross Signal Problem by Ernest Bramah

- The Problem of Cell 13 by Jacques Futrelle
- The Conundrum of the Golf Links by Percy James Brebner
- The Silkworms of Florence by Clifford Ashdown
- The Gateway of the Monster by William Hope Hodgson
- The Affair at the Semiramis Hotel by A. E. W. Mason
- The Affair of the Avalanche Bicycle & Tyre Co., LTD by Arthur Morrison

RESURRECTED PRESS CLASSIC MYSTERY CATALOGUE

Journeys into Mystery
Travel and Mystery in a More Elegant Time

The Edwardian Detectives
Literary Sleuths of the Edwardian Era

Gems of Mystery
Lost Jewels from a More Elegant Age

E. C. Bentley
Trent's Last Case: The Woman in Black

Ernest Bramah
Max Carrados Resurrected:
The Detective Stories of Max Carrados

Agatha Christie
The Secret Adversary
The Mysterious Affair at Styles

Octavus Roy Cohen
Midnight

Freeman Wills Croft
The Ponson Case
The Pit Prop Syndicate

J. S. Fletcher
The Herapath Property
The Rayner-Slade Amalgamation
The Chestermarke Instinct
The Paradise Mystery
Dead Men's Money

The Middle of Things
Ravensdene Court
Scarhaven Keep
The Orange-Yellow Diamond
The Middle Temple Murder
The Tallyrand Maxim
The Borough Treasurer
In the Mayor's Parlour
The Saftey Pin

R. Austin Freeman
The Mystery of 31 New Inn from the Dr. Thorndyke Series
John Thorndyke's Cases from the Dr. Thorndyke Series
The Red Thumb Mark from The Dr. Thorndyke Series
The Eye of Osiris from The Dr. Thorndyke Series
A Silent Witness from the Dr. John Thorndyke Series
The Cat's Eye from the Dr. John Thorndyke Series
Helen Vardon's Confession: A Dr. John Thorndyke Story
As a Thief in the Night: A Dr. John Thorndyke Story
Mr. Pottermack's Oversight: A Dr. John Thorndyke Story
Dr. Thorndyke Intervenes: A Dr. John Thorndyke Story
The Singing Bone: The Adventures of Dr. Thorndyke
The Stoneware Monkey: A Dr. John Thorndyke Story
The Great Portrait Mystery, and Other Stories: A Collection of Dr. John Thorndyke and Other Stories
The Penrose Mystery; A Dr. John Thorndyke Story
The Uttermost Farthing: A Savant's Vendetta

Arthur Griffiths
The Passenger From Calais
The Rome Express

Fergus Hume
The Mystery of a Hansom Cab
The Green Mummy
The Silent House
The Secret Passage

Edgar Jepson
The Loudwater Mystery

A. E. W. Mason
At the Villa Rose

A. A. Milne
The Red House Mystery
Baroness Emma Orczy
The Old Man in the Corner

Edgar Allan Poe
The Detective Stories of Edgar Allan Poe

Arthur J. Rees
The Hampstead Mystery
The Shrieking Pit
The Hand In The Dark
The Moon Rock
The Mystery of the Downs

Mary Roberts Rinehart
Sight Unseen and The Confession

Dorothy L. Sayers
Whose Body?

Sir William Magnay
The Hunt Ball Mystery

Mabel and Paul Thorne
The Sheridan Road Mystery

Louis Tracy
The Strange Case of Mortimer Fenley
The Albert Gate Mystery
The Bartlett Mystery
The Postmaster's Daughter
The House of Peril
The Sandling Case: What Would You Have Done?
Charles Edmonds Walk
The Paternoster Ruby

John R. Watson
The Mystery of the Downs
The Hampstead Mystery

Edgar Wallace
The Daffodil Mystery
The Crimson Circle

Carolyn Wells
Vicky Van
The Man Who Fell Through the Earth
In the Onyx Lobby
Raspberry Jam
The Clue
The Room with the Tassels
The Vanishing of Betty Varian
The Mystery Girl
The White Alley
The Curved Blades
Anybody but Anne
The Bride of a Moment
Faulkner's Folly
The Diamond Pin
The Gold Bag
The Mystery of the Sycamore
The Come Backy

Raoul Whitfield
Death in a Bowl

And much more!
Visit ResurrectedPress.com
for our complete catalogue

About Resurrected Press

A division of Intrepid Ink, LLC, Resurrected Press is dedicated to bringing high quality, vintage books back into publication. See our entire catalogue and find out more at www.ResurrectedPress.com.

About Intrepid Ink, LLC

Intrepid Ink, LLC provides full publishing services to authors of fiction and non-fiction books, eBooks and websites. From editing to formatting, from publishing to marketing, Intrepid Ink gets your creative works into the hands of the people who want to read them. Find out more at www.IntrepidInk.com.

www.ingramcontent.com/pod-product-compliance
Lightning Source LLC
Chambersburg PA
CBHW071326250626
47159CB00004B/1483